# CONTENTS

# INTRODUCTION

It all began with a short story. Well, two short stories, actually. For Big Red and Old Red Amlingmeyer, brothers/cowboys/wannabe detectives, "The Red-Headed League" got the mystery-ball rolling, introducing them to Sherlock Holmes and his unique approach to "conundrum-busting" (as Big Red calls it). But for me, writer guy, "Dear Mr. Holmes" is where it all began. That's the story that *shows* the Amlingmeyers discovering Holmes. I wrote it for this lofty reason: I really, really wanted to sell another story to *Ellery Queen Mystery Magazine* and I thought I'd have a better chance with a Sherlock Holmes tie-in. Classy, eh? But hey—it worked.

Thanks for the leg up, Sir Arthur! Where would Nicholas Meyer and I be without you?

Before "Dear Mr. Holmes," I'd been having good luck selling Christmas stories to *Ellery Queen*. The magazine puts out a holiday-themed issue every year, so I figured writing about poisoned fruitcakes and evil mall Santas and the like would give me a leg up. And since such strategic thinking actually seemed to pay off (a rarity for me), I stuck with it. "What other theme issues does *EQMM* do?" I asked myself. The answer: just one. An annual tribute to Sherlock Holmes.

So the question then was *how* to write about Holmes. I didn't want to do a pastiche or parody, but once you've eliminated those what's left? How can you have a Sherlock Holmes story without Sherlock Holmes?

# Steve Hockensmith

I'd been wrestling with that for days when my wife suggested we go on a hike. (It's perhaps closer to the truth to say "my wife informed me that we were going on a hike." I like hiking fine, but I enjoy reading and watching old movies even more, and those don't involve getting off the couch on a Saturday morning.) Soon we were winding our way up Mt. Tamalpais in Marin County, Calif. My wife, no doubt, was communing with God and becoming one with nature. Me? I was still trying to figure out how to sell another story to *Ellery Queen*.

That mountain trail gave me the answer. Being away from roads and telephone poles and all the noise of modern life put me in mind of the past. Specifically, the past of the West. (I was in California, remember. As Big Red points out in *The Black Dove*, that's about as far West as you can go without getting very, very wet.) So there I was thinking about the Old West and Sherlock Holmes, and it hit me: They overlapped. The Victorian Era we associate so much with Holmes coincided with the time we now think of as "the Wild West." While Holmes and Watson were solving mysteries in London, cowboys were roping steers in Texas! What would those cowboys make of men like Sherlock Holmes and John Watson?

*Et voila*. A series is born.

I wrote "Dear Mr. Holmes" in 2001, which means I've had Big Red Amlingmeyer yammering away in my head for an entire decade now. At times, I've felt a bit like his put-upon older brother: I've just wanted the big guy to shut up. He hasn't yet, though. At least never for long.

I'm not sure what he'll have to say next or when he'll chose to say it. While we wait to find out, I hope you enjoy these stories. This is where it all began. Where it's all going, I suspect, remains to be seen . . . .

Steve Hockensmith
Alameda, Calif.
February 2011

Steve Hockensmith

# DEAR MR. HOLMES

*The Strand Magazine*
George Newnes Ltd.
3 to 13 Southampton Street
Strand, London, England

Dear Mr. Holmes,

This is my third crack at writing this letter, and by God I'm going to get through it this time come Hell or high water. If Gabriel himself were to come down and blow on his bugle before I'm done, I'd just turn around and tell him, "Hold your horn, Gabe, I'm writing a letter to Mr. Sherlock Holmes."

Part of my difficulty with this chore is that my book learning amounts to six years in a country school and two years clerking for a granary in Peabody, Kansas. And my brother Gustav's got five years less on the schooling and not a day wielding a clerk's pencil, yet *he's* trying to tell *me* how to write this letter.

Somehow I doubt if you're looking over that Watson fellow's shoulder when he's trying to write about you. But my brother is not a refined gentleman like yourself. So if you notice any bloodstains on the paper as you read this, you'll know he stuck his big nose in one time too many and I had to give it a good punch.

Now I've read about your way with "deductions," so perhaps I don't need to introduce myself before I get to the nub of the matter. I can just see you taking one good whiff of this letter and saying to yourself, "This was sent by a cowboy—one who needed a good bath!" And you would be right. My name is Otto Amlingmeyer, I am what they call a "cowboy" working the Old Western Trail from Texas to Montana and, yes, I suppose I could use a dunking—but not until I've written "And that's how it all happened, I swear on my dust-covered soul. Sincerely, O.A. Amlingmeyer."

You being an uncommonly educated fellow and all, you surely don't put any stock in those dime novels about cowboy life. The way they tell it, your average drover spends his days fighting off fifty Comanche braves with one hand and untying a beautiful gal from the railroad tracks with the other, all the while with a lit stick of dynamite clenched in his teeth, pearl-handled six-guns in his holster and a horse that dances the Texas two-step when he whistles "She'll Be Coming 'Round the Mountain." Sure, we have plenty of adventures on the trail, so long as your idea of an "adventure" is pulling a steer out of a sinkhole or throwing rocks at coyotes so they won't sneak into camp at night and eat your boots.

But on our latest cattle drive, my brother and I finally have had a genuine dime novel-type adventure. And we only lived to tell about it because of you.

"Ahhh!" I can hear you say. "At last! The point!"

You'll have to excuse me. I'm used to yarning around a campfire, where the idea is to keep your lips flapping as long as possible so as to better distract your pals from how cold, tired and miserable they are. If I try to write this letter that way, they'll have to cut down all the trees in Kansas to make enough paper for me to get the job done. So I'd better just get to it.

Gustav and I first became acquainted with you and your reputation as a puzzle-breaker about three months ago. He and I had just made the trip down to Brownsville, Texas, to meet up with an old compadre of ours by the name of Charlie Higgebottom. Charlie was fixed to be caporal of a big drive—three thousand Mexican longhorns headed up through Texas, Oklahoma, Kansas, Nebraska and Wyoming to the Blackfeet Agency up around Billings, Montana. That's as long as the Big Trail ever gets, so Charlie needed the best cow and horse men he could lay hands on. Charlie's been on enough drives with us to know that we can both handle cattle, so naturally he sent word that we should come along.

Now to Charlie and most of the other bull nurses we know, Gustav and I aren't "the Amlingmeyer brothers." I guess that just doesn't slide off the tongue easy as it should. So instead we're "Big Red" and "Old Red," or just "the Reds," on account of our strawberry-red heads of hair. I'm Big Red for reasons a deep thinker such as yourself can surely work out. But my brother's Old Red not so much for his age (though at twenty-six he is a bit long in the tooth for a cowpuncher) as much as for his personality. Gustav's never cottoned much to japes or tomfoolery. He's a quiet fellow, always looking serious and a little down in the mouth—what you might call morose, like a dog you just kicked off the foot of your bed.

So to move along in the direction of that *point* I should be steering towards, maybe three days into this latest drive, when most of the hands were circled up around the fire after getting the herd bedded down for the night, Charlie pulled something out of his saddlebag and gave it to me. It was one of those story magazines, though not one I'd ever laid eyes on before.

"I've been holding onto this for eight weeks," Charlie said. "Found it on a bench at the railroad station in San Antonio and figured it was the hand of fate. I had to hold onto it till I saw the Reds again."

I didn't know what he was working his jaw about until I opened it up and started flipping through the pages. About half-way through the magazine, I came across a story you know well— "The Red-Headed League."

The title alone got a chuckle out of me. I read it out loud for Gustav (who can't tell his As from his Zs or anything in between), but he just grunted. The boys around the fire got a fine laugh from it though, and they called out for me to read the whole story. Now along the trail I've got a reputation for oratory and poetry reciting and song singing and such, being under-blessed on modesty and powerful over-blessed on lung power. So I grabbed a lantern off the commissary and cleared my throat and gave the fellows a regular night at the theatre.

Well, you'll have to tell that Dr. Watson he's a top-rail yarn spinner. The boys ate it up like it was hot doughnuts on Christmas morning. They were hooting and joshing me and Gustav fierce when they heard that burro milk about the locoed American tycoon giving away money to redheads. Not a one of them figured out it was just a bad man's scheme, and when you caught the rascal red-handed (so to speak) trying to dig his way into a bank they cheered and clapped like you were right there with us doing back-flips.

Now usually the flannelmouthed whopper-swapping you'll hear around a cowboy campfire puts my brother straight to sleep. And for a minute or two I thought "The Red-Headed League" would be just another lullaby as far as he was concerned. But when I got to the part where you told that pawnbroker everything there was to know about himself—where he'd been and what he'd done and who he was, just from looking at him—Gustav perked up right smart. His eyes got all wide in a way I'd never seen, picking up the light from the fire and glowing like the big eyes of a hoot owl. But though he was staring straight at me, I knew he didn't see me or the campfire or the boys gathered around it. What he saw was you and Dr. Watson and that pawnbroker and everything else in the story. When I finished he even applauded along with the rest of the boys, which was peculiar indeed since a show of enthusiasm from Gustav is about as common as a six-legged mule or an honest bartender.

That dreamy-like look stayed on Old Red's face all the next day. And when we were gathered around the fire that night, he asked me to read the story again. Well, I rarely turn down an opportunity to practice my elocution, so I pulled out that magazine and gave it my all. As you might imagine, the fellows didn't get quite so worked up about it the second time, though they did give it a good listen. Gustav, on the other hand, was mesmerized. The next night, he asked me to read it *again*, but (no offense now) the boys wouldn't stand for it. They got to stretching the blanket about ornery beeves they'd seen—a puncher by the name of Tornado Monroe even claimed a steer pulled a knife on him once—and Gustav got up and wandered away, as he will when the proceedings are not to his interest and he's not ready to sleep.

Now when you're tending to a herd all day long, you don't have time to work your gums at anybody who doesn't have hooves, which is why I hadn't had a chance to ask my brother why "The Red-Headed League" had him all google-eyed. So after listening to a few more whoppers from the boys, I got up and went looking for him. I found him out by the picket line, where we had our night horses hobbled. He was staring up at the black night sky like a coyote getting ready to let loose with a yodel.

"They're called stars," I said. "Don't worry—they ain't going to fall on you."

Of course, that didn't even get a smile out of Old Red, though sometimes I can get him tickled if no one's around.

"What are you out here pondering on, old-timer?"

He just shrugged, looking kind of embarrassed.

"Now come on, brother. You know you can unshuck your lips with me. That magazine story's got a fierce grip on your head, ain't it?"

He nodded slowly, real thoughtful-like. "Yup, I suppose it has," he said, speaking just as slowly. "It's that Holmes feller. His whole way of lookin' at things."

"What about it?"

"Well, you know I like a man can think straight. And he seems to be the straightest thinker I ever heard of."

"So you admire the man."

"More than that. Hearin' about him makes me wonder. You know . . . well, you know about my schoolin'. . . ."

Gustav got to looking all bashful again. He can be a mite prickly about his lack of letters. It's always seemed to sting him that our dear old mama had him working the fields while the younger kids got to go to school.

"I know," I said.

"Well, the thing about it is, he don't need no book-learnin' to do what he does. He didn't catch them bank-robbin' snakes with some trick he learned at a university. He caught 'em cuz he knows how to *look* at things. Look and really see 'em."

I shrugged. "I guess you're right. So?"

"So, seems any man could do the same, he put his mind to it."

Now I'm ashamed to admit I laughed when I saw what he was driving at.

"I know you're sharper than you look, Brother, but I don't think you could beat this Sherlock Holmes in any war of wits."

Gustav gave me his best scowl—the one that makes a rabid badger look downright friendly by comparison.

"I don't aim to beat him," he said. "I just think he's worth studyin' on, that's all. Seems like he don't do nothin' but sit around and cogitate and *whammy*—things happen. Whereas fellers like you and me and the boys back there, we never think at all, just *do*, and we don't get no whammy at all."

"Cowpunchin' ain't a thinker's game."

"Don't I know it."

The bitterness in his voice put a little cramp in my grin. I knew he longed for better things than riding herd on someone else's cattle. And part of the reason he couldn't get those things was because he'd always had younger brothers and sisters to look out for. Now most of them were dead, with only one left for him to nursemaid—the baby of the family, Yours Truly.

Looked at a certain way, I owed him everything I had, right down to the boots on my big feet. So who was I to poke fun?

"Tell you what, brother. Tomorrow night I'll borrow the lantern off the chuck wagon and you and I can come out here and visit with Mr. Sherlock Holmes again."

That got me a glimpse of that rarest of prairie critters, the Gustav Amlingmeyer Smile. I went back to the fire after that. He and I had second watch that night, which meant we'd be back up on our mounts by two o'clock in the morning. I wouldn't have time for forty winks, but I could still catch me maybe eighteen if I turned in right quick. I left Gustav there by the horses, looking up at the sky like he'd never seen it before. I found him there still when I came back a few hours later.

Over the next three weeks, I read him "The Red-Headed League" a dozen more times. I finally stopped when I noticed his lips forming the words before I could speak them.

"You've got this thing memorized!" I said.

"Only the important bits."

"Well then, you don't need to hear 'em anymore."

After that, we took a little holiday from Dr. Watson's story. Truth to tell, I'd become mighty sick of it myself, fine though it is. Reading it over and over was like having steak for dinner every night. Sooner or later, a man's going to pine for a plate of beans.

So for the next few weeks, there was no more talk of Sherlock Holmes—though every so often I would see Gustav's mouth working as he rode along, and at times it seemed like he couldn't keep his mind on his steers. That won my brother some jibes from the other fellows, who joshed him that he was going soft in the head in his old age. I knew what he was thinking on, of course, but I kept that to myself.

By this point we'd crossed the Red River and were deep into Indian territory. Now no matter what you may read over there in England, we don't have big Indian wars like we used to. That was all ironed out not too long after Custer and his boys got themselves turned into pincushions. But cowboys have still got to watch their backsides on Indian land—especially when there's Comanches and Kiowas on the prowl. They might not steal many scalps these days, but they do surely love to steal cattle.

Charlie Higgebottom doubled up the night watch the day we got across the Red River, so there were four of us out under the moon at all times while the rest of the outfit slept. Now "the rest of the outfit" amounted to just eight men, not counting Charlie and our cook, Greasy Pete Tregaskis. We weren't overstocked for hands, since delivering beeves to an Indian agency, as we were doing, is not the most profitable drive a fellow can undertake. So we were all of us a little droopy in the saddle, overworked and dying of thirst for a good night's sleep. Sometimes a nightmare would make me jump, and I'd wake to find myself on my horse, on watch.

That's just what happened this one particular night, except it wasn't any nightmare that woke me up. It was gunshots. And if that hadn't been enough to snap me out of the Land of Nod, the stampede would have done just as well, for you can't go firing off a six-shooter at night without spooking the herd something fierce. When they get spooked, they run. And when they run, we have to ride after them.

The chase took hours. I spent most of that time trying not to end up something sticky on the bottom of a thousand steers' hooves. This was only my third drive, you see, so I didn't have the stampede-breaking know-how of a Gustav or a Charlie Higgebottom. I spurred up toward the front just once, to make sure my brother wasn't already worm bait a few miles back. There he and Charlie were, riding right alongside the lead steers, trying to convince them the world wouldn't come to an end if they stopped running. That would be a difficult thing to do, I knew, since cows are second only to rocks as the dumbest things God ever created. So I left them to it, dropping back where it was safer and I could do more good, along the right flank with a couple of the other punchers trying to keep our big herd from turning into five hundred little herds.

When it was all over, the steers dropped down to the ground to take a much-needed nap. Pretty soon they were snoring under the early-morning sun like nothing ever happened. Cowboys aren't as lucky in such matters as cows, however. There's no rest for us after a stampede peters out. You've got to fan out and round up the strays. I was fixing to bear down on couple of loose steers when Gustav and Charlie rode up, both of them looking like they had a mouthful of something a dog wouldn't eat.

"Did you see what started all this?" Charlie snapped at me.

"Well, it's good to see y'all, too. Your concern for my well-being has me all teared up," I said. "And no, I didn't see what started this. I just heard someone set his gun a-goin' and before I knew it I was up to my neck in beef."

"How about Billy and Peanuts?" Gustav asked. "You seen 'em?"

"No. I haven't seen 'em since . . . . "

And then I realized why Charlie and Gustav looked so riled. Billy and Peanuts—alias Bill Brown and Conrad Emicholz—were the two fellows out on watch the same time as Gustav and me.

"Nobody else has seen 'em?"

Charlie shook his head. Gustav sighed.

"I'll go back and look for them," my brother said. He nodded at me. "Mind if I take him with me?"

Charlie looked thoughtful for a moment. "Yup, maybe you better." And he wheeled his horse and rode off after those longhorns I'd been aiming at.

"So. . . I'm glad to see you didn't get yourself killed last night," Gustav said.

"Well, that just about sums up my feelings upon seeing you," I said.

Gustav nodded. "Alright then." That's about as sentimental as he ever gets. "Let's go get us some fresh horses."

Once we had our new mounts, we headed back down the trail, Gustav riding the eastern side, me riding the western. We saw a few strays, but no Billy and no Peanuts. A couple miles back we ran into the commissary hurrying to catch up with the herd. We asked Greasy Pete, our outfit's biscuit rustler, if he'd seen the boys. He hadn't. Before we rode on, Gustav asked if he could get a shovel and a scattergun out of the wagon.

"You expectin' to use those?" asked Greasy Pete.

"Wouldn't ask for 'em if I didn't," Gustav said.

This shovel and shotgun talk was making me jumpy as a jackrabbit, but I tried not to let on. I never could hide a thing from my brother though. When Greasy Pete pulled out the scattergun for him, Gustav handed it over to me. He knew I'd take comfort from a piece of heavy artillery across my saddle.

About a half-hour after we left the chuck wagon, we found ourselves back where it all started—the spot where we'd had the herd bedded down for the night. The trail was plain as can be, being a quarter mile wide and flat as a river bed. There was some brush and trees on the western side, more brush and a small rocky bluff on the eastern side.

"I was round about here, up toward the point, when those shots went off," Gustav said. "How about you?"

"I'm not sure. It was mighty dark," I said, not adding that it was so dark because I had my eyes closed at the time. "I think I must've been up toward the point, too. Seemed like pretty near the whole herd tried to plow me under once they got runnin'."

Gustav took his horse to a slow trot. He was headed for the rocks to the east. That made sense to me. It was the best place around for jumping a man. I followed, my palms slicking up the shotgun with sweat.

As we rounded the bluff, I caught sight of something red pressed up against the gray rock. It looked to be a man. I stopped my horse and brought up the shotgun.

"Gustav," I said.

"I see him," my brother said. "Hey, Peanuts! I sure hope that's you!"

There was no answer—no sound, no movement, nothing. Gustav unholstered his six-gun and fired off a shot into the sky. The red shape was as still as the rock around it. Gustav climbed down off his horse.

"Come on," he said.

I dismounted and followed. I kept the shotgun leveled at the quiet fellow, though with the buzzing of flies growing louder as we approached I didn't much expect him to kick up any kind of fuss.

It was Peanuts alright. He was in the same red calico shirt he'd been wearing the past two months. The red was darker now though—soaked through with blood from his open belly and mangled scalp and empty eye-sockets. He was propped up against the rock like he'd just leaned back to enjoy a little siesta in the shade. Billy was next to him, barked up just as bad.

I did some colorful cursing of the Kiowas, the Comanches,

the Apaches and every other tribe under the skies. Gustav took it all more calm-like, which is his way when faced with the alarming or the unpleasant.

"Well," he said, "now we know why the buzzards couldn't lead us straight to 'em. If the boys had been left out under the sun, they'd be just about picked clean by now." He kicked a clod of chewed-up sod thrown up by the stampede. "Or they would've been churned into butter by all those hooves."

I turned, still cursing like thunder, and went to get back on my horse.

"What do you think you're doin'?" Gustav called after me.

"I'm gonna track down those murderin' sons of bitches and give 'em a taste of what they gave Billy and Peanuts. What do *you* think *you're* doin'?"

"I'm buryin' the boys and then I'm headed back up to join the outfit. And that's what you're going to do, too. That's what *I* think."

"But—"

"As long as you're headed over there, you may as well grab the shovel off my horse and get to usin' it. I think this is as good a place as any to lay the boys down."

I did as I was told, though I cursed and kicked about it. As I got to work piling up dirt, Gustav showed me the lay of things.

"Whoever did this has got a six-hour jump on us at least. They'll have some of our cattle with 'em for sure, and that'll slow 'em down. But it would still take us hours to track 'em and catch up. And then what? It's you and me and two exhausted horses against Lord only knows how many men. Nope. The only thing to do is give these two a proper burial and then go tell Charlie what happened."

I couldn't argue with the wisdom of it, but it didn't sit right, I can tell you that. I tried to work my anger into my shoveling, and I sure gave that ground a good beating. While I was digging, Gustav was hunched over the bodies, looking them over as casual as he would a couple of ponies he was thinking about buying. He even handled them, leaning them forward so he could see their backs.

# Dear Mr. Holmes

"Why are you pawin' at 'em like that?" I finally asked him.

"Well," Gustav said, kind of reluctant-like, "just between you and me and the boys here, I'm wonderin' what Mr. Sherlock Holmes would make of all this."

That put a twig up my snoot, I confess. I hadn't known Billy and Peanuts very long, had never worked a drive with them before, but they were comrades just the same and it seemed disrespectful to be thinking about some magazine story when they hadn't even been planted yet.

"That Holmes feller might be a sharp tack on paper, but he ain't no Indian fighter," I said.

"Maybe. But the thing is, whoever barked these heads cut 'em up bad. Their scalps must've come off in four, five pieces. And—"

"Now ain't that a scandal?" I cut in, snorting like a steer with a knot in his tail. "The Kiowas ain't gettin' enough practice with their scalpin'! I guess you better just write yourself a letter of complaint to the Bureau of Indian Affairs."

Gustav shot a sour glare my way, then went back to inspecting the bodies and the ground around them. I plunged the shovel back into the earth, and neither one of us said a thing until it came time to settle the boys into the shallow little hole they were going to share for the rest of forever.

Seeing as how I'd just about broken my back digging, I made Gustav do the dragging. He rolled Peanuts into the earth first, then went back for Billy. When we had the two curled up together, we piled on a load of rocks so the coyotes couldn't get at them. We didn't throw around any words of consecration, each of us still being vexed with the other and just Christian enough to know that men who hadn't been inside a church in 10 years don't have any business playing preacher.

Before we headed out to hook up with the outfit again, Gustav had us do a little ride south. We'd barely gone a hundred feet when we came to a fresh trail pushing east through the brush.

"You still wanna go get yourself killed, you just ride that trail good and hard," Gustav said to me.

Our little brotherly spats tend to live and die within the span of an hour. I'm just not good at grudge-holding. So I was ready to patch things up by now.

"So what do you figure happened, brother?" I asked.

"I'm still figurin'," Gustav said warily.

"Well, here's how I see it. A few wild bucks—renegades—they jumped Billy and Peanuts, cut out some cattle, then fired off a few shots to get a stampede goin'. They knew that'd scatter the rest of us while they skedaddled."

Gustav nodded slowly. "Makes sense."

"Sure it does. What other way would you reckon it?"

Instead of answering, Gustav pointed at the trail we'd just come across and asked a question of his own.

"What does that look like to you? Maybe a dozen head? Four or five horses?"

I'm not as good with trails as my brother. I can read English. He can read hoofprints. So it was best just to agree.

"That seems about right," I said. "So?"

Gustav just shook his head sadly, like he was puzzled how such a feather-brain came to be a blood relation. He turned his horse and kicked him into a gallop. I followed, and we were too busy riding to have any parlay until we caught up with the herd a few hours later.

Charlie and the rest of the boys had finished rounding up strays and were doing a count—a mighty big undertaking when you've got three thousand animals to throw a number on. We reported what we'd found, and everybody put together the same story I had. Naturally, there was some talk about hunting down the dirty redskins who'd cut up Billy and Peanuts, but Charlie put a bullet through that notion pretty fast. Dodge City was two weeks north of us. When we went in for supplies there, we'd spread word of what happened, but that was all that could be done. We'd lost only fifteen head to the raiders and the stampede, leaving three thousand steers to look after and just ten cowpunchers left to do it.

"If it were up to me, I'd let all you Indian fighters go get yourself bushwhacked," Charlie said. "But it's not up to me. It's up to our employer, the Lone Star Land and Cattle Company Incorporated. And we know what they want: They want the job done. That's what we're here for and that's what we're gonna do. Any arguments?"

There weren't any, but there was more than a little grumbling. My brother kept out of it, though. He was even more tight-lipped than usual. He didn't open his mouth unless it was to stick some beans and bacon in it at supper time. His eyes had gone kind of faraway and unfocused, like he didn't notice me, the boys, the cattle, the horse underneath his rump, nothing.

"Why's Old Red gone so quiet on us again?" Greasy Pete asked me the day after we buried Billy and Peanuts. "Did one of them Comanches cut out his tongue?"

All I could do was shrug. That very morning I'd asked Gustav what had him all hushed up and the only thing he'd say was, "I'm tryin' to introspect."

The next day, we *all* had something new to think on. Gustav and I were riding point up at the front of the herd, him on the right side, me on the left, both of us just behind Charlie, who as trail boss was usually a quick trot ahead leading the way. We were just loping along casual as can be, slouching low in our saddles, dreaming of rocking chairs and feather beds, when a sound bounced out of the air up ahead and straightened out our spines. It was a gunshot, not too far away by the sound of it. I turned to look at Gustav, and he was already yipping his horse into a gallop. I did likewise.

"What do you think?" Charlie asked once we'd come pounding to a halt next to him.

"Came from that washout up ahead there," Gustav said, pointing at something that didn't look like anything more than a streak of brown in the grass. But my brother's got eyes and ears as sharp as a razor blade, so I didn't doubt he was right.

Neither did Charlie. He pulled out his forty-five. "Alright, Old Red. You and me'll ride on into it and see what we see. Big Red, you stay up top and hug the edge. Not too tight, though. If this is some kinda ambush, you'll be our ace in the hole."

"Or you'll be mine," I said, drawing out my own six-shooter. "Kinda depends on who gets ambushed where, don't it?"

"Only one way to find out," Gustav said, and on those cheerful words of parting we rode off.

There was a washout up ahead, just like my brother said. I waited a minute while he and Charlie worked their horses down into the dried-out creek bed, then I wheeled my mount to the west and trotted off. I stayed just close enough to the washout to follow the sound of hooves and the cloud of dust they kicked up.

After maybe five minutes of riding, the dust cloud stopped and drifted apart on the breeze as the hoof beats came to a halt. I stopped, too, and heard words bounce up out of the gully.

"Easy there, mister," Gustav was saying. "No need to go pullin' out any hardware."

I knew my brother wasn't really talking to whoever was down there with him and Charlie. He was talking to me, telling me what he saw. I slipped off my horse and slinked over to the washout's edge. Down below, just a few feet away, was a man standing next to a prone pinto. The dirt around the horse's head was black-red with blood. A saddle sat on the ground near the man's feet. He had a gun in his hand, and it was all set to go off in the general direction of my brother's belly.

"Who're you?" the man growled.

"Us? Oh, we're nobody. Just drovers movin' through with some cattle," my brother said from up on his horse, sounding as cool as lemonade with ice. "Me and Charlie here—oh, my name's Gustav Amlingmeyer, by the by—we're headed up to Billings from Brownsville. Been on the trail nearly two months. And how about yourself? Where you headed?"

Of course, this was uncommonly chatty for Old Red. But he wasn't being sociable. He was giving me time to angle around behind the hombre with the gun.

"If you don't know, then it ain't none of your concern," the man said. The barrel of his gun wasn't angling down a hair. "Now why don't you two get offa them horses?"

Charlie and Gustav looked at each other, and Gustav gave a nod. "Alright," he said. "We'll come on down. Won't we, little brother?"

Well, you couldn't ask for a plainer signal than that. I jumped, landing next to the man like a bag of hammers. I only got one hand on him though, and he spun out of my grasp, off balance. But he looked a little dazed, and I managed to get my feet planted before he could bring his shooting iron back into the game. I threw a fist at him, and though it only seemed to graze his chin his head snapped back and his eyelids fluttered and his knees gave out from under him. He dropped the six-shooter and toppled backwards into the dirt next to the dead horse.

The stranger stayed down for a minute or two. By the time he sat up, shaking his head and rubbing his jaw, I had his own gun pointed at him.

"Hold on there, friend," he said. "Let's talk this over."

"Oh, I'm your friend, am I?" I said. "You sure are sociable now that the bullets are pointed in your direction."

"I didn't mean no offense before." He looked over my shoulder and tried an unconvincing smile on Gustav and Charlie, who had dismounted and stepped over for a closer look at our prisoner. "Y'all rattled me, that's all. I just got myself out of a mighty tough scrape and I didn't fancy the notion of another one so soon."

"What kinda scrape?" Charlie asked.

"The red-skinned kind," the man said. "I was headed up to Wichita and I ran into a war party. They—"

"War party?" Charlie broke in. "What kind? Kiowa? Comanche?"

"I didn't stop to ask. The way they lit out after me, I just figured they were the scalpin' kind."

Charlie and Gustav exchanged a glance. Charlie looked worried. My brother—well, he did a good job of not looking one thing or another.

"Go on," my brother said to the man. "What happened?"

"Well, they chased me half the night, poppin' off shots every time they got within a quarter mile of me. They finally dropped away somewhere, but I wasn't takin' any chances. I reckoned this here arroyo was as good a place as any to hole up. Only I slipped off to sleep while I was waitin' for my last stand. When I woke up, I noticed that ol' Jimmy over there had picked up a bullet. You know how a good horse is. He can go for miles without letting on he's about to die. Well, he was sufferin' pretty bad, so I did the only thing I could do. The next thing I know, I've got men ridin' at me and fallin' out of the sky on me and throwin' punches at me. Is it any wonder a feller would get a little jumpy?"

"Not at all, not at all," Charlie said. He reached out and offered the man his hand. "No hard feelings, I hope. My name's Charlie Higgebottom."

The man gave Charlie's hand a shake, then let Charlie help him to his feet. "I'm Joe," he said. "Joe Sweet." He turned to face me. "And you're the feller with the big fist."

I grinned and nodded. "Sorry about that. Otto Amlingmeyer's the name, but the boys call me Big Red."

"I can't imagine why," Sweet joked as we shook hands.

While Sweet and Charlie and I were getting chummy, my brother had wandered over to Sweet's horse. He was giving the animal a sour look, like he expected it to hop up and start calling him names.

"Oh, that's Old Red, Otto's brother," Charlie said when Sweet turned toward Gustav. "Don't worry about the introductions. You won't hear five more words out of him the whole time you know him."

"Well, it's nice to meet you anyhow, Old Red," Sweet said.

My brother just looked up and grunted.

Charlie chuckled. "See? What'd I tell you?"

"So what'd you boys say you were doin' out here?" Sweet sucked a lungful of air through his nostrils. "Shoot. That's right. It's a wonder I didn't notice it before. There's a herd headed this way, ain't there?"

"Yes, sir. Three thousand head." Charlie proceeded to tell

Sweet all about our drive, right up to and including what had happened to Billy and Peanuts. "You wouldn't be a cowpuncher, would you? We're a few hands down and we've got a long way to go."

"Well, I've roped me a few steers over the years," Sweet said. "Even worked a drive up to Cheyenne once. I'd be happy to ride with you for a spell."

"Good!" Charlie clapped Sweet on the back. "So here I am a foreman who needs himself a cowboy, and right here in the middle of nowhere I meet up with a cowboy who needs himself a horse. I guess I'm one lucky son of a bitch today."

Sweet grinned again. "That's what people always say after they meet me."

That got a good laugh out of me and Charlie, but my brother didn't even crack a smile. "Tell you what, Mr. Sweet," Gustav said once the guffaws had petered out. "You take my mount there and let Charlie show you what's what. My brother can grab me another horse from the remuda and ride it up here. I'll use your saddle for now and give it back to you tonight."

Sweet's grin slid off his face like eggs off a greasy frying pan. "Thank you for the offer, but I'd rather be the one to wait. I'm a touch particular about my saddles. The wrong one'll kink up my back somethin' awful."

"Oh, got yourself a special make, do you?" Gustav said. He crouched down next to the saddle lying in the dirt beside the horse. "Just looks like a regular California to me." He stretched out a hand toward the saddle bags. "Maybe it's these—"

"Get your paws away from there," Sweet snapped, taking a few quick steps toward my brother.

Gustav stood and turned to face him. "Somethin' the matter, Mr. Sweet? You're still actin' a mite tetchy."

It seemed to be a good thing Sweet's gun was in my hand instead of his. And if looks could kill, as they say, Sweet wouldn't have needed a shooting iron at all. But after staring death at my brother for a few seconds, Sweet relaxed with a shrug and a none-too-powerful smile.

"Awwww, you're right. Just look at me. Those braves gave me a permanent case of the jitters. Sorry. Didn't mean to jump ya' like that."

Gustav acknowledged the apology with a nod.

"All the same," Sweet continued, "I'd prefer it if people didn't handle my gear. I'm just . . . well, I'd prefer it. You know."

I did know. When it comes to superstitions, cowboys have got everybody beat but gypsies and Irishmen. I've never met an Irish gypsy cowboy, but I bet he wouldn't be able to pull himself out of his bedroll in the morning for all the bad omens he'd see in the wrinkles of his blanket. If this Sweet fellow got riled when folks touched his saddle, well, that wasn't so strange. I myself get the sweats whenever I see a white dog or a man in yellow trousers. Don't ask me why, for I don't know. Whatever the reason, it reminds me to be tolerant of other men's hoodoos.

"Don't fret about a thing, Joe," I said to Sweet. "You just wait here and I'll rustle you up a fine cow-pony in no time. That alright by you, boss?"

"Sure," Charlie said. "We've jawed long enough. It's time to see whether my new hand can keep his britches on the backside of a horse."

That brought three smiles out to shine on the world. But one of us didn't seem to be in a smiling mood. I'm sure a blue-ribbon deducer like yourself doesn't have to be told who that was.

Sweet made himself useful right quick. Charlie had him ride swing on the left side of the herd, not far behind me, so I got a chance to see if the man was as good as his mustard. He was. He cut in stragglers before they got five steps from the herd. And he did it easy, without getting too spicy about it in that way that can rile a steer up. It wasn't like he was stopping a stampede barefoot and blindfolded, but he was making my job easier, and the jobs of the flank riders and drag riders behind us. So that meant Sweet was hunky-dory as far as that half of the outfit was concerned.

After we had the herd bedded down for the night, Charlie

introduced Sweet to the rest of the boys. Everyone huzzahed him for showing up just when we needed the help, japing about how he was "sweet" to ride with us to Dodge.

"Nothin' sweet about it," Sweet joked back. "For one thing, I ain't got a horse." He reached up, removed his hat and ran his fingers through his hair. "And for another thing, I like my scalp where it is."

"You've kinda grown attached to it, huh?" called out Tornado Monroe, who earned his handle by being the biggest blowhard on the prairie.

That drew out a few chuckles, but poor Peanuts and Billy were still too fresh in the ground for anyone to laugh much. An awkward silence followed. As so often happened when Tornado met a moment of quiet, he endeavored to put an end to it as quickly as possible.

"'Joe Sweet.' Hmmmm," he said. "That sounds kinda familiar now I think about it. Any reason I oughta know that name?"

The friendly expression on Sweet's face suddenly pulled up lame. "No reason," he said.

"But I do swear I've heard that name somewhere before," Tornado said, not noticing the change in Sweet's disposition. "Where'd you say you was from?"

Sweet suddenly stopped worrying about living up to his name. "Is this fat-mouth accusing me of something," he snarled.

Every man in camp turned to stone.

"Well, is he?"

I'd given Sweet his gun back earlier that day, and he looked mad enough to use it if Tornado so much as blinked.

You never know which way Tornado's going to spin, but this time he chose to go easy.

"I didn't mean nothin'," he said.

Charlie stepped up now, trying out a friendly grin that was meant to calm Sweet down. He put a hand on the man's shoulder. "No need for a fuss. Far as we're concerned, you're—"

Sweet shrugged away Charlie's hand. "Nobody lays hold of

me. Me or my gear either one. You all understand that?"

Nobody said if they did or didn't. They just watched quietly as Sweet grabbed up his saddle and stomped off. When he was far enough away, one of the boys let out a low whistle.

"Feller's sure got a temper on him, don't he?" Greasy Pete said.

There were murmurs of agreement, and though Sweet came over to the fire later that night and tried to make nice, everyone was wary around him after that. We all fell into the habit of watching him out of the corners of our eyes. It was like having your sister marry a rattlesnake. He was one of us now, but we couldn't stop wondering who he was going to sink his teeth into next.

We were a mighty sulky bunch around the fire that night. Only one hand looked anything but glum. And it was the very fellow who usually went slinking off by himself the first chance he got.

Gustav was watching Sweet like the man was a fireworks display, looking a little amazed and a little amused. When I asked him why he seemed so perked up for once, all he'd say was, "As Mr. Holmes might say, we've got ourselves a real three-piper here."

Frankly, I couldn't make heads nor tails out of that, and a part of me worried that my brother had finally rounded the bend from "peculiar" to flat-out "loco."

Over the next few days, though, it was Sweet who had us all truly worried. The man's temper flared up every time the outfit gathered together. Somebody was always standing too close to his saddle or asking the wrong question or just remarking that the sky sure was blue in the wrong tone of voice. It got so bad that a few of the boys went to Charlie and asked him to just give Sweet a horse and tell him to clear out. Charlie shook his head.

"We've still got near two weeks on the trail before we reach Dodge," he said. "I need all the hands I can get, even if one of 'em is touched in the head."

So all of us had to keep right on tiptoeing around Sweet like he was a hornet's nest under a hat. But the more we bent over backwards not to stir him up, the louder he buzzed.

"What're you lookin' at?" he'd say. Or "You got somethin' you wanna ask me?" Or, more often than anything else, "One step closer to my gear and I'll shot your foot off."

As Sweet grew more and more ornery, my brother grew more and more excited, almost tickled even. Oh, he hid it from everybody else, but I could see it in his eyes every time Sweet fired off his mouth. He insisted on being mysterious about it all though, and eventually I decided to save my stomach the irritation and avoid talking to Sweet and Gustav both.

Sweet had been kicking at us for five days before we finally found the burr under his saddle. We were just finishing up supper when Tornado piped up with, "Don't throw out the whistle berries yet, Pete. We got us some company."

All the boys sat up straight and followed Tornado's gaze out toward the east, and lo and behold there was a rider heading in for camp. We gave him a few friendly yahoos, and he took off his hat and yahooed us right back. A visitor on the trail is usually a welcome thing indeed, for it breaks up the monotony, offers an opportunity to become acquainted with the latest events of the day and gives a man a chance to trot out all his favorite jokes, stories and songs . . . the ones his compadres grew sick of long ago. Since our only other caller in weeks had been less than a rousing success—that caller being Sweet—everyone was looking forward to doing some *real* socializing.

Everyone, that is, except for Sweet himself. There were no yahoos from him, and as the stranger rode up and dismounted Sweet pierced the man with that cactus-prickle stare of his.

"Hello there, fellers," the stranger said. "Mind if I hitch up my horse and join you?"

"Go right ahead," Charlie said. "Fix yourself up with a plate off the commissary there and come grab some beans."

"Thank you." The man wrapped his reins around a wagon wheel and pulled a plate out of the chuck box. "My name's Les Pryor." He started toward the fire, a friendly smile on his dirt-covered face. "I'm—" The plate slipped through his fingers, and the smile followed it toward the ground.

His gaze was stuck on one man. Joe Sweet.

In the instant it took us to realize something was wrong, Pryor had already filled his hand with a gun.

"Nobody move," he said.

Charlie being the trail boss, we all left it to him to ask the obvious question.

"What in the hell do you think you're doin'?"

"My job." Pryor reached up and gave his chest a couple of swats. Prairie dust billowed off the front of his shirt, and something pinned there took to shining in the firelight. It was a badge.

"George Sweetman," Pryor said, aiming the words straight at Sweet, "you're under arrest."

Sweet muttered a curse that would make a bear blush.

"No use complain' about it, Sweetman," the lawman said. "It's the rope for you for sure this time."

The rest of us looked back and forth between the two men, so slackjawed we couldn't form words. A dime novel was suddenly playing out right in our midst, and we were filled with awe. True to form, it was Tornado who was able to get his mouth working first.

"We don't know this feller," he said to Pryor. "He just joined up with us a few days ago."

"That's right," Charlie added. "His horse was dead. He said he'd run across a war party. A few of my men lost their scalps about a week back, so we let him ride with us."

Pryor flicked a skeptical look in Charlie's direction. "You the leader of this outfit?"

Charlie nodded. "Yes, sir."

"You got any papers to back that up?"

"I sure do. They're in that saddlebag right over there."

Charlie pointed at his saddle. It was sitting just a few paces from the fire.

"Alright. Go get 'em. But if there's anything in there other than travelin' papers . . . "

Charlie got up and started moving slowly toward his gear, his hands spread out before him. "Don't worry about that. We'll have this all sorted out in a trice."

A moment later, Pryor was flipping through the papers as best he could one-handed. The other hand still had a gun in it. And it was still pointed in our general direction.

"What's your name?" Pryor asked.

"Charlie Higgebottom."

"Who do you work for?"

"The Lone Star Land and Cattle Company Incorporated."

"Where are you headed?"

"Montana. The Blackfeet reservation up on the Yellowstone."

Pryor handed the papers back to Charlie, favoring him with a grin. "Well, looks like I owe you gents an apology."

The whole outfit heaved such a big sigh of relief it's a wonder we didn't blow out the fire.

"No need for apologies," Charlie said. "Just tell us what's goin' on here."

"First things first. Would one of you fellers be willin' to hold a gun on that coyote over there?"

Seeing as how he meant Sweet, there were plenty of enthusiastic volunteers. Pryor holstered his gun.

"Mind if I borrow me some rope?" he asked Charlie.

"Now hold on, sheriff or deputy or whatever you are," Charlie said. "Sweet there might not be the most easygoin' feller I've run across, but he's part of my outfit now, and I personally don't know that he's committed any crime."

"Oh, he has. Just about every kind you could think of," Pryor said. "And his name's 'Sweetman,' not 'Sweet.' George Sweetman."

Sweet finally spoke up for himself then. "My name's Joe Sweet, I swear it. I'm not an outlaw. This feller's crazy."

"Well," Pryor said. But before he could get out another word, a different voice spoke up.

"Look in the man's saddlebags."

We all turned toward Gustav. He was sitting a short hop away from the fire, leaning back against his saddle. His face was serious, but his eyes had a little chuckle in them.

"Sweet's saddlebags. Why don't we see what's in 'em."

Tornado clapped his hands. "That's right! He was always so damned touchy about them bags. Must be somethin' in 'em!"

There was a little stampede to Sweet's gear, but Tornado ended up at the front of the herd. "Well, lookee here," he said, pulling out a handful of yellow papers.

One of the them was a handbill. Tornado held it up for all to see. The word "WANTED" was printed across the top. Underneath was a drawing of a rat-faced man with dark eyes and a bushy mustache.

"If I didn't know any better, I'd say this was our pal Joe Sweet," Tornado said. "Except the poster here says his name is George Sweetman."

"Awww, it couldn't be Joe anyhow," one of the other boys added with a grin, "seein' as how this Sweetman's wanted for cattle rustlin', horse thievin', robbery and murder. Why, our sweet Joe would never get mixed up in such goings-on! Ain't that right, Sweetie?"

A thunderclap of guffaws rolled out across the plains, and the boys began passing the other papers around and reading them aloud. You might have heard that some frontier outlaws are so stuck on themselves they save their "clippings." Well, I can tell you now that it's true. The saddlebag was stuffed with stories torn out of newspapers, each of them recounting the misdeeds of one George Sweetman.

We all knew we'd be talking this one up around many a campfire in the years ahead, so we were making the most of it, giggling and firing off japes and jabs at "Sweetie" as Charlie brought Pryor the rope he'd asked for. The only one who didn't get any digs in was my brother, who was still leaning back against his saddle, watching us caper around like kids.

"I hate to tell you this, Mr. Pryor," Tornado said, "but there ain't a sturdy branch within twenty miles of here."

"No need for a tree," Pryor said. He led Sweetman over to the wagon, sat him down and proceeded to tie him to the same wheel he'd hitched his horse to. Sweetman cursed under his breath the whole time but didn't kick up any real trouble.

"Well, if you ain't gonna stretch his neck, what're you gonna do?" I asked.

"I'm takin' him in," Pryor said. "And you're all gonna help me."

That ended the party straight away.

"What are you talkin' about?" Charlie asked, though the sudden chill in his voice said he already knew the answer.

"I'm talkin' about deputizing all you fellers. I'm based out of Vinson, and my posse packed it in three days ago. If I'm gonna get him back to town I'm gonna need help."

"Vinson?" Charlie shook his head. "That's south of here, friend. Three or four *days* south. We're headed north."

"I know that. But look . . . we had a regular army out after Sweetman and his gang a few days back. He was ridin' with five, six other men at the time. I don't know where they got to, but if I try to take him in alone—"

"Oh, don't worry about them, lawman," Sweetman broke in, smiling for the first time since Pryor rode into camp. "They up and left me after your posse put a bullet in my horse. They're probably half-way to Mexico by now. You won't get any trouble out of those boys."

The words seemed right enough, but the smile undercut them somehow. Sweetman looked like a spider trying to coax a fly into a kiss.

"We're cowhands, not gunmen," Charlie said to Pryor. "We've got a herd to look after. That's our job. We can't help you do yours. I'm sorry."

Pryor eyed Charlie scornfully, then looked past him at the rest of the outfit. "There's a reward," he said. "I'll give a share to every man who comes with me."

Tornado held up the handbill with Sweetman's face on it. "It says five hundred dollars here. Divide that up between us all and you ain't got enough for a haircut."

"That poster's a month old," Pryor said. "Sweetman here's caused so much trouble along the Old Western Trail the Kansas Cattlemen's Association threw in another two thousand last week."

Sweetman grinned, looking pleased that his worth had increased five times. Tornado whistled. The rest of the men mumbled at each other, all of them saying more or less the same thing: "That's a lot of cash."

Charlie could sense that the outfit was pulling away from him. "Now, fellers, think about this. Vinson's gotta be a hundred miles out of our way. We can't just—"

"You say you'll cut up the reward equal? One share for every man?" Tornado asked Pryor.

Pryor shrugged. "Why not? If I try to collect the whole kit and caboodle myself, I'll just end up with a bullet in my back. But with you boys behind me—"

"Won't be none of my boys behind you, Pryor," Charlie growled, squinting and digging in his heels and straightening up his spine and generally trying to look like the kind of trail boss a man doesn't argue with.

Tornado wasn't spooked. "Oh, shut your trap, Charlie," he said. "I say we help the man."

"We can't."

"Says who?"

"Says *me*!"

"Well, I don't give a damn!"

And the shouting match got going full steam. There was no way Charlie could win, him being outnumbered something like ten to one, but he gave it a good try nonetheless, screaming out insults until his face was red as any Apache's. I noticed in a sort of a back-of-the-mind way that my brother wasn't jumping in on Charlie's behalf, but I was too busy shouting my way into the debate to wonder where he stood on things. Pryor got into the mix of it here and there too, saying "You'll have more waitin' for you in Vinson than you will in Billings" and "It'll only be a week out of your way" and "We live in a democracy, fellers. Just put it to a vote and be done with it." That last one sounded mighty reasonable to most of us.

"Everybody stop your yappin' and we'll settle this quick with a show of hands," Tornado called out. "Now then, raise your hand if you think we oughta—"

Just about every man Jack of us was about to shoot his paw into the air and send us riding off to Vinson. But before Tornado could finish calling for the vote, a familiar voice piped up again.

"Whoa now! Hold on there!"

Gustav was standing by Pryor's horse, and as we turned to face him, he said something that made me wonder if we needed to have him trussed up next to Sweetman.

"Boys," he said, "I think we need to ask ourselves a very important question: What would Sherlock Holmes do in this situation?"

It had been weeks since I'd read out "The Red-Headed League" for the whole bunch, so it took a few seconds for the words "Sherlock" and "Holmes" to come together in their heads. When it did, the boys either snickered or shook their heads in confusion.

"Who's this Holmes feller?" Pryor asked.

"An Englishman," Charlie said with a sad sigh. "One of them 'detectives.'"

"Well, what's he got to do with us?"

"Plenty, Mr. Pryor," my brother said. "Looked at the right way."

Charlie and Tornado shared a little glance that said they'd struck on something they could agree on: Old Red had left his sanity along the trail somewhere in North Texas.

Gustav smiled grimly. "I know what you're thinkin'. But just hear me out. If you still wanna take us chargin' off to Vinson after I've had my say, well, I'll forfeit my part of the reward."

I could see lips moving soundlessly in the flickering light of the fire. The boys were doing some quick mathematics. My brother's share wouldn't mean too much when spread around the group, but it must have been enough.

"Go ahead," Tornado said.

Gustav took a deep breath, cleared his throat and had his say. For a man unaccustomed to speechifying, he did a whiz-bang job of it. His voice quavered once or twice early on, but once he built up a head of steam there was no stopping him.

"Fellers," he began, "you know me. I'm the kinda cow puncher who likes to keep both boots square on the ground or firm in the stirrups. I'm not one for flights of fancy or unnecessary gum-flutterin'. So I'm not just mouthin' off here for my own amusement. If I don't miss my guess, each and every man in this outfit has a bull's-eye on his back, and we better get 'em off lickety-split or there won't be anyone left to do the buryin'.

"Now a month or so back we heard how Mr. Sherlock Holmes cracked up a gang of bandidos over in London, England. He didn't do it with fast guns or quick fists. He did it with sharp eyes. He saw the hidden connections 'twixt this thing and that thing— connections that were there for any man to see if he just tilted his head a bit and found the right angle of lookin'.

"That kinda thinkin' made a powerful impression on me. I have to admit, there was a part of me that was hopin' for a chance to try it out myself. Well, boys, I got my chance and I took it. You can rest assured I wasn't too happy about it, though.

"If you'll recall, it was me'n'Big Red that went back for Billy and Peanuts after we lost 'em in that stampede. What I saw put me in mind of Mr. Holmes right off. Somethin' didn't sit right, and I did my best to work out what it was.

"First thing was how the boys was killed. They were each of 'em stabbed in the gut and chest. Now think about that. Where's a man gotta be to poke someone that way? Why, right in front of him, that's where. But Billy and Peanuts were doin' their rounds. They were mounted. How's a Kiowa or Comanche kill a man on horseback? With an arrow or a bullet or by hoppin' right on the horse with him and stabbin' him in the back or reachin' around and slicin' his throat.

"And then there was where the bodies were left. They were propped up against a bluff, nice and tidy. Now you can't tell me they died that way—sittin' side by side while two somebodies went to work on 'em with blades. No, sir. They were killed somewhere else and moved.

"But why? Well, here's one thing to ponder on: If they'd been left where they died, what would have happened? A few hundred head of cattle would've run over 'em, that's what, and there wouldn't have been so much as a fingernail left for us to find.

"So what are we to think? A gaggle of renegade Indians talked Billy and Peanuts down off their saddles, knifed 'em, scalped 'em, dragged 'em out of the way so their bodies wouldn't get mussed up any further, then made off with . . . how many head did we lose? Just a dozen or so? No. Uh-uh. It just don't figure.

"Of course, I was chewin' on this as we moseyed up the trail. But I was doin' it quiet-like cuz I didn't have enough conclusions sewn together to make half a hankie. And then we ran across Mr. Sweetman there, and suddenly I had me a whole new mouthful to chew on.

"I knew he was nothin' but venom and manure practically the minute he opened his mouth. He said his horse got shot and lamed up so he had to put it down. Well, I took care to get up close to that pinto of his. There were two wounds alright: one in the head, one in the flank. But it was clear as day which one came first. You get a horse shot in the hindquarters, run it across the prairie, it's gonna be soaked in sweat and blood. But that carcass was dry as desert dirt, and the blood around its head was already baked to a crust. That horse had been dead over two hours before we showed up. The shot we heard—the one into the haunch—that was just to draw us in.

"So we ride up, and this crafty outlaw gets the drop on us. Fine. Makes sense. But then my baby brother—who, try as he might, ain't exactly Comanche material when it comes to stealth—is able to sneak up and lay him out with one swat? A swat that's half air? You don't need a hound dog's smeller to know that stinks.

"Then once Sweetman's back on his feet he doesn't waste two minutes before he's hissin' like a wildcat cuz I'm strayin' too close to his saddlebags. And when we join up with the rest of the outfit, every other thing out of his mouth is, 'My saddlebags! My saddlebags! Touch 'em and die!'

"Well, it was easy enough to figure out what that really meant. Tell a boy fifty times an hour not to look in the cellar and you know he'll be creepin' down there with a lantern first time you turn your back. Sweetman was desperate for us to look in those damn bags.

"Only he didn't count on how easily buffaloed you fellers are. I finally lost my patience yesterday morning and sneaked me a look when I came in off watch. Sweet made it easy for me by gettin' up to make water when I strolled into camp. Why, he practically handed the saddlebags to me and said, 'Have at it.'

"It seemed mighty curious to me that an outlaw named 'George Sweetman' would come up with an alias as wispy thin as 'Joe Sweet' then practically wave a wanted poster under the nose of every man he met. I figured if I sat back and watched a little while longer, Sweetman's real plan would come into view soon enough. So I kept my trap shut and pretty soon our lawman here arrived, and there the whole thing was, stretchin' out before me like a wide open valley.

"Billy and Peanuts weren't killed by Indians. They were killed by the only folks who could somehow coax 'em off their horses before planting a knife in their guts—white men. They were scalped and left to find so we'd blame a raidin' party off a reservation. The killers only took a few head of cattle cuz they were gunnin' for bigger game.

"We might've set off after the raidin' party—leavin' the herd sittin' out there on the trail with hardly a hand around to greet whatever rustlers might happen along. Or, with the outfit down a couple men and a band of scalp-hungry braves on the prowl, we might've put in at the nearest town. That would have been Vinson.

"But Charlie, he chose to push on, so we kept headin' north. Then a few days later, Sweetman falls into our laps, and he does everything but hand-deliver a telegram tellin' us he's an outlaw with a bounty on his head. And if we wanted to collect that bounty, where would we go? Again, the nearest town. Vinson.

"But none of us gets the message . . . or so Sweetman thinks. So a sheriff's deputy just happens across our trail and spots Sweetman right off. Takes him without a fight, too. And where does this lawman want us to go? Where else? Vinson.

"And it's a funny thing about this lawman. Quite a coincidence. His horse's wearin' the Diamond T brand. And that just happens to be the same brand I saw on Sweetman's pinto.

"What am I to make of that? Well, there's only one thing to make. Both those horses were stolen from the same place by the same gang, and this feller callin' himself 'Pryor' is no more a deputy than the beans I ate for dinner. He and Sweetman want us to turn southeast toward Vinson. I suspect they've got a crooked buyer there just waitin' for our herd—and probably a few gunmen sittin' up in the hills, whittlin' the hours away till we get our steers close to town and they can pick us off at their leisure.

"That's how I reckon it all, anyhow. As my brother's reminded me a few times, I ain't no Sherlock Holmes, so I could be seein' things all cross-eyed. But I've been workin' hard to see it straight, the way Mr. Holmes would, and if I've got it wrong . . . well, I invite you boys to tell me another way to figure it that makes half the sense."

Nobody said a word for nearly a quarter of a minute. We all just stared at Old Red in a trance of glassy-eyed stupefaction. It was Pryor who broke the spell with a dry chuckle.

"Whoooeee," he said. "I think your friend here must've been ridin' without a hat today. The sun cooked his brain right through, eh, fellers? Now to get back to the business at hand . . . . "

Every man in the outfit turned to face him, and those faces didn't look thunderstruck any longer. They looked mad.

"Don't tell me you think that crazy little coot's onto somethin'?"

Pryor didn't get an answer in words. He got it in action. Charlie and Tornado stepped up together to grab his arms. He tried for his six-gun, but I got a fist upside his skull before he was half-way to the grip. It was a good, solid punch, too. Pryor sagged in Charlie and Tornado's hands, and when they realized he'd been knocked cold they simply let him plop to the ground like a patty out of a bull's backside. I bent down and unholstered Pryor's gun and handed it to Charlie.

He thanked me with a little nod, then turned to glare at the rest of the boys. "Anyone here still feel like holdin' a vote?" he grumbled.

Everybody stared down at the dirt, suddenly looking mighty ashamed of themselves.

"Alright then."

Charlie turned toward my brother, and his scowl blossomed into a big grin.

"Well, Old Red, looks like that Sherlock Holmes has got hisself some competition."

He gave my brother a shake of the hand so enthusiastic it nearly tore his arm off, and suddenly the rest of the boys were pushing in around them both, slapping my brother on the back and huzzahing his world-class smarts. Gustav withstood it all in bashful silence for a moment before he held up his hands and called for everyone to quiet down.

"Thank you, fellers, thank you. But before y'all go and elect me president, someone needs to get over to the chuck wagon and tie up Sweetman before he can cause any trouble."

I looked past my brother and the men gathered around him. "Ain't he already . . . well, I'll be damned!"

Sweetman was on his feet next to Pryor's horse. He had a rifle half-way out of its saddle scabbard. In a flash he had nearly a dozen guns on him. He let go of the rifle butt and kicked at the dirt.

"How'd you know he wasn't tied up proper?" Charlie asked.

"Who was doin' the tyin'?"

Charlie nodded. "Pryor."

"That's right. I figured he might want his partner free to lend a hand, so I put an eye on the rope he'd wrapped around Sweetman.

It was done up with a timber hitch knot, so Sweetman could slip it any time he chose. He had to wait and see if his play was gonna come off, but once Pryor was down he was bound to pull somethin'."

Everyone shook their heads, marveling at how simple all that deducifying seemed once it was talked out. Over the next few weeks, the boys had Gustav go over the whole thing again and again. It got to be torture for Sweetman and Pryor, who had to hear over and over how my brother had tripped them up. Sweetman would get to swearing a blue streak whenever the subject came up, which naturally inspired everyone to reminisce about it all the more.

The two outlaws rode with us as far as Dodge City. We kept both of them out in the open, and not a second passed when there wasn't a shotgun stuck in Sweetman's face. If the rest of his gang trailed us, looking for a chance to spring him, we never knew it. Should they have tried, he wouldn't have done them much good as a mastermind, not having a head and all.

When we got to Dodge, it turned out the reward on Sweetman was still good—five hundred of it, anyway. Pryor was just dripping a little honey when he said it was up over two thousand. We picked up some extra dinero, though, since Pryor had a bounty on him too, only it was under the name "Frank Adams."

The boys took a vote on it and decided to give all the money for Sweetman to Old Red. My brother's too retiring a fellow to argue with such gestures, so he just slipped me a big wad of the cash and told me to treat the outfit to the biggest rave-up Kansas had ever seen. Charlie had consented to give us two whole days to live it up before we hit the trail again, so I used the money to indulge the fellows in every pleasure Dodge City had to offer, which is plenty.

Gustav didn't partake of the fun, though. He used some of his newfound fortune to rent a hotel room and hire a working girl to spend the days there with him. It was all purely gentlemanly though, I assure you. You see, he managed to dig up a copy of *A Study in Scarlet* somewhere around town and he needed someone to read it to him.

If only that gal had the patience to write for him, too. Gustav tried putting this letter together with her, but she kept interrupting his yarn-spinning with questions. The man can't even read, for Pete's sake, and she's asking *him* how to spell "Sherlock." He finally came and grabbed me out of the Blue Boar Saloon and forced me up here practically with a gun in my ribs.

But even though I lost the chance at a few more drinks, a few more hands of poker and a few more hours of sleep, I'm actually sort of glad it turned out this way. Writing this all down was a mighty big chore, and it helps me feel a little bit of extra ownership in my brother's world-class conundrum-busting. I reckon your pal Dr. Watson probably feels the same way sometimes. You might want to ask him about that.

Well now, looks like I finished up just in time. Charlie's started pounding on the door threatening to set fire to the hotel if we don't saddle up pronto. We've still got a thousand miles of ground to cover before those Blackfeet get their steers. Wish us luck, Mr. Holmes.

Anyway, that's how it all happened, I swear on my dust-covered soul.

Sincerely,

O.A. Amlingmeyer
Dodge City, Kansas
July 2, 1892

# GUSTAV AMLINGMEYER, HOLMES OF THE RANGE

*Harper's Weekly*
Harper & Bros., Publishers
325 to 337 Pearl Street
Franklin Square
New York

Greetings to whichever Harper I have the pleasure of addressing!

First off, let me slather on a bit of butter by telling you how much I appreciate your family's fine magazine. Out here in Montana, a person can get to thinking the world isn't anything but grass, sky and cow pies. *Harper's Weekly* is one of the ways we Westerners remind ourselves that there's still a thing called "civilization" out there and that supposedly we are a part of it. That's an important idea for folks to keep a rope on, I can assure you, for I've been to a few places where they didn't, and it was almost enough to get me believing all that science talk about men being nothing more than monkeys who traded in their tails for trousers.

As much as I admire your publication, however, I do have a notion as to how it could be improved. It has come to my attention in recent months that there are two kinds of stories much in demand by the reading public: yarns about cowboys and yarns about detectives. I know about the first because, until a few weeks back, I was a working cowpuncher myself. Many's the time I've pulled out a copy of *Buffalo Bill Stories* or *Deadwood Dick Library* and tickled the boys in the bunkhouse by reading out the most outlandish bits of balderdash contained therein. Detective tales, on the other hand, I never troubled myself with until recently, when my brother got himself a craving for them worse than a rummy craves rotgut. In the past two months, he's read dozens of the damned things—or, to be more accurate, he's *heard* dozens of them, because I do all the reading, my brother having discontinued his schooling before he could discover what follows A, B and C.

It occurs to me that cowboys being popular and detectives being popular, a cowboy detective would be twice as popular as each. And I just happen to know one, for there are lessons to be learned from detective yarns, and my brother has put them to use. An account of how he's done so is what fills the next few pages— pages that I propose you reprint in *Harper's Weekly* under the title "Gustav Amlingmeyer, Holmes of the Range." (If that title is not to your liking, feel free to brand it with another. I'm also rather partial to "Old Red's Deadly Dilemma" myself.)

Gustav Amlingmeyer, as you might have guessed, is my brother, although those who know him by his Christian name are few and far between. It's much more common to hear him hailed by the handle "Old Red." This he earned both for his sunset-red head of hair and his midnight-black disposition. My name is Otto Amlingmeyer, though I've been rechristened "Big Red" because I've got the same hair as my elder brother but about a foot more of spine and leg beneath it.

It was only natural that Old Red and I should become cowboys, as we grew up with ample supplies of the profession's two most important requirements: poverty and desperation. Though drovering is hardly the best way to go about ridding yourself of either, somehow we've managed to build up a small stake—though Old Red might argue with that "we." Like many a hand, I'm a man who likes to cut his wolf loose at the end of a trail, and no doubt wine, women and song would claim every penny if the purse-strings were mine alone to draw tight or pull open. Gustav, on the other hand, manages to keep his wolf hog-tied at all times, and he's insisted on squirreling away almost all of our pay.

"Pushin' other men's cows ain't gonna get us nowhere," he would tell me when I fussed over this. "We gotta save up and buy somethin' of our own if we wanna end up anything more than a couple saddle bums."

I always assumed that the "something of our own" Gustav talked about would be a little ranch or farm somewhere. So you can imagine my dismay when my brother informed me we were going into the restauranting business. I was in a saloon here in Billings at the time, and though I was the one doing the drinking I asked Old Red whether he was drunk or crazy, for surely it had to be one or the other.

"Nothin' crazy about cookin' for folks," he said. "People always need food."

I didn't bother asking him if he was joking, seeing as how he cracked a funny about as often as a coyote yodels "Onward, Christian Soldiers." "How much?" I asked instead.

"Two hundred."

That was nearly half what we had saved. I yelled out to the bartender to bring me some of his best whiskey, pronto, as soon enough I would not be able to afford it. Once the first shot was tickling my liver, I nodded at Old Red.

"Alright," I said. "I'm ready. Tell me the rest."

And that he did. It seems he'd bumped into a fellow name of Starchy Baker who'd been one of the belly cheaters on a big West Texas roundup Gustav had ridden in '88. Starchy had tired of doing all his cooking out of the back of a chuck wagon, so he'd traded in his dutch oven for the real thing. He had himself a little lunch counter out near the stockyards, and there were always enough outfits coming through to keep his griddles hot. Only Starchy couldn't hardly keep up anymore on account of the rheumatoid arthritis that had driven him off the trail in the first place. It was getting worse now, and Starchy figured he needed a long soak in the Arkansas hot springs to uncurl his boogered-up bones.

"So you bought him out for two-hundred dollars."

"He wanted three at first," Old Red said. "I haggled him

down pretty good."

I tossed back another gulp of tonsil varnish. "We'll see about that."

We walked out to the edge of town and Gustav showed me what two-hundred dollars could buy a man in Billings: a rotting shack, twenty rickety chairs, a couple wobbly tables and an ancient cast-iron stove.

"It ain't the looks that count. It's the location," Gustav said, probably just blowing back at me something Starchy had said to him.

"Well, let's not forget another little certain something there, Brother," I replied. "How about the damn *food*! You can hardly tell salt from pepper, and the last time I tried fixin' up any grub I nearly killed six men and a dog."

Now my brother's temper is a strange and unpredictable creature. Some days he might snarl at you for pouring your coffee too loud, other days you could tie the ends of his mustache together and he wouldn't say boo. This happened to be one of the latter kind of days, for he didn't take to screaming back at me or even raise his voice.

"You and me, we won't have to so much as crack an egg," he said. "Starchy had him an Irish gal that filled in from time to time. There's no reason we couldn't hire her on to do all the cookin'. All we'd have to do is take the orders, tote the food and tally up the money."

That took some of the bite out of me. Old Red had thought it through fine enough. Still, I felt pretty strange about trading in my chaps for an apron.

"What do you say we fire up that oven and just shovel the rest of our money straight in?" I said. But Gustav was still feeling charitable, and he didn't take the bait.

Two days later, Starchy cleared out his gear, said his goodbyes and left us to it. At last, the Amlingmeyer boys were respectable businessmen. Or at least we were as respectable as you can be when you're running around in a greasy apron fetching beans and bacon for cowboys. We had other customers too—railroad men, soldiers, drifters who'd come into a charity nickel. We certainly weren't catering to the town's leading citizens, but Gustav and I didn't mind so long as folks paid for their food and ate it without getting into a fight.

Our clientele coming from the rougher classes, we did have a tussle on our hands every so often. Some Texas drover would get salty with a buffalo soldier, hot words would lead to flying fists, and lickety-split grown men would be poking each other with forks and trying to spoon each other's eyes out. Now as I've got an uncommon amount of flesh to bring to bear, it at first fell to me to settle any dust-ups. But we quickly learned that imposing size was a less reliable peacemaker than questionable sanity. If I couldn't break up a fight quick enough to suit her, our cook would come flying out of the kitchen with a meat cleaver in her hand, a scream on her lips and a bloodthirsty look in her eyes. She'd take to swinging that blade around, and everybody in the place would duck for cover. By the time she'd calmed down and headed back into the kitchen, we'd all of us forgotten who'd been punching who in the first place. Pretty soon, I didn't bother stepping into customers' tangles, as word spread that Starchy's Cafay was under the protection of Crazy Kathy McKenna, and all she had to do was lay hand on that cleaver to restore order.

Now you might think it would hurt business, people having the impression they could end up with cold steel in their belly along with their beef stew. But cowboys being cowboys, it was the best advertisement our little establishment could have. Fellows would come in straight off the trail and order up a batch of fried chicken just so they could sit there and gawk at Crazy Kathy. Every now and then a couple of them would try to get a rise out of her by playacting they were headed for a fracas, but I soon learned to spot our amateur thespians early on and would politely suggest they take their food and their foolishness outside.

Of course, there were some townsmen who didn't find all this a real tickle, and one of them would drop by from time to time to remind us that he still wasn't laughing. Seeing as he was the town marshal, we didn't have any choice but to listen.

"That dirty mick cook of yours ever hurts anybody, I'm holdin' you two responsible," he'd say. Then he'd grab him a couple of biscuits and walk out. He was a big, boulder-headed son of a mule name of Ben Nickles, and men who opened their mouths too wide in his presence often found a gun barrel where their teeth used to be. So we just nodded, said a silent goodbye to our biscuits and then got back to work. Old Red would store up his curses until the restaurant was closed for the night, then he'd start pouring them out all over me.

"He's a disgrace to his badge," he'd say. "If there's a problem he can't solve with fists or guns, then that's a problem don't get solved at all. The man's all muscle, no method."

That last bit was considered by Gustav to be the ultimate insult to a lawman's skills. He'd made a study on "method" after stumbling upon accounts of one Sherlock Holmes of London, England. This Holmes fellow's sort of a gentleman layabout turned sleuth who solves crimes by means my brother describes as "observation and cogitation." Driving cattle's a true test for nerves and muscle, but you might as well deposit your brain in a bank before you hit the trail, for you won't be needing it until you get back. My brother being a man with little learning but much smarts, I believe drovering had become a kind of mental torture for him. His mind was dying of thirst, and this Sherlock Holmes was a cool drink of water.

Whatever the explanation for it, my brother's fascination with Holmes drove him to snatch up every detective magazine he could lay hands on. Nick Carter, King Brady, Old Cap Collier, even Madge the Society Detective—we've read about them all. It didn't take long for Gustav to turn sour on these American crimebusters, though. All muscle, no method, he said. But we were stuck with them, as a yarn about Holmes is harder to find than a Mormon in a whorehouse. Gustav's only managed to rustle up two Holmes tales so far: one called *A Study in Scarlet*, the other "The Red-Headed

# Dear Mr. Holmes

League." We end every day the same way, in the bed we share in the storeroom at the back of the shack, me reading out the story of Old Red's choice. I say a quiet prayer before we turn in that he won't ask to hear about Holmes, as I've read those two stories so many times the words are practically tattooed on my eyeballs.

Now let me warn you, spending the last waking hour of each day in the company of a dime novel detective will do strange things to your sleep. My dreams are stuffed to bursting with black-caped kidnappers and bomb-lobbing radicals and skulking Chinamen with ruby-handled daggers hidden up their silky sleeves. It's almost a relief when Crazy Kathy barges in before the break of dawn to fire up the oven, making enough noise to wake the deaf and the dead alike.

Not long after she shows up, the first customers come banging through the rickety door out front. Sometimes it's cowboys, sometimes it's railroaders. Either way, they want the same thing—coffee, biscuits, bacon, eggs. When they start asking for beefsteak or beans, I know it's getting on toward noon. Every now and then some big-mouthed bull nurse will try to cut a shine on Crazy Kathy by calling out that he wants roast goose with oyster stuffing and he wants it now. If she's in good mood, Kathy will ignore him. If she's not, she'll step out of the kitchen with that cleaver of hers and let the fellow know he's a catfish-faced son of a bitch and he's going to get beans.

For pure *mean*, we figured our cook was pretty near the hands-down champion of the Plains. But eventually a customer came along who gave her a real run for her money. His name was Jack G. Johnson, and for two weeks solid he ate nothing but Crazy Kathy's cooking—breakfast, dinner and supper. Why he did so was a mystery to us all, for he announced time and time again that it was the foulest hog-slop he'd seen heaped on a plate since his days in the Confederate army. Of course, Kathy came out to challenge this notion the first time she heard it, but this Johnson fellow called her bluff.

"Get your ass back in that kitchen before I put my boot on it, you poxy Irish slattern," he growled at her. "And the next time you make me stew see to it you put some damn salt in it."

Every man in the place got set to jump when they heard that, for surely anyone slow on his toes was about to end up with old Jack's brains in his hair. But Crazy Kathy just sneered, spat at Johnson's feet—not *on* them, you understand, *at* them—and stomped back to the griddle. It seemed Kathy had met her match, and those of us there to witness it could only gape in silent wonder. Johnson wasn't one to rest on his laurels, however.

"Hey, pimples," he said to an especially young puncher a couple chairs down from where he sat. "Stop your gawking and make yourself useful." He pointed at a salt shaker and snapped his fingers impatiently until it had been handed to him. Needless to say, the cowboy got no thanks.

Whereas Crazy Kathy added the kind of color our customers appreciate, no one appreciated Jack G. Johnson. Politics, religion, personal hygiene—no subject was taboo to him. He said men who wanted to keep Benjamin Harrison in the White House ought to have their heads examined, and men who wanted to put James Baird Weaver in Harrison's place ought to have their heads *removed*. Labor agitators should be shot on sight, but the real enemy were those Jew bankers in New York and the "mongrel races" flooding our shores from abroad. Sweep out the Chinese, the Irish, the Italians, the Poles and the Russians—and exterminate the Indians down to the last suckling child while you're at it—and then this country might really stand for something again. Or so Johnson told us.

Every so often, there would be a fellow who agreed with every little thing he said, which seemed to annoy the man more than all those labor agitators and bankers and "mongrels" combined. He'd get to ripping into the poor chowderhead's crooked teeth or ratty clothes or big feet or some such thing, and before long his one potential ally would turn against him, and Johnson would be happy again.

But where Johnson's capacity for cussedness really took the

prize was on the subject of negroes and the Civil War. My brother and I hailing from Kansas and being of German stock, we have our own feelings on this matter. Gustav was born a year after the war ended, and I didn't mosey along until six years after him, but sometimes it felt like we were both of us at Chancellorsville and Gettysburg for all the talk we heard on it in our younger days. We were much aware that we'd lost three uncles, five cousins and an aunt in the war. The uncles and one of the cousins died wearing blue. The others were cut down by rebel Bushwhackers.

We'd also known a number of negro cowboys over the years, for though you'll see nary a one in *Buffalo Bill Stories*, you'll find plenty working the trails. As with all men, some are good, some are bad. We didn't feel any hesitation about befriending the good, and one and all were welcome to spend their money in our little cookhouse.

But Johnson would get to fussing and cussing every time he found himself in the company of a negro. And if he discovered you were a Union man—or, worse yet, a Union *veteran*—he'd lay into his Northern aggression, carpetbaggers, race mixers and scoundrels speech. And if that didn't get a rise out of you, he'd wheel out the heavy artillery. The first time he did it, every customer in the place nearly emptied the stomachs they'd been trying to fill. Johnson had been storming away at Ricky Hess, a kid soda jerk who took his meals with us so he could hear the punchers blow some wind about life in the saddle. I think Ricky wanted to prove he had some eggs in his basket, for he was needling old Johnson right back, saying how Abraham Lincoln was a saint and your average Confederate soldier was nothing but a shoeless hillbilly fighting with a bent-barrel musket and a rusty butter knife.

"You want to see what the average Confederate soldier could do?" Johnson asked.

Ricky stiffened up and leaned back, getting set to dodge the old man's swing. But instead of throwing a punch, Johnson just smiled. His lips didn't stop at a simple grin though. They kept on going, pulling back until his whole face was stretched into an open-mouthed grimace, like he was screaming without making a sound.

And then the damnedest thing happened. Johnson's teeth began to *move*. They shifted to the right, shifted to the left, shifted to the right again, then wriggled themselves all the way free of his face. Johnson caught them in his hand as they fell and then held them up at Ricky.

"You see these, boy?"

Ricky nodded, staring slack-jawed at Johnson as if the man had just produced Jeff Davis from his mouth instead of a pair of dentures.

"Well, these ain't porcelain teeth. They're *Yankee* teeth, pulled from blue-bellies at Antietam." Johnson winked, and his pruned-up lips wormed themselves into another smile. "I do believe some of 'em weren't even dead yet. Those Northern boys weren't much in the way of soldiers, but I'll give 'em this much—they had some mighty fine choppers. These dentures were made for Major Dick Wheeler, my commanding officer, in 1862, and they served him well for twenty-four years. When he died, his widow was kind enough to give 'em to me. I had my son do 'em over to fit my mouth, and they've been chawin' up biscuits for me ever since."

Johnson glanced around the room and, satisfied that he had everyone's full and utterly horrified attention, got to opening and closing those dentures so it looked like his hand had itself a working mouth.

"Glory, glory Hallelujah," he sang. "Glory, glory Hallelujah. Glory, glory Hallelujah. His truth is marching on."

Ricky ran out of the place pale as a Klansman's sheet, Johnson cackling at him like some loco old squaw.

Now my brother typically adheres to a strict neutrality when it comes to customer disputes. "As long as folks can keep eatin', it ain't no business of ours," he'd say to me. But Gustav looked about ready to chuck that neutrality in favor of a public horsewhipping.

"Mr. Johnson," he said, and his voice sounded completely calm and respectful despite the words it was about to pronounce, "I'm advising you to keep those filthy things in your mouth when you're on my property or they're gonna end up . . . . "

Well, the locale my brother suggested might offend delicate sensibilities, but it should suffice to say that depositing a pair of dentures there would be an unpleasant experience for all concerned.

Johnson didn't bat an eye. He just sucked in those teeth of his and got back to work on his chicken and dumplings. And come suppertime he was back again.

Gustav was glad enough to have the old man's money, if not his company. But I had to wonder why Johnson had to spend any money on grub at all. Certainly, he didn't come to Starchy's every day out of necessity. He had both an able-bodied daughter-in-law and a prosperous son, so home-cooking or a better class of restaurant were not beyond his reach. George J. Johnson, the son, was the top dentist around, the only competition in Billings being an opium-addled old quack name of Huggins who had the devil of a time convincing folks to call him "Painless" instead of "Brainless." As a result, Doc Johnson was doing enough business to make himself a real pillar of the community, the proof of which was his recent marriage to Elsa Mueller, the daughter of one of Billings' resident preachers (Lutheran in this case) and a pillar in her own right as a leader of the town's growing temperance movement. Though it had been known that Doc Johnson was a Southerner, no one had known quite *how* Southern until Papa Johnson stepped off a train whistling "Dixie." The elder Johnson caused quite a stir, being as rude and hard-headed as his son was courtly and mild-mannered. The local tongue-flappers whispered that the old man had come West for his health, for he was a gnarled little lizard, and every day he seemed to turn more mottled and rashy-looking.

Now all this was but distant gossip for us no-accounts out on the edge of town until the day Johnson limped into Starchy's to plague us with his patronage. Despite the old man's constant complaints, *something* about our place agreed with him. He dragged himself in looking like a fellow not only at death's door but with one foot firmly inside the house. Within a few days, however, his color improved, his back straightened and he was digging into

Kathy's "hog-slop" con mucho gusto. Some folks joked that Kathy's cooking had restorative properties and should be bottled as a patent elixir. Others said Johnson would thrive in any environment in which he could make himself a nuisance. Either way, he quickly became our most loyal—and loathed—customer.

He minded Gustav's warning though, keeping his dentures perched on his gums where they belonged. But from time to time he'd brag on his "little Yankee prisoners" and set them to squirming around so much behind his smile it looked like he kept a snake in there.

While Johnson was fixed to Starchy's tight as a tick, Ricky Hess we didn't see for a while. It took him a week to work up the nerve to come back. But when he did return, he did it big, striding in puffed up like a rooster and taking an empty seat to the left of the old man.

Johnson didn't notice at first, for he had already divided his forces on two fronts, firing insults into the kitchen where Kathy was frying him up a steak while aiming the occasional barrage at the fellow to his left, a black puncher by the name of Feathers Purnell.

Though Ricky was trying to come off tough, I noticed him fiddling nervously with a salt shaker as I walked up to take his order.

"I'll have whatever he's havin'," he said, jerking a thumb at Johnson. When the old buzzard turned to point his beak at him, Hess gave him a hearty slap on the back. "How ya doin' today, reb? What's the latest news from Richmond?"

Johnson gave him a squint hot enough to bake a cake. "I'd thank you to keep your hands off me, you miserable little piss-puddle," he said.

I got set to haul myself over the counter and pull him and Ricky apart, but before either man could fire off a punch toward the other's face, Kathy stomped out of the kitchen and threw a plate down in front of Johnson.

"There's yer steak," she said. "May ya choke on it and catch the first coach to Hell."

Kathy's curse brought a smile to the old man's lips, and he turned away from Ricky and called after her, "If it tastes as bad as your cookin' usually does, chokin' to death will be sweet mercy."

Johnson snatched up his fork and knife, and for a second there everyone watching expected one or the other to end up in Ricky's throat. But the old man got to sawing away at his beef instead. He stuffed a big, bloody strip of it into his mouth, gave it a couple of chews, then winced and swallowed.

"Damn, woman," he said, bringing a hand up to rub the left side of his face. "I asked for steak, not fried rope." His cheeks bulged on one side, then the other as his tongue probed around inside his mouth. He slid a finger in there and fished out a small, yellow sliver. "I've eaten shoe leather more tender than this. Ain't nothin' on this plate but gristle and bone."

But as much as he complained about that first bite, it didn't stop him from carrying on with a second and a third and so on. In between chews he cheerfully badgered Kathy and Ricky and Feathers, squeezing off affronts at each one in turn before starting around the circle again when he'd made a full rotation of it. Kathy and Feathers took it quiet, her busying herself with her cooking and him busying himself with his fried oysters. But young Hess sparred back, and whenever he and Johnson swallowed their last mouthfuls I figured we'd be right back where we started, with the two of them ready to throw around fists instead of harsh words.

After a few minutes, however, Johnson seemed to lose his taste for fighting and steak both. He went all quiet half-way through a remark about Feathers' mother and dropped his knife and fork on the counter-top with a clatter that turned me around from the dirty plates I'd been handing to Gustav. Johnson had gone sweaty slick since the last time I'd glanced his way, and he proceeded to wrap his arms around his stomach and let out a moan like a motherless calf on a cold night.

"You alright, mister?" Feathers asked.

"Do I . . . look . . . alright?" Johnson gasped, managing to be nasty even when it appeared he hardly had the strength to stick out his tongue. He pushed his chair back and stood up. "I just . . . need to . . . go outside and . . . ."

He didn't get anywhere near outside. After three wobbly steps, he swooned and hit the floor, managing to turn over a table and cover himself with other men's dinner in the process.

Feathers made it to him first, rolling Johnson over and brushing cornbread crumbs and butter off his face. The old man's eyes rolled back in his head, the lids fluttering, and a breathy whisper slipped through his trembling lips.

"What's he sayin'?" I asked.

Feathers leaned his ear in close. Then he put his hand up to Johnson's face again, this time wrapping the palm and fingers across the old man's eyes and nose and sort of giving a little squeeze. Then the cowboy stood up, a look on his face like the kind a fellow gets after taking a sip of rancid buttermilk. But he didn't say a thing.

Gustav piped up then. "Frank," he called out to one of our regulars, "go get Doc Snow. Anvil, I think you oughta fetch Doc Johnson. And quick, boys."

"You think he's dyin'?" I asked as Frank and Anvil darted out the door.

Gustav gave me one of those stares that tell me he's not altogether convinced he and I could come from the same bloodline.

Johnson took to heaving and purging after that, and soon he and the dirt floor around him were far from a pretty sight. As much as I might have cursed the man in my heart the past few weeks, it still stung to see him squirming like a gut-shot dog.

Now one thing you've got to understand about a town like Billings: Entertainment and spectacle are in mighty short supply. Not having an opera house, a music hall, a zoo garden or any other modern place of amusement, folks out here have to make due with shootings, hangings and fires. Misfortunes of all sorts being popular viewing, a man dropping a hammer on his foot is just about all you need to draw a crowd. So by the time Frank got back with Doc Snow, the two of them had to push their way through a swarm of spectators that had gathered around to witness the infamous Jack G. Johnson's final moments. Thanks to that crowd, Frank and the doctor missed those moments by about a minute, for when they finally wriggled past the last onlooker, Johnson was dead.

That didn't keep Doc Snow from hunkering down and giving the man's twisted-up corpse a good going over. Snow was an altogether over-educated, over-mannered and over-efficient fellow to have landed in a place like Billings without some trouble back East sending him our way. Folks viewed him as the gift horse you don't look in the mouth, however, so nobody asked questions about his past. They just listened to what he had to say and thanked the Lord they didn't have to get all their medical advice from strangers selling miracle cures off the back of medicine show wagons.

So it hit the crowd like lightning when the town's one and only respected physician stood up, brushed off his frock coat, and announced, "This man was poisoned."

While everyone else was still sputtering out things like "What?" and "Did he say 'poisoned'?" and "Hooo-whee! Murder!" Old Red was bending over the body asking the doc how he'd come by his conclusion.

"The symptoms," Snow said. "And you'll notice crescents of white on the fingernails and a whiff of garlic still on the tongue. All signs of *poudre de succession*."

Gustav looked up at Snow. "All signs of what now?"

"*Poudre de succession*," Snow said again (and I'll admit right here I only know how to spell it out because I tracked him down this morning and asked him).

Before Snow could lay out for my brother and the rest of us rabble exactly what he was talking about, Anvil Hayes elbowed his way to the center of the room.

"Couldn't get Doc Johnson. He's out to the Lazy P pullin' teeth. Won't be back 'til tonight," Anvil said. "I told his wife the old man's sick, though." He looked down at the body, and I couldn't tell if the chagrin on his face was because Johnson had died or because he'd missed the dying.

Just then the crowd began to part like the Red Sea for Moses, and I knew before he even stepped into my sight that Billings' top lawman had arrived to irritate my brother with his enthusiastic application of muscle over method.

"Damn it all, is that man dead?" Marshal Nickles asked as he pushed past Anvil.

"As dead as the proverbial doornail," Dr. Snow replied.

"Doc said it was poison," I added, trying to be helpful. "Poodrey dee zoo-zay-zion or some such."

"Arsenic," Snow finally explained.

That sent another lightning bolt through the place, and half the men there seemed compelled to shout out "Arsenic!" like it was "Hallelujah!" and they were at a tent revival. But none of them hollered louder than Nickles, who immediately whirled off toward the kitchen and backed Crazy Kathy up against the stove.

"Alright," he said to her. "Let's go."

"What're ya talkin' about?" Kathy asked, a tremor of fear in her usually commanding voice. "Where would I be goin' then?"

"You're comin' with me to the jail, that's where you're goin'."

"Hold on, Marshal," my brother said, following Nickles into the kitchen. "We don't know who slipped Johnson the poison. There ain't no proof it was Kathy."

"You shut your trap. And while you're at it, shut your doors." Obviously pleased by the rare (for him) experience of making a clever remark, Nickles let his mouth tilt over into something that was half sneer, half smile. "I've warned you about lettin' this crazy Irish hag do your cookin'. Far as I'm concerned, you and your brother are practically murderers yourselves. So I'm orderin' you to close this fly-trap down 'til we can get this in front of a judge. And don't give me any back-talk about it. Just be glad you ain't under arrest . . . yet."

Then Nickles turned back to Kathy, locked a big paw on her wrist and yanked her toward the door. She unraveled a string of curses on him that would make a sailor's ears bleed, but I saw terror in her eyes. The crowd moved back to let them through, then flowed in around them like quicksand, swallowing the two up and blocking our view.

I heard Gustav sigh and start rooting around for something in the kitchen. When he stepped out, he was strapping on his gunbelt.

"Better get yourself heeled, Brother," he said to me. "We don't want poor Kathy runnin' into a lynchin' bee between here and the jail."

I dusted off my iron and strapped it on, wondering all the while if the mob wouldn't see fit to string us up too, guns or no.

As it turned out, there was no need to fret about a lynching just yet. Quite the opposite. Everyone seemed to take Johnson's murder as an excuse for a holiday, and Kathy wasn't in jail ten minutes before there were fellows outside selling boiled peanuts and ginger beer. Some folks even began spreading out blankets and setting out picnics.

Gustav and I tried to get inside the jail to have a word with Kathy, but one of Nickles' deputies encouraged us to amble along. As this encouragement came from the business end of a Winchester, we ambled. We could hear Kathy somewhere inside the jail though, still telling Nickles his head was packed full of the stuff you pay a man a penny to shovel off a stable floor.

We sparked a good bit of commentary as we weaved our way through the throng, everybody trying to play Eddie Foy with cracks like "Hey, boys! I hear the cookin' at your place is to die for!" and "Mind if I send my mother-in-law over for supper tonight?"

"Well, Old Red," I said once we'd escaped the jeers, "what do you think? The five o'clock or the eight-thirty?"

"The five o'clock or the eight-thirty *what*?"

"Train, brother. Five o'clock east, eight-thirty west. I vote for east, myself. From Miles City we can head all the way down to—"

Gustav gave me a look of disappointment and dismay he'd inherited from our mother. "We ain't goin' anywhere," he said. "Kathy needs our help."

"Oh, come now. There ain't no helpin' crazy folks. You know that. Hell, she probably did it."

"Well, then you just think of it as helpin' ourselves. It'd look mighty bad, us skeedaddlin' now. Like maybe Kathy had some help curling Johnson up. And what about Starchy's Cafay? We can't just walk away from that."

"I ain't sayin' we walk away. I'm sayin' we *run*. You heard those fellers back there. Starchy's ain't nothin' worth stickin' around for. The place was ruined the second Johnson hit the floor."

"We're stayin'," Gustav said, using the tone of voice that told me he was pulling rank. There would be no more debate. The elder brother had spoken.

"Alright. We stay. For now. But how in God's name are the two of us supposed to help Kathy?"

"It won't just be the two of us. We've got an important friend on our side."

"Oh?"

I ruminated for a second on our friends in Billings, none of whom you could label "important." "Penniless," perhaps. Or "powerless." "Drunk," "rowdy" and "smelly" would also fit just fine on most. But there wasn't an "important" in the bunch.

"Just who are you thinkin' of?"

"Why, Mr. Sherlock Holmes, of course."

My brother gave me a sly little wink, and I took to wondering if crazy is something you can catch. After all, he'd spent a lot of time in the kitchen with Kathy. Maybe she'd given him a bad case of the locos.

Not that Gustav can't do up a fine display of detective-style thinking every so often. Mr. Holmes has this way of spinning little details into big "deductions," and my brother had taken a pretty fair whack at it on a few occasions. Then one day he pointed out a fellow slurping on some soup in Starchy's and told me he'd deduced that the man was a Hebrew butcher who'd served in the army and just returned from California. Turned out he was an Italian tailor two months off the boat from Europe, and he was as far west as he'd ever been in his life. My faith in my brother's grasp of "method" was never quite the same after that.

And anyway, even Holmes himself couldn't prove trees can sing, dogs have wings and extra glue makes for tasty doughnuts. Kathy's innocence I saw as being much the same. I figured she'd walk free about the time I saw a flock of beagles flying south for the winter. Which meant Starchy's was finished, and so were we.

I was pulled free of these gloomy thoughts by an even gloomier sound—that of a woman weeping. It was Elsa Johnson, the old man's daughter-in-law. She was in our shabby little shack looking about as out of place as a pearl on a plate of baked beans. Her white silk dress could just about blind you it was so gleaming clean. She was sitting with her back to the body, her slender shoulders shuddering slightly with delicate, ladylike grief. Doc Snow held one of her hands in his and whispered quiet comforts in her ear as Howard and Andrew Gould, the paunchy namesakes of Gould Brothers Funeral Parlor, hovered over the corpse like a couple of fat-bellied vultures in thirty-dollar suits. A simple wooden box lay near the corpse. It was just for toting stiffs, I assumed, being too plain for burying the father of an honorary member of the thriving merchant class.

We'd put on hats before running off after Nickles and Kathy, and I swiped mine off my head and elbowed Old Red to remind him to do the same.

"Ma'am," I said. "I would like to convey our most sincere condolences to you and your husband in this time of loss. If there's anything we can do to be of assistance, I just ask you to let us know and it will be done."

It was my thinking that a little honey could sweeten Mrs. Johnson's disposition towards us, which might help us sidestep reciprocations of a legal nature. But when that woman stood and turned to face us, she looked at me like I'd dumped a bucket of cold water on her head.

"You've already done enough," she said, her voice icy calm despite the tears she'd been shedding just a moment before. She looked at the Gould brothers and nodded her head. "It's time we left."

"Hold on there, ma'am," Gustav said. "Someone needs to examine the body before it's moved."

"Excuse me?" If she'd looked at me like I'd been throwing water around, the glare she gave my brother suggested his bucket was full of vinegar—or worse.

"That's how . . . "

I cringed, knowing the words "Sherlock Holmes would do it" were about to come from my brother's mouth. He seemed to sense what a damn dumb thing this would be to say, and he managed to get his lips pointed in a different direction before the damage could be done.

" . . . police back East handle this kind of thing."

It was an improvement, but it still didn't get a warm reception.

"I don't care how 'police back East' do things. My husband's father is dead, and I will not have strangers pawing over his body."

She nodded at the Goulds again, then walked briskly into the kitchen and out the back door. Doc Snow was a step behind her, fixing to catch her should she faint, I suppose. The Gould brothers followed too, after loading up Jack G. Johnson with the dainty touch of a woman packing away fine china—which was a tad funny, seeing as the man wasn't in any condition to complain should you yank off his ears. Out back they slid the box up on a wagon, then proceeded to cart away the Johnsons both living and dead.

Dr. Snow started to drift off after the wagon, but Gustav shouted out "Doc!" and waved him back. He seemed a touch reluctant to step foot inside our humble establishment again, and he stopped just short of the door.

"That was rather indelicate, your request to the lady," he said to Gustav. The few times I'd run across him in the past, Snow had struck me as a rather stiff, crusty fellow, and now it looked like his contact with Mrs. Johnson had put even more starch in his collar.

"Ain't nothin' delicate about murder," my brother replied with such confidence and bravado you'd think he'd been a New York constable all his days instead of a farmboy, drover and dishwasher.

"Anyway, I thought you were a man of science."

Now a fair enough response would have been, "What do *you* know about being a 'man of science'? You can't even spell the words." Instead Snow blinked and kind of harrumphed and said, "I am."

"Good," Gustav said. "Then you can tell me if there's a test for arsenic."

Snow nodded. "The Marsh Test. It's simple enough. Through the application of heat one can convert arsenic into arsine gas, which can be precipitated on a surface such as a mirror or a porcelain dish as a—"

There was more, but I can't get it straight even after more talk with the Doc. Suffice it to say the answer was indeed "yes," and Gustav disappeared into the lunch room and came back a moment later holding a plate topped with a half-eaten serving of steak and potatoes.

"You think you could apply all that who-ha you just talked up to this here chow?"

"Certainly."

Gustav held out the plate. "Alright then."

Snow took hold of the plate reluctantly, like he was being handed a bowl of scorpions. "This was Johnson's dinner?"

"That's right."

"I have to warn you: I'll feel obligated to report my findings to Marshal Nickles."

"That's what I'm countin' on," my brother said, sounding like he already knew what those findings would be and the test itself was practically beside the point. "When can you have an answer?"

"Tonight maybe. Tomorrow morning at the latest."

"Good. I'll leave you to it."

As Snow went on his way, looking buffaloed to find himself walking across town with a plate of steak in his hand, I asked Gustav what exactly he expected this "Marsh Test" would prove.

"I've been practicin', Brother," he replied. "Tryin' to shape myself into a real top-drawer observationalist, just like Mr. Holmes.

And let me tell you—I was in the kitchen when Kathy was frying up that food for old man Johnson, and I didn't see her doctor it up with anything but salt and pepper."

"Yeah, you were in the kitchen alright," I said. "Washin' dishes. You tellin' me you could scrub a pot and keep the eagle eye on Kathy at the same time?"

Though I half expected Old Red to take to barking at me for my lack of faith, he actually smiled and almost—*almost*—peeled off a chuckle.

"That's good, you askin' questions like that. I do believe you've picked up a thing or two from Mr. Holmes yourself. A first-class detective ain't gonna trust nobody's observations but his own."

"I ain't no detective," I said. "I'm a cowboy, and so are you. Now let's act like it and just saddle up, hit the trail and forget this whole ugly . . . . "

It was no use. He wasn't even listening to me anymore. He'd turned away and picked a frying pan up off the stove, and now he was staring into it like a sideshow gypsy stares into her crystal ball.

"What do you see there?" he asked me, flipping the pan around and shoving it under my nose.

I shrugged. "Grease and gristle."

"That's right."

He clanged the pan back on the stovetop and snatched up a salt shaker from a shelf nearby.

"Every order of beef and taters Kathy did today got fried up in that pan—including a couple for fellers who moseyed in *after* Johnson." Gustav's words came out slow and quiet as he upended the shaker and sprinkled some salt in the palm of his left hand. "If she'd put any arsenic on the old man's food while it was cookin', we'd have ended up with more than one corpse clutterin' up the place."

He ran a finger over the granules in his hand, and I leaned in to get a closer look myself. Growing up I had more experience with arsenic than with salt. The former we kept in ample supply to deal with rats and coyotes. The latter my mother guarded like it was gold dust, doling out about a pinch a year for the seasoning of food while hording the rest for pickling and preserving.

"Salt," I said.

"Salt," said my brother.

He clapped his hands clean then ran through the same business with the pepper.

"Pepper," I said.

"Pepper."

We spent the next half-hour peeking into every canister, prodding around all the corners and poking away at anything that looked even the tiniest bit like arsenic powder. By the time we finished up, our hands were chalk white with flour and sugar and baking soda, but there was no arsenic to be found.

"Alright," Gustav said, wiping his hands clean on his trousers. "The food wasn't poisoned in the kitchen."

"I don't know. Kathy might still have the poison on her. In one of her pockets, let's say. She could've slipped it out when the food was ready and sprinkled on a touch before I took it to Johnson."

"Just sloppin' it over the top? 'Here's your steak, Mr. Johnson. Hope you like it extra *powdery*.' Even you would've noticed that."

"What do you mean even me?"

But once again I was just giving my mouth muscles some exercise, for my brother had closed up his ears and moved on. He headed into the lunch room and walked up to the chair in which Johnson had eaten his last supper.

"Ricky Hess," he said, pointing to the seat to the left of it. "Feathers Purnell." He pointed to the seat on the right.

"You think one of them did it?"

"'It is a capital mistake to theorize before you have all the evidence,'" Gustav said. "'It biases the judgment.'"

I recognized the quote right away, coming as it did from *A Study in Scarlet*, a tale I've read so many times I'll still have bits and pieces of it bouncing around my skull if I live to be older than Noah.

"Well, before you go gettin' any ideas, I'll just point out that it's also a capital mistake to run around accusin' people of murder," I replied. "Folks tend to take that kind of thing rather personal."

I may as well have been warning the sun not to come up in the morning. My brother just said "Grab your scratch paper" and headed for the door. I followed after snatching up the tattered old envelope and pencil I sometimes used to take orders when too many fellows got to shouting out their druthers at the same time.

I didn't need any of Mr. Holmes' method to figure out who Gustav was going to put the eyeball on first. When I caught up to him, he was headed for the stockyards over by the railroad depot. Feathers had been there for days helping the Triple T boys load up a herd of beeves bound for Chicago.

"So what am I supposed to do with this paper?" I asked Gustav.

"Write on it."

"My word, what a notion. You mean like . . . . " I pulled out the pencil, gave the lead a lick and began moving it over the envelope. "'My . . . brother . . . is . . . a . . . horse's—"

"I can't very well take notes myself, now can I?" Old Red snapped, grumpy that he had to come right out and say it. "I need you to kind of . . . chronicle things."

My reading and writing were a gift from my elder siblings, as they worked extra hard so at least one member of the family—the baby, yours truly—could stay in school long enough to get some actual use out of it. I'm ever mindful of this, which is why I don't buck too hard when Gustav needs use of the skills he was too busy farming and driving cattle to collect for himself.

"I understand," I said. "I'll be like your Doc Watson."

Gustav gave me a hard look, and I knew I was being compared—none too favorably—to Dr. John Watson, the fellow who writes up Sherlock Holmes' adventures for the magazines.

"All you gotta do," my brother said, "is keep track of the clues."

"How am I supposed to know what they are?"

Gustav shook his head. "I'll let you know. Now button your

lip. There's Dave Ryan."

Ryan was the Triple T's trail boss. He gave us a big grin as we approached and let us know he'd be eating his meals over at Blythe's Restaurant from now on. We took the joshing the only way we could—by shrugging and pretending to chuckle—and Gustav quickly moved things along to the point of our visit. Ryan told us where Feathers was and let us know it was alright to talk to him for a while . . . long as we didn't try to slip the man any food. We laughed again, thanked him and walked away cussing him under our breath.

"You know it's just gonna be more of the same long as we stay in Billings," I said to Gustav once we'd corked up our curses.

Old Red made a noise that might have meant "Ain't it a shame?" and might have meant "We'll just see about that" and might have meant "That corn on my toe sure is painin' me today." I didn't bother asking which, as he probably wouldn't have told me. Sometimes I think if words were water, my brother would be Death Valley.

We found Feathers with a couple other punchers, all of them using prod-poles to convince a group of bellowing beeves they ought to move on up into a cattle car. We got more japes thrown at us by the other two hands, but Feathers didn't even light up a smile. When we called him over for a parlay, he came slow and wary, like a dog approaches a man with meat in one hand and a switch in the other. That struck me funny, the relations between us being normally friendly, if not overly familiar.

"What do you want?" he asked us.

"Just wanted to ask you a few questions about what happened at the Cafay," Gustav said.

Feathers squinted at him. "Why ask *me* questions?"

"Cuz you were there."

"Lot a men were there."

"But you were up close."

"Not really."

"Well, you were the first one to get to Johnson when he fell.

Looked like he even whispered something in your ear."

Feathers shook his head. "No words. Just noises. Like he was gasping for breath."

"But then after that I saw you kind of put your hand on him. Across his eyes. I thought maybe he'd already—"

"I don't know what you're talking about."

That stopped Gustav cold. He just stared at Feathers for a few seconds, a little twitch kicking up around his eyes. When he spoke again, he sounded bona fide bewildered.

"Now, Feathers, I saw you place your—"

"You're a damn liar. I never touched the man." Feathers began to back away from us, eyes spitting fire. "Now you two just clear on out. I ain't got nothin' more to say to you."

He walked back to the cattle chute and grabbed up his prod-pole. Then he glanced back and gave us a look that said he was ready to use that big, mean stick on steer or man alike. That was enough to prod *us*, and we left.

"So," I said as we walked away, "you just let me know which clues I should be jottin' down and I'll—"

"Oh, shut up."

I don't always listen to my brother when he gives me this little nugget of advice, but I did so now. I figured he was discovering detectiving isn't as easy as he'd made it out to be, and a man's got a right to be a mite tetchy when his daydreams get cut down and used for kindling.

But Gustav wasn't ready to light up that particular bonfire just yet. From the way he steered us through the streets, I reckoned our next stop would be C.V. Kramm Drug & Variety Store, where Ricky Hess spent his days jerking sodas. But as we passed by another store, Bragg & Company Dry Goods, Gustav froze up, spun on his heel and marched inside.

We got a right warm welcome from Bragg and company. There were eight or nine people in the place, and they all greeted us with a smile. Several were even so kind as to point out exactly where the rat poison was stocked. I rode it out just fine, being accustomed to both making sport and being sported in turn. But Gustav's face turned almost as red as his hair, and the more folks pulled his leg the closer he got to kicking them with it.

"I'd like to have a word in private," he said to Mr. Bragg, a cheerful old backslapper with muttonchops so big they practically drooped out over his shoulders like a gray shawl.

"Why certainly, Old Red." Bragg peered over my brother's head to wink at his customers. "There's something I'd like to ask you, as well."

Bragg stepped out from behind the counter and waved us back to a dark corner of the store.

"I'm wonderin' if Kathy McKenna, Ricky Hess or Feathers Purnell have bought any arsenic off you in the last week or so," Gustav asked, his voice low, once the three of us were circled up away from our audience.

The face under Bragg's carpet of whiskers turned mock serious. "I thought that's what you'd be asking," he said. "Well, I don't know this 'Feathers Purnell,' but I understand he's a negro cowhand, and we haven't had any trade with the likes of that. As for Hess, I haven't had any business from him either, though his aunt and uncle are regular customers. Kathy comes in often enough as well, but I can't recall selling her any arsenic recently. Which isn't to say she hasn't purchased any in the past. I'd be surprised if she hadn't."

"Oh? Why's that?"

Bragg chuckled. "Because it's easier to say who *hasn't* bought rat poison than who has. I can barely keep the stuff on the shelves."

Like most cowtowns on a railroad line, Billings has rats like a dog has fleas. As even I could see, that meant mere possession of rat poison could hardly be considered a black mark against you. If it did, nearly everyone in town would be a candidate for the noose.

Gustav seemed to come to the same conclusion, as he thanked Bragg and turned to go. But Bragg reached out and snagged hold of his arm before he could take a step.

"Hold on. I've got a question for *you*, remember?"

My brother nodded curtly. "So ask it."

Bragg cleared his throat, then spoke in the loud, clear tone of voice men reserve for delivering either sermons or digs that are meant to be overheard.

"When you're on the stand, I'd appreciate it you'd testify that you bought the poison here," he said. "That kind of word-of-mouth advertising can't be beat."

Gustav jerked his arm from Bragg's hand and stomped from the store, followed by both me and the guffaws that nipped at our heels. I pulled out my envelope and pencil again.

"Now what exactly should I write down? 'Nothing,' 'squat' or 'diddley'?"

My brother didn't break stride, just bolted once again toward C.V. Kramm Drug & Variety Store. I pocketed my note-taking gear and trailed along behind him. When we got to Kramm's, we found the fellow Gustav wanted to see hunched over a dime novel.

"Well, howdy there, pard," my brother said, taking a seat across from Ricky Hess and his gleaming brass soda fountain. Gustav's words had a casual, joshing quality about them I'd never heard him use before.

Ricky looked up and smiled. "Old Red! Big Red! What are you two doing here?"

At the sound of our nicknames, C.V. Kramm himself poked his head around the corner. He was in a back room, no doubt grinding up a treatment for vapors or shingles or some unpleasant thing. He took a short break from his important work to shoot us a glare.

"Good day to you, Mr. Kramm," Gustav said with uncommon cheer. "My brother and I thought it was about time we tried one of these here 'cola' drinks folks've been talkin' about."

Kramm couldn't quite muster a smile, but he did at least gives us a nod. Then he was gone.

"I do believe your uncle doesn't care for us," Gustav whispered to Ricky.

The boy gave the back room a disdainful wave of his hand.

"Awww, he doesn't like me going down to Starchy's."

Gustav winked. "Full of bad influences, huh?"

"So he says. Did you really want a cola?"

"Sure we do. Show us your stuff."

Ricky grinned and made a big show of scooping up our glasses, juggling them around, squirting in some syrup and playing that soda fountain like it was a church organ. Gustav pretended to find the boy's display a right fascinating sight indeed, but I saw his eyes flicker this way and that when Ricky was too caught up in his performance to notice.

"Here you are, fellers," Ricky said, sliding the glasses down smoothly onto the marble countertop. "Don't drink 'em too fast. They'll give you hiccups."

Though personally I can't see the sense in paying out good money for anything in a glass that won't get you drunk, both I and Old Red had sampled our share of fountain drinks over the years. Yet my brother took to smacking his lips over that cola like it was rib-eye steak after a week on hardtack, so I did the same. There followed perhaps a minute of conversation on the unfortunate events at Starchy's, but my brother playacted like this topic was already a terrible bore and his only concern was finding us a new cook. He changed the subject by asking Ricky what he'd been reading when we came in.

"Oh, nothing," the boy replied bashfully.

I leaned over and took a peek at his magazine. "'Jesse James and the Cheyenne Treasure,'" I read aloud.

"Jesse James?" Gustav sputtered in mid-sip. He slapped his glass down and shook his head with fatherly disappointment. "I'm surprised at you, Ricky. Readin' one of them rags that make *Jesse James* out to be some kinda hero. The man was just a dirty reb thief and nothin' more."

"I know. But . . . well, I just—"

"Who's that feller up there?"

Leaning up against the long mirror behind Ricky were three portraits—Abraham Lincoln, U.S. Grant and a middle-aged fellow in dress uniform I'd never laid eyes on before.

"That's my grandfather. Colonel D.L. Kramm. He was killed at Shiloh."

"Oh, was he now? Well, what do you think old Colonel Kramm would think of 'Jesse James and the Cheyenne Treasure'?"

"I . . . I don't know . . . he . . . I never . . . . " Ricky began fiddling with an empty glass as he stammered, and something about the nervous fluttering of his fingers caught my eye and tickled my memory.

"Is that any way to honor your granpappy?" Gustav prodded Ricky. "Lookin' up to some mad-dog bushwhackin' murderer?"

"I do honor my grandfather. I do. I even—"

Gustav perked up so much at these words he practically took to floating above his chair. But at just that moment C.V. Kramm stepped out of the back room again and shouted for Ricky. He was holding a small package wrapped in brown paper.

"Take this over to Mrs. Gluck and come straight back with a dollar and two bits and not a penny less."

"Yes, sir."

Ricky whipped off his white soda jerk's apron, took the package and gave us a half-hearted wave as he hurried out the door. He almost looked relieved to be escaping from us.

Instead of skulking back off to his pills and powders, Kramm took Ricky's position behind the soda fountain.

"I couldn't help overhearing some of your conversation," he said to us. "It's not so much Jesse James that boy idolizes. It's no-account saddle tramp cowboys."

Gustav didn't even look at the man he was so lost in thought, so I took the liberty of answering for both of us.

"Oh, don't you fret, C.V. We was the same way when we was his age and just look how good we turned out! It's goin' on six weeks since I last shot a man in the back, and Old Red here hasn't rustled any cattle in months!"

"Drink up and get out."

My brother didn't bother to finish his cola, but I wasn't about to let Kramm kick me out without first getting my nickel's worth. So I threw my head back and drained the rest of my drink so fast I was hiccupping before I could even set the glass down.

"So, brother—what *hic* do you want me to *hic* chronicle for you *hic*?" I asked as we headed back toward Starchy's.

"If you want to 'chronicle' the fact that you're a flannelheaded fool, then go right ahead. Otherwise, don't bother."

"Now *hic* don't tell me we *hic* don't have any clues."

"Most likely we've already got all the clues we need." Gustav kicked at the dirt, and when he spoke again all the backbone was gone from his voice. "I just don't know what the hell they are."

"Well, *hic* I bet even Sherlock Holmes *hic*—"

"Otto."

"Yes *hic*?"

"Don't talk to me 'til you're over those damn hiccups."

"Al-*hic*-right."

Hiccups being hiccups, of course, I couldn't keep quiet even though I wasn't saying a word. Gustav could only take it so long. Cursing "these infernal distractions" that cramped up his cogitations, he banished me from the restaurant practically the moment we arrived.

"Go on over to the jail and make sure that mob ain't gettin' restless. And don't come back until you've stopped making that blasted noise!"

As it turned out, the mob at the jail was nothing to worry about, as it had broken apart and drifted off when it became clear no necks were going to get stretched just yet. They'd be back tomorrow though, when Kathy went before the justice of the peace for a hearing. If he said Yea, there would soon be a trial. If he said Nay, Kathy would be released—though that would hardly be a victory for her, as it was as likely as not that a makeshift Vigilance Committee would quickly decide a trial wasn't really all that necessary anyway. The oddsmakers had a Yea as an even money bet, as Thomas Fraser, Billings' justice of the peace, was known to be friendly with the Johnsons—so much so that Mrs. Fraser had been sipping tea with Mrs. Johnson when news reached them of the old man's death.

I learned all this from the deputy marshal who'd threatened us with lead poisoning when we'd asked to see Kathy earlier in the day. He still wouldn't let me in to speak with her, but he was a far more agreeable, talkative fellow without a bloodthirsty crowd around. Also I credit myself with having a way with putting folks at ease, though my silk-tongued ways were sorely tested by those hiccups.

By the time I finally ambled back to Starchy's, both the hiccups and the light of day had faded away. Old Red seemed to have faded as well, for I found him in bed with a pillow over his face.

"You asleep?" I asked.

"Nope," Gustav said, his voice muffled by burlap and feathers. "You hiccuppin'?"

"Nope."

"Good. I need to talk to you."

I eased myself down onto a corner of the tattered soogan we treat like a double bed. I'd been anticipating this talk for hours. In fact, I'd already decided how to play it. If my brother couldn't quite bring himself to give me a flat-out apology for this whole restaurant fiasco, I'd be gracious about it. All I cared about was putting it behind us. But I was firmly opposed to sneaking out of town in the middle of the night. We still had more than two-hundred dollars in the bank, and I didn't intend to leave Billings without it.

"I've been thinkin'," Gustav said from under his pillow. "Thinkin' and thinkin' and thinkin' in circles. And I keep endin' up in the same place."

"I understand," I said (since he couldn't see me nodding sympathetically).

"There's somethin' I've overlooked—somethin' Mr. Holmes would see that I don't. I need you to help me get a bead on it."

"I understand," I said again, though I wasn't entirely sure I did. This was not the talk I'd been hoping to have.

"Somehow somebody got that poison into Johnson a few minutes before he died. Now I wasn't out front at the time to see who was doin' what where. But you were. I need you to think hard—brain-bustin' hard, brother—and tell me everything you recollect from the time Johnson walked in to the time he keeled over."

"Alright. But you gotta do somethin' for me first."

"What's that?"

"Well . . . do you think you could have this conversation without a pillow on your face?"

After a long, quiet moment, my brother brought up his hands and pressed them down on the pillow—and kept them there. "It helps me think," he said.

So I spent the next hour talking to a pillow and a pair of hands. I started out with what I'd seen before Johnson died. Then, just out of sheer momentum maybe, I carried on through the rest of the day, laying out my impressions of our attempts at Sherlocking.

I half-expected to hear snoring coming out from under that pillow when I was finally done, so still were my brother's hands, but instead Gustav just said, "Thank you. You go on to sleep now." I was mighty tired by then, and I gave him no arguments. Soon I was the one doing the snoring.

One thing you learn when you're working the cattle trails is how to sleep light when you need to and heavy when you can. Since I no longer have any stampedes or rustlers to worry about, I can go as heavy as I please. So once I start catching my winks, almost nothing on earth can keep me from collecting all forty—not even Old Red sitting bolt upright and shouting, "Of course!" Or the sound of my brother jumping out of bed and banging around that restaurant like a bronc kicking his way out of a corral. Or the curses that soon followed. Or, a little later, what seemed to be the scuffing steps of a not particularly graceful man dancing a happy jig. All these noises came to me like echoes in my dreams, and when I awoke the next morning I could hardly be sure I'd really heard them at all.

I hefted myself out of bed and shuffled off in search of my brother, intending to round up a report on the night's happenings. I found him in the front room freshly shaved, dressed in his cleanest clothes and sunny as a California July. Yet while he seemed uncommonly cheerful, he was no more chatty or charitable than usual.

"If you wanted explanations, you should've tracked 'em down yourself, cuz you saw all you needed to see to put you on the right trail," he said. "I ain't got time to walk you through it now. I need you to get busy makin' yourself presentable. You look worse than a sharecropper's scarecrow."

When I was shaved, combed and dressed to Gustav's satisfaction, he finally let me know why we needed to dude ourselves up.

"While you were in back there sawin' logs, I was out arrangin' a little meetin' over to the Gould Brothers Funeral Parlor. It's set for quarter to nine. I need you to make sure Marshal Nickles and Judge Fraser are there."

"How am I supposed to do that? Ben Nickles would just as soon hang us as wave hello."

Gustav gave me a sly look of the sort that usually precedes a wink. "If you need to give Nickles a prod, you just tell him I've got Jack G. Johnson's *real* murderer hog-tied and ready for a brand. And I don't care if the brand's his so long as justice is done. If that don't do it . . . well, I'm sure you can polish it up right with that slick talkin' you do."

It made sense to send me for Nickles and Fraser. I'm the talker. Gustav's the thinker. But looking at my brother then, I had to wonder if all that thinking hadn't overheated his head, like a fast horse that's been baked by a hard rider. After all, the man had taken to lying around with a pillow over his face.

"Alright," I said reluctantly. "I'll try."

I found Nickles and Fraser in the judge's office. The hearing wasn't supposed to start until ten, but those two fellows looked so chummy I reckoned the judge wouldn't feel the need to hear a single word by that time. His decision would've been made hours before.

Now if there's one thing in this tale in which I can take a personal kind of pride, it's this: Not only did I *try* to lure them over to the Goulds', I *succeeded*. As their minds were firmly closed to persuasion, I went by way of their hearts. Which is not to say that I appealed to their compassion, since I have my doubts as to whether Nickles has any to which one could appeal. Instead I needled both men mercilessly, alluding to the ridicule and shame that would befall them should Old Red Amlingmeyer capture a culprit they were too stubborn to do anything about themselves. This fanned in them a tiny ember of doubt and a blazing fire of annoyance, and I believe they followed me primarily so they could later have the satisfaction of arresting me.

We arrived at the funeral parlor just a few minutes late. Howard Gould met us at the door, his round face sagging with strain, and he escorted us into the main viewing room mumbling about improprieties and irregularities. There were three men waiting for us. One of them was laid out in a beautiful maple-wood box. The other two were Doc Snow and my brother.

"I'm surprised to see you here, Dr. Snow," Judge Fraser said. He's a short, bushy-browed Scot with his clansmen's natural gift for ladling out scorn. "I hope you're not going to tell me you're mixed up in this nonsense."

Doc Snow's not the kind of fellow to brook much in the way of sass himself, and he responded first by dismissing Gould, then by brushing a bit of imaginary fluff off his sleeve and finally by looking up at the judge as if he'd almost forgotten the man was there. "I am," he said.

"Damn it all!" Nickles exploded. "Somebody better get to explaining or Crazy Kathy's gonna have some company in her cell!"

Doc Snow looked at Gustav, so I looked at Gustav, so Nickles and Fraser looked at Gustav. Jack G. Johnson didn't look at anything but the insides of his eyelids.

My brother cleared his throat and pulled himself up to his

full height, like a preacher getting set to rain down some fire and brimstone.

"Alright," he said. "I can do the explainin'. But you gents might want to seat yourselves before I set into it. It's gonna take a good bit of talk to spool out.

"Now I don't know if any of you have heard of Mr. Sherlock Holmes of London, England. If you haven't, Marshal Nickles, I suggest you acquaint yourself with him at your earliest convenience. For when it comes to puzzle-bustin', he's the cock-a-doodle-doo. And he said somethin' once that I've been tryin' to keep in mind ever since I watched Johnson here cash in. 'In solving a problem of this sort, the grand thing is to be able to reason backward.'

"It occurs to me that layin' the blame on Kathy McKenna is reasonin' *forward*—and skippin' a few steps as you go along. It's true enough that she and Johnson weren't exactly cordial with each other. And it's also true that Kathy can be quite the wildcat when she's riled. But there's a big difference between breakin' up fights by wavin' a knife and seasonin' a man's vittles with arsenic. Poison is a sly, sneaky way to lay a person down, and there ain't much sly and sneaky about Crazy Kathy. If she had a mind to kill Johnson, she wouldn't plot it out beforehand. She just grab up a blade and sink it into the man's skull.

"But when you're known as 'Crazy Kathy,' I suppose people are liable to jump to conclusions. Even so, I would hope there would be some kind of search for what the experts call 'data' or 'clues' or 'evidence,' but I don't mean to call into question the abilities of anyone present, so I won't dwell on that now. I'll just move along by mentionin' the thought that struck me as I watched Kathy dragged away to the hoosegow: If someone were to slip a dose to Johnson, Starchy's would be the place to do it, as Crazy Kathy's reputation would ensure that the hand of the law would quickly fall on her.

"If, that is, the poison got noticed at all. I'm proud to say my brother and me haven't passed any bad meat or butter or eggs since we've been runnin' Starchy's, but we all know it's easy enough to get doubled up on rotten grub you buy from someone else's kitchen. On top of that, Johnson was an old man, and not a very fit one to see him a couple weeks ago. If Doc Snow had been attendin' to sick folks outside town or tied up with some other business—or even if he'd just been a less book-smart and sharp-eyed feller than he is—we wouldn't be here talkin' about murder at all. We'd just figure the reaper finally caught up with the ornery old snake, and he'd be planted without a second thought or a single tear.

"So I got to thinkin' there's a slippery side to these goin's-on that folks aren't gettin' hold of. Havin' studied on Mr. Holmes' way of doin' things, I thought maybe I could. The way to start, I figured, was to cut the likeliest suspects out of the herd—'suspects' bein' detective lingo for folks you *suspect* might be guilty of something. But I'm sure you already knew that, Marshal.

"Now there were really only two suspects to be had, far as I could see: Ricky Hess and a puncher name of Feathers Purnell. They were the fellers sittin' on either side of Johnson when he got that arsenic in him. The old man had given each of 'em a taste of his venom in the past, so maybe it wasn't no accident they were nearby when someone slipped him a taste of poison.

"I went to see both of 'em yesterday, and afterwards I had a devil of a time figurin' which one had done it, for I came away convinced it had to be one or the other. You see, Feathers was the first feller to try to help Johnson after he hit the floor. The old man whispered somethin' to him, somethin' he didn't seem to like at all. And then Feathers laid his hands on Johnson kinda peculiar-like—though he called me a liar for sayin' so later, and I saw it all with my own eyes. And Ricky, he runs orders for his uncle. I've heard tell them druggists use arsenic in some of their medicines, so who's to say Ricky couldn't borrow himself a sample?

"Well, I set about to ruminatin' on all this last night, and damned if I didn't just about melt down my brain like so much candle wax. But I kept at it, and Mr. Holmes' advice about reasonin' backward finally gave me my first step ahead. I was thinkin' about Feathers puttin' his hands on Johnson's face the way he done. What's the use of such a thing? And why deny it? Johnson was already plenty sick, so it's not like Feathers needed to get any more poison in him by then. So maybe it was because of whatever Johnson said—not that it would make much sense for him to tell Feathers, 'I'm fadin' fast. Would you mind stretchin' your hands 'cross my face before the death rattle commences?' In fact, wouldn't he say just the opposite, seein' as how Feathers is a negro and Johnson had made his hatred of that race plain time and time again?

"Once I hit upon that, I knew exactly what Feathers had heard and why he'd reacted the way he had. You see, the old man's last words on this earth were in keeping with all the nastiness he'd spread around before 'em. He said, 'Get your hands off me, nigger.' And Feathers decided to show the old bastard that his days abusin' black folk were over, so he gripped a hand right to Johnson's face. But this wouldn't go down too well with some—a negro actin' in such a fashion with a dyin' white man, even one as hated as Johnson. So Feathers wisely decided to keep all this to himself.

"Now this didn't put Feathers in the clear, but it did explain some of what needed explainin', and that freed me to concentrate on Ricky. He'd let the old man sorta run him out of Starchy's a week or so back, and when he finally showed his face again yesterday he seemed to be tryin' to live that down. I was back in the kitchen at the time, but I could hear him and Johnson tradin' stings somethin' fierce. Though the boy was tryin' to act tough, he had him a touch of the jitters—or so it would seem from something my brother told me. Like a lot of fellers, Ricky likes to get his hands to workin' when he's nervous. I noticed that when I was puttin' a little fire under his saddle-warmer yesterday. And it appears his fingers were plenty busy when he was ribbin' the old man, for Otto here saw Ricky playin' with the salt shaker on the counter in front of him.

"I was lyin' down when I first got to ponderin' on that salt shaker, but soon enough I hopped up and tried to work out a way to kick myself in the pants, for surely I'd been lookin' right over something that was as hard to miss as a cougar in an outhouse. Johnson liked his food with a dash of pepper and a fistful of salt, and everyone around Starchy's knew it cuz he'd get to screamin' for the seasonings before the first bite even got off his plate. If there was something you wanted on the man's food, here was a guaranteed way to get it there. When I realized this, I went chargin' out to the counter and grabbed up that salt shaker and turned it right over. And do you want to know what happened?

"The top came off. The whole thing emptied out in about two seconds. Ricky had been up to something alright, but not murder. He'd been lookin' to catch Johnson with a trick boys have been pullin' since the day a shaker first put salt on food. Just to be sure, I spent a good amount of time sifting through that salt, and I assure you it was all crystals, no powder.

"Well, I sat there starin' at the mess I'd made for a good long while. I put the quirt to myself all night, and this was the best I could do. I was about to give up and go to sleep, but then I noticed something else lyin' there on the counter where Johnson had been sittin'. A teeny yellow-brown ditty, not much different than a thousand other little things my brother and I sweep up and throw out every day. But it told me everything I needed to know. You see, I hadn't really been reasonin' backwards at all. I thought I knew the who, and I'd been tryin' to use that to get to the how. What I needed to do was go the other way. The how could tell me the who. And it did."

Out in the funeral home's foyer, chimes began to ring. It was nine o'clock, which meant my brother had been working his lips more than ten minutes straight. I wondered that those lips didn't drop right off, as sometimes a month went by without so many words passing between them. But unaccustomed as Gustav might have been to speechmaking, he had all of us there in his spell. Even Nickles seemed more than a little awestruck when he piped up to ask, "What was it you saw?"

"That's a fair enough question, Marshal. But before I answer, I'd like Dr. Snow to tell you what he told me this morning." Gustav turned to Snow. "About Johnson's food."

Doc Snow nodded, then looked to Marshal Nickles and Judge

Fraser. "There's a way to test for the presence of arsenic—the Marsh Test. Old Red asked me to try it on what was left of Johnson's meal. I did, and it came up negative. I couldn't find the smallest trace of poison."

"But you said yourself Johnson died of arsenic poisoning!" Nickles blustered.

"That he did."

"But if it wasn't in his food—?"

I heard a door open in the front hall. Footsteps and low, murmuring voices followed. The sounds seemed to be some kind of signal for Gustav, for he quickly fished something out of his vest pocket and handed it to Nickles, and when he spoke again his words were running at a gallop.

"This is what I found on the counter, Marshal. Now what would you say that is?"

Nickles held up a small, dirty-yellow sliver no bigger than a pebble. I leaned forward to give it a stare and suddenly remembered the ugly little something Johnson had pulled from his mouth after his first bite of steak the day before.

"Looks like bone," Nickles said.

Gustav shook his head, then turned and walked to the casket that held Jack G. Johnson. What he did next knocked a gasp out of Nickles, Fraser and myself—though our gasps were nothing compared to the *scream*. Howard Gould had opened the doors into the viewing room just as Old Red plunged a hand into Johnson's mouth, and the sight of my brother rooting around in there like a bear after honey set Mrs. George J. Johnson into a fit of hysterics. I glanced around to see her husband and Gould steering the woman into a chair as her head rolled back and her legs went all wobbly. Then a horrible *shlurp* kind of sound pulled me back in the other direction. What I saw there was my brother yanking the old man's dentures right off his gums.

Well, as you might imagine, there was quite an uproar, with cries of outrage just about peeling the paper off the walls. But though Gustav was talking more slowly and softly than anyone else, his voice seemed to cut through, and before long folks were actually listening to it.

" . . . chip of tooth, not bone," he was saying when everyone piped down enough for me to hear his words. He brought the dentures over to Nickles and Fraser and pointed at one of the Yankee teeth old Johnson used to brag on so much. "You can see the tooth it came from. It's been hollowed out. It's one of the big ones in the back, too. What do you call these, Mr. Johnson?"

Johnson had a fresh face of sun from his ride out into the country the day before, but even with the red there he somehow looked pale. "How dare you—"

"It's a molar," Doc Snow interrupted, looking so unruffled by this strange turn of events I had to figure (rightly, I learned later) that he'd helped my brother arrange them.

"Thank you, Doc. You think you could run that Marsh Test on this here 'molar'?"

Snow nodded, his eyes fixed on the Johnsons. "Certainly."

"Good. Though I don't know if it's even all that necessary, for if you gents take a good look you'll see there's still some powder crammed up in there."

Both Fraser and Nickles took that good hard look, and once they did they shifted their glares over to young Johnson and his half-conscious wife.

"One thing I could never figure out about old man Johnson was why he kept comin' back to our place," Gustav said. "But you know, as much as he complained about the grub, it seemed to do him good. For if you'll recall, he had the color of a scabby toad a few weeks back, but he looked to be gettin' better with each passin' day. And I wonder now if that's because there was something about Mrs. Johnson's cookin' that didn't agree with him—something that sent him out lookin' for the cheapest food in town that wouldn't leave him feelin' sick as a dog. And if that certain something couldn't be got to him through his food, well, maybe there was another way. It wouldn't be that hard to do if you had yourself a drill and a skill with teeth. You could fix it so your handiwork wouldn't show, then just wait for something tough—like one of our ten-cent steaks, for instance—to pop off a bit of tooth and let the poison inside get to seepin' out. And doin' it roundabout like that had a big advantage, in that you could make sure you wasn't within a mile of the old man when he—"

Mrs. Johnson woke up enough then to start balling and carrying on something awful.

"God help us!" she sobbed. "The old man was a monster! A demon! He—!"

"Elsa!" her husband roared, leaping to his feet to tower over her.

The woman's words choked to a stop with a weepy whimper. When he was satisfied that she would say no more, young Johnson turned to face us again.

"This disgusting spectacle has unhinged my wife," he said. "I'm going to take her home. If you insist on continuing with these hideous insinuations, you can call on me later. But now I'm leaving."

He and Gould helped Mrs. Johnson to her feet, and the three of them moved with slow, shuffling steps out of the room.

"You're gonna let 'em go?" I asked Nickles.

It was Fraser who answered. "They'll be dealt with in due time," he said. "I see no reason not to allow them the opportunity to face this with dignity."

I thought back to the way Nickles had dragged Crazy Kathy off to jail and didn't recollect anything dignified about it. But I suppose pillars of the community have to be removed with special care. Or so think other pillars.

As it turned out, the Johnsons removed themselves, for when Marshal Nickles went to question them again an hour later they were both dead. There was no mystery as to the cause, as the tea cups and rat poison were left in plain view. What they hadn't seen fit to leave out, Nickles reported, was a letter of explanation—though of course the town was soon awash in rumors that this was a lie. The suicide note had been destroyed by Nickles and Fraser, folks whispered, as it revealed shocking improprieties old Johnson had taken with his daughter in law—improprieties her family wanted hushed up.

Gustav shrugged off such talk, saying he had no "data" with which to judge its merits. When I asked him about the *why* of Johnson's murder, he shrugged.

"Could be he really did take liberties with the lady. Could be his cussedness was bad for business. Could be he was an embarrassment for such fine, upstanding citizens," he said. "Could be he snored. Could be his feet smelled bad. Could be they just got sick of the old goat. All I know is I've got dishes to wash."

And that he does—more than ever, for the Johnsons' misfortunes seem to have made ours. Though the appeal of it entirely escapes us, everyone else in Billings has gone out of their way to eat at least one meal at the scene of the town's most famous murder. Some even ask to sit in Johnson's chair and order up exactly what he was chewing on when the arsenic did its work. We've been so busy, I've hardly had time to set this down on paper, which is why it heads out to you nearly three weeks after the fact.

I will now do my best to wait patiently for your response, though I'll admit that the thought of appearing in your publication has me wound so tight I could bust a spring. I certainly hope that you share my enthusiasm now that you've reached the end of my tale. I can't say whether your readers would embrace detective adventures of the sort experienced by Mr. Sherlock Holmes, but give them a native-born sleuth employing the same methods on our own Western plains, and they'll surely holler for more.

Sincerely,

O.A. Amlingmeyer
Billings, Montana
October 14, 1892

Steve Hockensmith

# WOLVES IN WINTER

*Harper's Weekly*
Harper & Bros., Publishers
325 to 337 Pearl Street
Franklin Square
New York

Dear Mr. Harper (or Bros.):

Well, here I am again. I was disappointed to learn that the story I sent your way a few months back—"Gustav Amlingmeyer, Holmes of the Range"—didn't "meet the magazine's editorial needs at this time." But now that you've started printing detective yarns on a regular basis, I thought I'd try again. So what you'll find below is another possible story for your magazine. If *this* tale doesn't meet your editorial needs, just look on it as the longest change-of-address notice you'll ever get.

Not that you'll find me on your subscriber rolls. The name you'd be looking for belongs to my brother, Gustav—or, as he's known out here in Montana, "Old Red" Amlingmeyer. In recent weeks, Old Red's become your magazine's most loyal listener. I would say your most loyal *reader*, except the only things Gustav can read are trails and the metaphorical writing on the wall. If there are letters and words and such involved, the reading falls to me. And lately, what I've been reading most is *Harper's Weekly*.

I can't claim that we've been regular readers of your publication in the past, since my brother and I have spent the last few years as cowboys working the Western cattle drives, and both magazine racks and mailboxes are far from plentiful on the open range. But last fall Old Red decided it was finally time to do something with our trail money other than squirrel it away in a bank. So we cracked open our nest egg and bought a cookshack near the railroad stockyards in Billings, Montana, rebranding ourselves as respectable businessmen.

And our business was indeed rather respectable the first few months. We sold everything we could dish out to the cowboys bringing herds in off the trail. Drovers are hungry fellows by nature—they never really get their fill on the job, and no matter how good their outfit's cook is they still want something other than beans and vinegar pie when they hit town. Things slowed down to a molasses drip when winter came on and the cattle drives stopped, but by then we'd made back half our investment and had plenty of money in the bank with which to ride out the snow months.

It was shaping up to be the warmest, dryest, most quilty-cozy winter I ever experienced in all my days. Not that the weather was good—it was so cold out a single breath was all it took to coat your lungs in icicles. But I was staying snug indoors, reading and playing solitaire at the café waiting for customers while Old Red went off to mustard every book peddler and dry goods merchant in town for detective stories. Though my brother had us settled down in the cookshack, he didn't see himself slinging taters and steaks forever. He dreamed of detecting.

The previous summer, Old Red ran across accounts of the great English crimebuster Mr. Sherlock Holmes, and they kindled in him the burning desire to become a sleuth himself. As a result, he had me reading out every mystery magazine he could find, from *Secret Service* to *Nick Carter Library*. Though my brother wasn't much impressed with the deducifying skills on display in their pages, he had to make due, since you could dig a hundred needles from a haystack before you'd find even one new Holmes tale.

That all changed thanks to you, of course. While my brother's usually a gloomy sort of fellow—like bears and badgers, his smile spends much of the year in hibernation—a couple weeks after Christmas he came charging into the café giddy with glee.

"Otto! Otto!" he shouted, waving a copy of *Harper's* over his head. "Look at this! What's this say right here!"

He pushed the magazine into my hands. It was folded open, and Old Red pointed at a boxed announcement across the top of the page.

"'*Harper's Weekly*, through special arrangement with George Newnes, Ltd., of London and Arthur Conan Doyle, literary agent, will be presenting in the months ahead Dr. John Watson's newest stories chronicling the astounding adventures of his friend, the consulting detective Mr. Sherlock Holmes. We trust that our readers will be as amazed as our cousins across the waves by Mr. Holmes's celebrated feats of deduction.'"

Below all that was an illustration of a lean, dapper-looking gent I recognized immediately as Holmes. The title of the story running with it was "The Cardboard Box."

"All I gotta do now is . . . what ya' call it? Inscribe to the magazine!" Old Red proclaimed, hopping from foot to foot with excitement. A prospector with a fistful of gold in his pan couldn't have looked much happier. "Then I can just sit back and let the stories come straight to our door!"

I'm not sure what excited my brother more: finding a new Holmes yarn or the realization that he could *subscribe* to a magazine to get more. If he could have stories coming straight to his door, you see, that meant he finally had a door they could come to.

Old Red had been on the move about 10 years before we settled in Billings. He left home after our dear old *Vater* died of smallpox, and my *Mutter* would get letters from him stuffed with greenbacks, the return address—when there was one—saying "Brownsville, Texas" or "Abilene, Kansas" or "Ogallala, Nebraska," always in handwriting we'd never seen before and hardly ever the same place twice. He came back to get me when the Cottonwood River overflowed, sweeping away the Amlingmeyer farm and the rest of the Amlingmeyers with it, and after that I guess the only home he really had was me, drifting around with him the next horse over.

So the thought of sitting still and letting the good things come to him must have seemed pretty sweet to Old Red. It's just too bad it couldn't last.

A few days after Gustav's first *Harper's* showed up in the mail, what folks are calling "The Panic" hit town. According to the newspapers and your very own magazine, it started back in New York when the big-money boys suddenly decided an ounce of silver was worth about as much as a bag of cow chips. Loans were called in, stocks fell, and suddenly the silver boys were scrambling for gold or cash. Once upon a time I would've figured all this wouldn't mean doodly to me and Gustav, us not being mining magnates or Wall Street kingpins. But I'm a sadder, wiser, poorer man today, and I know better. When giants fall, little folks get squished.

Of course, we had no idea those giants were even feeling woozy—or that they'd quietly drained just about every penny from every bank in the West. No, the first we heard of it was when our Irish cook, Crazy Kathy McKenna, came running in one morning yelling, "Wake up and get yer asses to the bank! They're makin' a run on the son of a bitch!"

We'd taken to sleeping in the back of the café, this saving us money on rooming while discouraging any light-fingered nighthawks from helping themselves to our canned goods. Unfortunately, that put us a good half-mile from the First People's Bank of Montana. So by the time we'd thrown on our clothes and splashed through the icy-muddy streets without even the benefit of a cup of coffee for fuel, the crowd was breaking up and the "CLOSED UNTIL FURTHER NOTICE" sign was already in the window. Some of the folks in the mob looked a little less distressed than others. These, we soon figured out, were the ones who'd managed to get out some of their money before the doors were barred shut. Our luck wouldn't have been any better had we done our banking elsewhere, however, for directly across the street the exact same scene was playing out at the First National Bank of

Billings.

"Alright, Gustav—tell it to me straight," I said, even though my tight-lipped brother wasn't in the habit of delivering bad news any other way. (He never beats around the bush when he can simply trample right over it.) "How much we got left?"

I knew it was a bad sign when Old Red answered me by reaching into his pocket. He pulled out a few coins and a crumpled greenback.

"Looks like about two dollars," he said.

I dug around in my own trousers and came up with another thirty cents. "How much in the till?"

"The usual."

That would be another five dollars, plus change.

So that was that. We might not be what you would call financial wizards, but Old Red and I knew what "CLOSED UNTIL FURTHER NOTICE" meant. It meant "CLOSED UNTIL HELL FREEZES OVER." Our money was gone. We were down to our saddles.

"Oh, that's a shame, it is," Crazy Kathy said when we got back to the cookshack and told her our woes. "I'd have come ta fetch ya sooner if I could, only I had to get out me own money first."

"What?" I said, yelping as if I'd been splattered with hot grease off the griddle.

"I have me little ones to look out for, ya know," Crazy Kathy replied with a casual, dismissive shrug. She reached into her apron pocket and pulled out a small handful of bills. "Twenty-one dollars I've been able to save with me cookin' and washer-work. It was damned hard to come by . . . ." Her gaze wandered around the café. "Which isn't to say I wouldn't part with it under the right conditions."

"We'll take it," Old Red sighed.

"What?" I said again. (I beg you to remember here that I still hadn't had a chance to wash the bed-fuzz out of my brain with a cup of coffee.)

My brother ignored me, as is often his preference.

"Can we stay on here a while?" he asked Crazy Kathy. "Help out during the day, sleep in back at night?"

"No," Crazy Kathy replied flatly, not even giving him the courtesy of pretending to think it over. "I'll be movin' me kids out of that drafty shack we've been rentin'. Joseph and Maura can take orders and clear tables while Kitty looks after the wee one in back. We won't have room for a couple of grown men clutterin' up the place. I'll need ya out of here within the hour."

Old Red shook his head sadly.

"Lord, Kathy—at least give me the money before you kick us out."

"What is . . . ?" I turned to Crazy Kathy. "Are you . . . ?"

She ignored my mumblings, too.

"At least I gave ya a chance to get to the bank," she said to Old Red as she handed him the cash. "Ya can't say I didn't do that."

"Come on, Otto," my brother said to me. "We've got us some packin' to do."

It all finally sank in for me when Old Red started rolling up his soogan and stuffing his magazines into his warbag.

"I can't believe it! We've done that woman more than one good turn, and this is how she pays us back?"

Gustav looked at me just long enough to offer up a shrug. "Hard times are comin', brother—for everybody. Folks are gonna do what they think they have to."

"Well, what the hell are *we* gonna do? It'll be months before the big outfits start hirin' for the spring roundups, and we've got . . . what? Not even thirty dollars? That ain't enough to ride out the winter."

Old Red heaved a mighty sigh. Obviously, I wasn't telling him anything he wasn't well aware of already.

"Let's get this packin' done," he said. "We'll figure out what to do next over at Henihan's Saloon."

If my brother was aiming to shut me up—and I figure he was—he sure hit the bull's-eye. Aside from me, his only constant companion has been hardship, yet I'd never known him to seek out the kind of comfort that comes in a bottle. If things were so bad Gustav Amlingmeyer needed a drink, that meant I needed three. So I got to packing as quick as I could. I'd forgotten all about coffee by then. I needed whiskey.

When we got to the saloon, Old Red let me do the ordering, and I had the barman set us each up with a shot of redeye—with another shot for a chaser. Once our tonsils were good and scalded, we got to hashing things out. There really wasn't much to hash, though.

Around us were a good two-dozen customers all trying to drown out the same sorrow as us, and more newly broke merchants and tradesmen were drifting in by the minute. There wouldn't be any work for us around Billings for months—and even if there was, we'd have to fight off hundreds of hungry men desperate for the same jobs.

"We can stay here and starve," I summed it up, "or we can move on and hope things ain't as bad in the next town."

"Yup."

"So which one'll it be?"

"Why don't we put it to a vote?" Old Red said.

This was something Gustav proposed only on those rare occasions when he truly has no earthly idea what the hell we should do.

"Well," I said, "it wouldn't cost us much to ride the grubline to Miles City, whereas stayin' here we'll have to pay room and board just for the privilege of sittin' around goin' broke. So we may as well try our luck somewhere else. I vote we go."

Old Red voted likewise. We've never had a tie on such votes, actually. They're just Gustav's way of letting me make the occasional decision without having it go to my head.

After warming our bellies for the journey with another round of shots, Old Red and I stocked up on light provisions (costing us a precious two dollars from our meager kitty), collected our horses from the livery (thanking god we hadn't sold them off when we settled down in the café) and headed out of town. We didn't take the straightest route to the trail east—Old Red wound us through Billings first, down toward the stockyards. He wanted one last look at our little cookshack. We rode past it in silence, like mourners filing by the body at a wake.

Up until then, it had been a typical Montana January—which is to say, a miserable one. But though there was still snow on the ground as we set off, the day was uncommonly bright and warm, and the 150-mile ride along the Yellowstone River to Miles City got off to a downright pleasant start. In fact, being back in the saddle bucked me up a bit, and once we got on the trail the pure joy of riding the range again was almost enough to make me forget our misfortune. If Old Red was cheered any I can't say, for all I saw was his back, and I heard from him not a thing until we stopped to rest and water the horses hours later.

"There's a Crazy B line camp just north of that rise—we can make it there by nightfall," he said, pointing at a rocky bulge up ahead. "I'll let you do the talkin'."

"Like you could stop me."

Gustav just grunted, and a few minutes later we were riding again.

As my brother had predicted, we reached the line camp just as the sun was going down. It was nothing more than a shack, a shed and a barn—a remote outpost for keeping an eye on cattle and fence-wire far from ranch HQ. The lonely men working such camps are glad to have any company they can, and so-called "grubline riders" can usually count on a meal and a place to sleep. We were offered just that by the two hands we met that night.

There's always a toll to be paid for such hospitality, however: news from town. Being as overblessed with jawbone as my brother is underblessed, I was happy to oblige, gabbing on about the run on the bank and anything else that popped into my head while Old Red sat quietly in a corner sucking on his pipe. When we'd been living in the cookshack, he'd had the luxury of ending each day with a detective tale read out by yours truly, but he had to make due with stale gossip that night.

The gossip grew even staler as we made our way east, as each night I doled out the same old news to a fresh group of line camp hands or homesteaders. I got so bored with it, in fact, I started making things up around day four, and there are probably still a few folks back along the trail who think General Custer turned up alive in a New Orleans cathouse and Tom Edison sailed a balloon to the moon. On the fifth day, however, things got plenty interesting without any embellishment from me.

We'd stayed the night at a small, independent ranch about forty miles southwest of Miles City, sleeping on the floor by the fire while the four Texans who owned the place nestled up in tiny bunks against each wall. They were early risers, so we were on our way again before light.

As it turned out, light never came that day at all—at least not that we could see. Clouds had rolled in overnight so thick and grey the whole day was smothered in a smoky haze. The snow started in after we'd been in the saddle maybe two hours, greeting us tenderly at first with a swirl of delicate flakes before pelting us with wet clumps as big as nickels.

There were already a few inches of old snow on the ground before all this started, so it didn't take long for the accumulation to add up to something alarming. By mid-afternoon, the drifts were reaching up well past our horses' shanks, and Old Red and I had to keep slapping at our slickers to keep the sticky-soggy snow from coating us top to bottom. If we hadn't constantly brushed ourselves off, it would've looked someone set a couple horses loose with snowmen on their backs.

And the storm didn't just bring snow to the party: It brought biting-cold air that seemed to arrive all at once in a big gust that nearly knocked my hat off. All the new, wet snow got to icing over, and the clomp of hooves beneath us took on a harder, brittle, crackling sound. When we stopped to water the horses late in the day, we had to stomp our way through ice before they could even wet their muzzles.

"We need to put in soon," I said, trying to rub some warmth

into my mount's haunches.

Old Red was doing the same for his horse. "Gotta find somewhere to put in first, don't we?" he shot back, the words leaving his mouth in a thick cloud of frosted breath. "We've been movin' too slow."

"Slow but steady. Snow or no, we put some miles behind us today. I bet we run across someplace we can stop any minute now. It'll be good timin', too—my stomach tells me it's almost suppertime."

This optimistic chatter was aimed squarely at myself, as the growing chill and ever-encroaching dusk had me in desperate need of the kind of look-on-the-bright-side cheer my brother finds it hard to muster even when things are going *well*. Of course, Gustav stayed true to his look-on-the-dark-side ways, throwing me a dubious grimace before hauling himself atop his pony.

"Well, one thing's for sure—we ain't gonna run across squat standin' around gabbin'," he said, and he wheeled his mount around and set off.

My snowball caught him in the back of the neck before his horse had taken ten steps.

Old Red didn't even look back.

The day continued to wane while the snow most definitely did not, and an unhappy choice loomed larger and larger before us. We could keep fighting our way along in the hopes of reaching safe haven, only to get caught in full-on dark before we could find a decent spot to build a windbreak to ride out the night. Or we could stop now and throw together a crude shelter from branches and rotted-out logs . . . only to freeze in the night a hundred feet from a cabin we never saw.

I was chewing these options over—and finding the taste of each profoundly bitter—when my brother suddenly reined up his horse.

"What is it?" I brought my mount to a halt behind him. "You see somethin'?"

Old Red gave me such an explosive shush it almost sounded

like a sneeze. His right arm came up slowly, the glove-covered index finger stretched out to point at a long, rocky slope ahead. About half-way up, low, dark shapes were circling a large mound in the snow.

"Wolves?" I asked, my voice just a half-notch above a whisper.

"Wolves," Old Red whispered back.

"Ain't neither of us got a Winchester."

"I know."

"Our Colts ain't gonna be any use if they make a run at us."

"I know."

"And if we keep followin' the trail, they're sure to spot us."

"I know."

"But if we stop anywhere around here, they'll sniff us out."

"I know."

"This ain't good."

"God damn it, Otto, I *know*."

Old Red slumped in his saddle, and it was hard to know which was weighing on him more—his predicament or his big-mouthed brother. I gave him a moment to think in peace before I prodded him again.

"What are we gonna do?"

"Only thing we can do. Try to ride around 'em and hope that's a fresh kill they got up there."

"Cuz if it ain't—?"

Old Red steered his pony off the trail into the trees without giving me an answer. I didn't really need one, though. I knew what he was saying.

Those wolves would probably leave us alone . . . so long as they weren't *hungry*.

Most of the year, you wouldn't find wolves who'd willingly come within a mile of a man. But when the cold set in and the game grew scarce, there was no predicting what they might do. Whatever it was that usually kept them from attacking people—caution or courtesy, one predator to another—wolves could overcome it if their stomachs were empty long enough.

We were moving slower than ever once we left the trail, with brush and rocks to work around as well as the snow. I rubbed my right hand over my slicker nervously as we rode, unhappy indeed that the forty-five on my hip was buried beneath several layers of canvas, cotton and wool. And even if I could whip off my glove and dig out my hogleg in a moment of need, it probably wouldn't do me any good: Gun oil freezes quick and thaws slow, and there was every chance the trigger wouldn't even budge. If those wolves tried to jump us, my shooting iron would be about as much protection as a rolled-up newspaper.

It wasn't long before the ponies started acting as jumpy as I felt, snorting and straining at their halters, and that's when I knew we'd gone from trouble to *Trouble*. The horses could smell the wolves. Which meant, of course, that the wolves could smell us. Which meant that sooner or later—most likely *sooner*—Old Red and I were going to be making some new acquaintances.

I spotted the first one off to our right. He came loping up casual as you please, keeping pace with us from about forty feet out. As wolves go he was pretty unimpressive, looking almost like a scruffy farm dog or an overgrown coyote. But scraggy or not, you can bet I didn't care for his company.

"Gustav . . . ," I began.

"I see 'em," my brother growled.

It took a couple seconds for his words to sink in. Did he say "him" or "them"? A flurry of movement to our left answered my question.

It was another wolf, and there was nothing unimpressive about this specimen. He was as brawny as his friend was scrawny, and I could see thick muscles working beneath his heavy, gray coat as he tracked us. He gave me every opportunity to get an eyeful, too, for he was more daring than his packmate, moving in so close I could've pelted him with a snowball if I'd had one to throw.

"Watch your rear," Old Red said.

"Gee, thanks for the advice, Brother," I replied sourly. "But maybe you should've thought of that before we left Billings."

"I don't mean watch your ass, you idjit. I mean look out behind you. They'll come for your horse the way they go after cattle—from behind, tryin' to hamstring the straggler."

I swiveled around and looked behind me, and the word that escaped my lips would've landed a bar of lye soap in my mouth had I spoken it in the presence of my dearly departed mother.

"Another one?" Old Red asked.

"Not exactly," I said. "Another *two*."

They were only about twenty feet from my horse's tail, and though neither one of them was as big as the hairy brute off to our left, they scared me twice as bad. I got a look right into their eyes, and what I saw there was fear and something like hate—and most definitely hunger.

I couldn't help but think back on the stories I'd heard about cows picked off by wolves in winter. How they sometimes lived for minutes, even hours, while they were eaten by the pack, wailing in helpless misery until their suffering was finally ended by snapping jaws ripping out some vital organ. It was almost enough to make me hope for a quick slash of fangs across my neck. At least that way it would be over fast.

These uplifting musings were interrupted by my horse suddenly surging again against the reins. At almost the same instant, Old Red's mount did the same.

"The horses are gettin' spooked pretty bad," I said. "If one of us is thrown—"

"I ain't so sure they're spooked," my brother cut in.

"You can't tell me they're *happy*."

"Look at the wolves."

I glanced to my right. The first wolf had his thin muzzle up in the air. Over to my left, the big fellow was doing the same, snuffling and starting to whimper.

"They smell somethin'."

"Oh, Christ," I moaned. "What's it gonna be now? Bears?"

I heard Old Red take in a long, deep breath through his nose. I tried it myself, but my nostrils were frozen so solid you couldn't have gotten a nail up inside them with a hammer.

"Smoke," Old Red said.

It was but one not-particularly pretty little word, but it sounded like a beautiful melody to me just then.

"Smoke?" I repeated. "Smoke like a fire? Like a chimney? Which way? Where?"

"Loosen up your grip on the reins. The horses'll show us the way. Believe me, they're as anxious to get to that smoke as we are."

"No one could be as anxious to get there as *me*."

The crunch of quick movement through heavy snow spun me in my saddle, and I saw that one of the wolves riding drag on us had crept up so close I could almost lean down and touch his silver fur.

"Shoo!" I yelled at him. "Go on! Get, you mangy son of a bitch!"

But this was no slinking mutt out to raid the henhouse. Mere shouts wouldn't run him off. He bared his teeth and snarled, and just when I thought he was going to make a jump for me he stretched out his neck and nipped at my horse's hocks.

He missed, his sharp teeth snapping down on empty air that had been full of pony leg but a moment before. His aim was bound to improve, though, so I had no choice but to hit him with the only weapon I had: my hat. It was a nice hat, too—a new-ish white Boss of the Plains that was still clean and stiff. Within seconds, it was torn to a thousand pieces. I couldn't really mourn its loss, of course, for as long as that wolf was feasting on my hat, he wasn't feasting on my hide.

"Just hang on another minute, Brother," Old Red called back to me. "We're comin' up on a clearing. Soon as we're out of these trees, you dig your heels in hard."

The wolf who'd just made scrap of my hat was moving up on me again, and this time his friend was coming with him. I didn't even have to look at their hunting buddies on the flanks to be certain they were creeping closer, too. They knew we were headed toward a fire, and they aimed to pick off the laggard of our little herd—me—before we could make it to safety.

Just as the two wolves in the rear drew close enough to try for another bite at my mount, Old Red cleared the woods. He gave a "Yeehaw!" and got his pony moving as fast as he could. You can bet I did the same. It would be a race now, pure and simple.

The finish line was maybe a quarter-mile away: a small camp comprised of a cabin, a corral and a ramshackle barn. The horses charged toward it, working hard but moving slow through the thick snow, as if they were swimming in molasses. Fortunately, the wolves were having an even harder time of it, forced to take great leaping bounds to make any progress at all. A fifth member of the pack, who'd apparently been skulking out ahead to cut off any escape, came hurtling out of the trees at an angle, but he quickly got as bogged down in snowdrifts as his chums.

When we finally reached the barn, the wolves were a mere fifty feet behind us, yet Old Red risked his neck swinging down from his saddle and struggling to pull the doors open. It was hard work given all the snow piled up against the wood, and I jumped down to help. We got the horses inside and the doors shut behind us just as our escorts arrived. They sniffed and scratched at the wood outside while I clapped my brother on the back and took in a deep, relieved breath of painfully cold air.

"That's as close as I ever want to cut it," I said. "I thought we were wolf feed for sure."

"We don't play our cards right, we still will be."

"Sweet Jesus, brother . . . can't you let yourself be pleased for a minute?"

"I'll be pleased when them wolves are gone and we're in front of a fire."

It was full-on dusk outside by now, and inside the barn it was as black as midnight aside from soft streaks of light that shot through the looser boards and shingles to form a dim gray spider's web around us. Soon enough we'd lose even that to see by, so Gustav and I got to hunting for a lantern. When I came across one hanging from a nail pounded into a post, Old Red dug out a match and lit it up.

I'd already heard horses snorting and stomping in the dark, so I knew ours weren't the only ponies inside. By lamplight, I could see four others in stalls along the walls. They obviously sensed the wolves that were being kept at bay outside by nothing more than an inch of rotting wood, and they were whinnying and kicking nervously.

"We need to calm them ponies or one of 'em's gonna bust right through the wall and let our friends in," my brother said.

He approached the nearest, tetchiest of the horses, a big calico mare, and reached up slowly toward her.

"There, there, girl," he murmured soothingly. She let him place his glove on her nose, and he began stroking her gently. "Everything's fine. Everything's fine."

I could've asked Gustav why he found it so easy to calm and comfort horses and so difficult to offer an encouraging word to *people*—most especially his own brother. But I had work to do. I snatched up some hay from a bale nearby and walked it toward a chestnut gelding.

"Here you go," I said. "Why don't you—"

The gelding stretched out his long neck and chomped down on my handful of straw, ripping it from my grip.

"Watch out there, pal. You almost got some hand with your hay."

I brought the gelding more straw, and he tore into it like that wolf had torn into my hat a few minutes before.

"I don't think these horses are just scared," Old Red said, offering the mare a bouquet of straw that she eagerly yanked away and swallowed with barely a chew. "They're starvin'."

He swung the lantern around until he spotted bags of oats in one corner, and after we'd unsaddled our own horses and berthed them in a couple of empty stalls, we dipped into the feed and gave all the ponies a decent dinner. Strangely, it turned out only two of them were frantic with hunger: the gelding and the mare we'd tried to comfort first. They sucked up their food in a flash and whinnied for more while the others were but half-way done. Even our tired mounts didn't act near so famished, and they hadn't eaten more than a hatful of dried corn all day.

The food and attention had the desired effect, and soon all six horses were chewing placidly in their stalls, the wolves forgotten. And it appeared the wolves had forgotten us, as well, for the only sound outside was the howling of the wind, with no other kind of howling to be heard.

"Think we oughta make a run for that cabin yonder?" I asked Old Red. "It's mighty cold out here and it's gonna get a damn sight colder before the night's over."

As is often his habit, my brother didn't deign to reply. He was staring at the mare's stall, which was pocked with turds and iced-over slick with frozen piss.

"Sloppy," Gustav grumbled. He turned to look at the gelding's stall and found it in the same condition. "Damned irresponsible."

"Well, I'd say the folks around here have had good cause to stay indoors, what with the blizzard and the *wolves* and all."

"These stalls ain't been cleaned out in at least two days. And it looks to me like the horses that weren't gettin' fed weren't gettin' fresh water, neither." Old Red shook his head, scowling. "That just ain't right."

Before my brother stumbled across the science of detection and deduction via Mr. Sherlock Holmes, there were only two subjects upon which he had much of an opinion: drovering and ranching. And he had *much* of an opinion. He'd spent years in the saddle as both a cattle-drive cowboy and a top-rail ranch hand, so he had the experience to know how things ought to be done—and the orneriness to gripe when things were done any other way. For him, encountering incompetence or carelessness was like taking a big bite of sand, and either one would get him spitting mad.

"Yeah, yeah, true, true," I said. "But lazy or not, whoever's in that cabin has got himself a nice fire goin', and you yourself said you'd like to thaw your ass by it. So maybe you'd best pack your complaints away for now. If we live through the night, I promise

I'll listen to your belly-achin' all day tomorrow."

Old Red glowered at me a moment before accepting that there was some wisdom in my words.

"Alright," he said with a curt nod. "Let's get a look at that cabin."

After searching along the wall of the barn, we found a knothole that allowed us a peek outside in the right direction. There was a near-full moon above the trees by now, and it cast a silver light that bounced up off the new-fallen snow and gave the world an eerie glow. Of the wolves we saw no sign. All they'd left behind them was a creepy tingle that played up and down my spine as I peered out wondering which tree or mound of snow they might be hiding behind.

When it comes right down to it, though, a creepy tingle's no match for a rumbling stomach or the slow-spreading numbness that warns of encroaching frostbite.

"The cabin's not so far away," I said. "I bet we could make it over there in less than thirty seconds."

"Wouldn't take but *five* for one of them wolves to run up and rip your throat out," Old Red replied. "Then again, a few more hours out here and we'll freeze our huevos off. So I suppose we may as well take our chances."

"Good Lord—you'd make a hell of a general, wouldn't you? 'Well, boys, I reckon we're all gonna get ourselves killed . . . but what the hell? Anybody wanna charge up that hill with me?'"

"Come on," my brother mumbled.

As we headed to the barn door, Old Red pulled off the glove on his right hand, reached beneath his slicker, coat and sweater and pulled out his Colt.

"That thing won't be any use except for throwin'," I said.

"Maybe. Maybe not. But it's better than nothin', ain't it?"

After a bit of reflection, I yanked off my glove and pulled out my forty-five. It was so cold the metal stuck to my flesh, and the trigger seemed to be locked up solid. But I have to admit, the weight of the gun in my hand did help me feel better about what was to come next.

"What's the plan?" I asked.

Old Red shrugged. "I open the door. You run. I close the door. I run."

"Alright," I said, giving my brother a salute. "You're the general."

Gustav had put the lantern out by then, so I couldn't see him rolling his eyes. I knew he was doing it just the same, though.

A moment later, the barn door swung open, and I charged out into the snow. All my momentum was leeched away in an instant, and I quickly found myself wading with all the speed and grace of a cockroach stuck in a bowl of oatmeal. I heard a ragged huffing and puffing behind me, and I turned to see that Old Red, being possessed with legs a good sight shorter than my own, was having an even harder time of it. My pace wasn't so slow I couldn't slow it up a little more, so that's what I did, hanging back to make sure my brother wouldn't have to face our furry friends alone.

And it appeared that a reunion was indeed at hand, for when we were but ten feet from the cabin one of the wolves—the scrawny one with a taste for fine cowboy headwear—came slinking around the side of the building. We were so close to the door we had no choice but to continue our mad dash toward it, the barn being by then unreachably distant behind us. The wolf stood there and watched us run past, merely offering a snarl instead of jumping for our jugulars.

Now it's a custom along the grubline trails to leave one's front door unlocked as a show of hospitality to any hungry travelers who might happen by. Of course, such travelers are still expected to knock politely and only let themselves in if no one's around to play host. As you can imagine, however, my brother and I weren't overly concerned with social niceties at that point, being considerably more concerned with saving our butts. Which is why the two of us threw ourselves at that door without so much as a knock, a "Please" or a "How do you do?". As we hoped, it was unlocked, and Old Red and I came crashing into the cabin side by side.

"What the hell?" I heard someone shout as I closed and barred the door behind us. The words were phlegmy and slurred, and when I turned to get a look around I saw why.

Two men were stretched out on ratty old buffalo blankets on the dirt floor. They were leaning back against saddles with their feet up to the fire, and between them sat a half-empty bottle of whiskey. One corner of the cabin was littered with shards of brown, broken glass—apparently the remains of bottles they'd already polished off.

That seemed to settle the question of those hungry horses and the disgraceful state of their stalls. My brother and I had stumbled across a couple of line camp hands on a mid-winter's bender.

"Well, god damn it," one of them spat, and he surprised me by raising his hands up over his head. When his companion did likewise, I finally figured out why: Old Red still had his gun drawn.

"Relax, fellers," I said, working to stretch my lips into a friendly grin. I had a few days' growth of beard on me, and I could practically hear my frosty-stiff whiskers crackling and snapping like shattering ice. "You ain't bein' held up. You got company!"

This didn't cheer our new companions as much as I'd anticipated, and they gaped at us with bleary-eyed distrust even as Gustav lowered his six-shooter.

"Sorry to crash your little party, but we didn't have much choice," I explained. "It's cold enough to freeze fire out there, and the only other spot we could warm up was inside a wolf's belly."

Our hosts exchanged a wary glance before one of them—the man who'd cursed and put his hands up first—finally smiled back at me.

"Don't mean to seem inhospitable," he said. "We ain't seen another soul since back before Christmas, and then the two of you come chargin' in . . . it surprised us is all. Go on and make yourselves comfortable. I'll get coffee goin'."

I was layered up like an onion, so it took me a couple minutes to shrug off my slicker, sourdough coat, sweater, vest and flannel shirt and get down to regular wearing clothes. Old Red seemed to be in no worry to unbundle himself, simply standing there taking in our new surroundings as I peeled down.

There wasn't much light to see by—just the flickering from the fireplace and the dim glow of an oil lamp hung from one of the crossbeams in the low ceiling. Yet even in the shadowy gloom of the one-room cabin, it was easy to see that our new acquaintances hadn't been whiling away the quiet winter hours with housekeeping. As in most drafty camp cabins, the "wallpaper" came from newspapers and magazines, and ragged yellow pages had been pasted on all four walls—though in several spots the paper had been torn down and turned into crumpled balls that littered the hard-packed sod floor. Clothes, boots, tools, even plates of half-eaten food could be found there, too, and there was hardly an inch of floor that wasn't buried beneath debris.

The cabin's occupants weren't any neater themselves. Removed from the civilizing influence of women, most men will do away with such (by their reckoning) effete and pointless practices as shaving, bathing and regularly changing clothes. Our hosts seemed to have embraced this philosophy, as both had the wild, greasy hair, stubble-covered faces, grimy hands and wrinkled, stained clothing that are the official uniform of bachelors alone in the wilderness. They were roughly the same age as my brother and myself—neither one appeared to be north of twenty-five—and were equally mismatched. Although Old Red and I vary by height, with me towering over my "big brother," these other two fellows varied by width.

While the fat one fixed us up some coffee, the skinny one tried to blink us into focus from his spot on the floor.

"Where'd *you* come from?" the thin one muttered, the words coming out so garbled I could barely understand him. Even when I was able to shape his mumbled sounds into a sentence, his meaning wasn't plain: It seemed like something you'd ask a devil who'd just popped up before you in a puff of smoke.

"We were out on the trail when the snow kicked up," I said. "Got off to try and work our way around a pack of wolves and here we are."

"No, no," the skinny fellow grumbled, waving his hand and scowling. "*Where'd* you come from?"

"Jonesy's asking what town you boys started out from," the big man explained. He was heading toward us with steaming hot cups of coffee. "Sorry he's so mush-mouthed. You've probably noticed we've been doin' a little drinkin'.." He stopped a few feet off, and his grin stretched out so far it threatened to push his cheeks out past his shoulders. "Say, why don't you fellers have a nip with us? Sounds like you've got plenty to toast, dodging them wolves and all."

"I like the way you think, friend," I said. "Some whiskey would be just the thing to warm me up."

"Just drip a drop in my coffee," Old Red said. "I'll toast with that."

"To each his own," the fat fellow chuckled. He put the coffees down, then plucked the whiskey bottle from the floor and got to doling out shots. While he was busying himself playing bartender, my brother finally slipped off his slicker and coat, but he didn't bother stripping down beyond that.

Buck—for that was the fat man's name, he told us as he poured—brought over a generous dose of firewater for me and a liberally adulterated cup of coffee for Old Red.

"To the wolves," Buck said, raising up his own cup, in which he'd poured little more than a splash. "May their stomachs stay empty all winter!"

"To the wolves," Gustav and I repeated.

Jonesy didn't bother with the toast. He just slammed back his booze and wiped his mouth with his sleeve.

"Now," he croaked, "*where the hell did you come from?*"

I had to appreciate the man's single-mindedness. In that regard he reminded me of my brother, who could gnaw even the biggest questions down to size like a beaver slowly working his way through a redwood.

"Billings," I said. "We had a few clouds roll in on us there, so we're headed up to Miles City to see if the sun shines any brighter thataway."

"Billings, huh?" Buck mused. "You must've been on the trail . . . what? Four days now, at least."

"Five."

"So what was the talk over to Billings when you left?" Buck asked, leaning in to spill another slug of whiskey into my cup.

"The banks. Ain't nobody talkin' about any other thing." And just as I'd done the previous four nights, I got to acting like a newspaper with lips, talking through all the news I could think of. For a change of pace that night, I almost entirely restricted myself to the truth, perhaps because I was so particularly grateful to Buck and Jonesy for offering safe haven.

Buck kept me well lubricated as I rattled on, encouraging me with laughs and nods in all the right places. I sensed that he wasn't particularly interested in what I was saying, though. His eyes, wide and glassy when we'd first arrived, took on a sharper, dryer look. But while they seemed to gain focus, that focus wasn't so much on me as behind me, beyond me, maybe somewhere back up the trail.

"Damn, if that wasn't a closer shave than you'll get from any barber," he said after I'd moved from the news to a detailed (and only slightly exaggerated) account of our run-in with the wolves. He turned toward Old Red, who'd been perched silently on a rickety chair near the door the last few minutes, and gave the whiskey bottle a suggestive waggle. "I'd think you'd be more in a mood to celebrate your escape."

"Oh, don't mind my brother," I said. "He usually leaves the talkin' *and* the drinkin' to me."

Gustav surprised me by holding out his cup and favoring Buck with a small smile.

"I think tonight I'll make an exception. Hit me again," he said. "You'll have to excuse me if I seem on edge tonight, boys. I spent some long, hard winters workin' line camps alone, and bein' here now I can't help but feel a touch of the old cabin fever. I used to think they'd find me in the spring dancin' naked in the grass bitin' the heads off sparrows."

Buck nodded as he filled Old Red's cup with a glugging flood of redeye. "I know exactly what you mean. I'd surely lose what little mind I've got if ol' Jonesy wasn't around to keep me company."

Jonesy snorted from his spot on the floor and held up his cup for another refill. He didn't strike me as much in the way of company, but I figured he might be better than nobody. For a while, anyway.

"Where are your manners?" Buck joshed his friend. "We're almost a full bottle ahead of our guests. Least we can do is wait for them to catch up." And with that he handed me the bottle with a broad wink.

Gustav took a sip of his "coffee" (which was surely more whiskey now than java) as Buck took a seat on the cabin's sole bed, a narrow, poles-and-canvas bunk that was little more than a travois laid flat. I wondered if our hosts had to flip for it each night or if Buck just waited for Jonesy to pass out on the floor.

"Mighty nice of your outfit to spring for two hands here," Old Red said. "I once worked a winter for the Cross J with no company but a grouchy old tomcat and a family of fleas."

Buck looked put off, as drovers usually will if they think someone's saying they've got it soft.

"Well, I wouldn't call it 'nice.' I'd say it was practical. We got plenty to keep both of us busy out here—miles of wire and hundreds of head out on the range."

From the looks of things, of course, Buck and Jonesy hadn't been busying themselves with anything other than strong drink. But, as is usually my inclination, I aimed to keep things amiable, so not only did I not bring up that particular point, I made sure to jump back into the conversation before Old Red could.

"Which outfit you fellers with, anyway?"

"Our outfit?" Jonesy snorted. "Why, we're with the Crazy 3." He made an exaggerated show of keeping a straight face—which lasted all of two seconds before he guffawed, spewing out a mouthful of spittle along with his laugh.

"That's one I ain't never heard of," Old Red said.

Buck waved a hand at his friend dismissively. "Oh, that's just Jonesy's idea of a joke. We work for the Double Bar D."

As I fancy myself to be a fellow blessed with an especially keen wit, I took what you might call a professional interest in Jonesy's stab at humor.

"What's the joke?" I asked him.

Jonesy just giggled and rolled his eyes, so I tried Buck.

"I don't get it."

"That's cuz it ain't funny," Buck said, and he launched a kick that caught his friend in the back of the head.

"Hey!" Jonesy yelled, and when he swiveled around to glare at Buck he lost his balance and fell over sideways.

"Now *that's* funny!" Buck roared.

Jonesy was rubbing his head as he pulled himself upright, and he attempted to cultivate an air of wounded dignity that was rather hard to pull off with bloodshot eyes and a chin glistening with whiskey and drool.

"You didn't have to go and *kick* me," he growled.

Buck just looked at his friend with a placid, superior sort of amusement that seemed to say, "Yes, I did."

"If you're Double Bar D boys, you must know Les Foster," Old Red said. "He's an old pal of mine."

Buck opened his mouth to answer, but I couldn't resist cutting in line ahead of him. It's not often I catch my brother in a mistake, and I try to make the most of such opportunities when they arise.

"You must have frostbite of the brain, Gustav. Les Foster's the foreman down on the Circle 7. Tommy Sullivan runs the Double Bar D."

"Yeah, Sullivan's our boss man. Don't know him well, though," Buck said, pushing himself up further on the bed and leaning back against the wall. His head bumped into a gunbelt drooping down from a peg behind him, and he scooted over so the leather and steel were hanging just to the right of his ear. "Never heard of that friend of yours, neither."

"My brother's right. Guess I got some frost between my ears,"

Old Red replied with a little chagrined smile.

Buck snaked a hand up the wall and began idly peeling off one of the magazine pages pasted next to the holster. Gustav stared at Buck's fingers—and his smile winked out like the flame of a snuffed candle.

"So you don't know Les Foster," he said, his voice so cold all of a sudden I felt as chilled as I had outside in the snow. "But it looks like you know my friend Mr. Sherlock Holmes."

"Who now?" Buck asked, his fingers freezing mid-peel, his voice even icier than Old Red's.

I did my best to work up a chuckle I hoped would bring a little warmth back into the room.

"Now you're the one who ain't funny, Gustav. What makes you think the boys here have even heard of Sherlock Holmes?"

"What the *hell* are all y'all babblin' about?" Jonesy rumbled as he pushed himself slowly to his feet.

"Look at what's pasted up on the wall by that gunbelt," Old Red said, and though he didn't take his eyes off Buck I knew he was talking to me. "Don't it look familiar?"

I could barely make out the paper Buck had been picking at, but somehow I knew better than to step in for a closer look. Instead, I merely squinted and stared, and after a moment I realized that the page did indeed seem strangely familiar.

It was practically all text, printed too small for me to read from across the room. But smack-dab in the middle was an illustration. After a long gawk I could make out two gentlemen—one bare-faced, wearing a bowler, his mustachioed companion in a top hat. They were gazing down intently at something the smooth-faced man held in his hand.

"Well, I'll be," I said once the full light of recognition finally dawned. "That's a page from the new Holmes story in *Harper's*."

Old Red nodded. "'The Yellow Face.' That there's Mr. Holmes and Dr. Watson themselves."

"Mr. Who and Dr. What?" Jonesy spat.

Buck puffed out a series of quick breaths, and it took me a

moment to figure out that he was trying to work up a chuckle.

"Oh, we ain't bothered to read all the magazines and newspapers we got pasted to the walls. Some stuff's only good for keepin' out drafts, know what I mean? If you want something worth a gander, try lookin' behind you. That's where we put up the corset pictures from the Montgomery Ward catalog."

Gustav didn't turn for a peek. Instead, he moved his hand closer to his gun.

"We just got that story in the mail a little over a week ago," he said, and again I could tell his words were meant for me alone. "But remember what Buck here said. He and Jonesy ain't seen another livin' soul since *Christmas*. That's a month back."

"So?" I said, not taking the time to puzzle it out.

"Yeah, *so?*" Buck repeated—and then his hand was flying up and grabbing for the holster hanging above him.

Old Red's not much on quick draws, but he managed to get his shooting iron out first. Not that it made any difference. For all the squeezing he gave the trigger, nothing happened. The Colt was still frozen solid.

I grabbed for my forty-five, praying it had warmed up faster than Gustav's, just as Buck got off a shot that spit fire and smoke at my brother, sending him to the floor. The trigger on my Peacemaker didn't want to give, so I slapped at the hammer with my palm. The gun kicked and roared, and Buck fell back onto the bed.

Out of the corner of my eye I caught a whirl of motion through the gunsmoke haze, and I pivoted to find Jonesy staggering drunkenly toward a carbine propped up in a far corner of the cabin.

"Don't do it, Jonesy," I said.

He kept on going.

"For Christ's sake, don't do it!"

He groped for the rifle, muttering drunken curses under his breath. My bullet caught him in the side of the head as he turned around to face me, and he spun like a top before slumping to the floor, the wall beyond him splattered with gore.

I'd killed before, of course. I grew up on a farm, so I was

slicing throats and lopping off heads not long after I could walk. But there's a big difference between getting a chicken ready for the stewpot and blowing a man's brains out. I stared at Jonesy—all of him, even the bits that weren't inside him anymore—and the gun in my hand suddenly seemed so heavy I could barely hold it.

Shooting six-guns in a cabin's a bit like firing off a cannon in a closet, and it took a few seconds for my ears to stop ringing. When they did, I heard a sound that made me wish to be deaf again.

It was the sound of a man screaming.

I spun around to find Old Red sitting on the floor, looking stunned. A few feet behind him was his Stetson, blackened with soot and torn through with a brand new bullet hole in the crown. We'd both of us had the damnedest luck with hats that day.

Buck was writhing on the bed nearby. He'd been gutshot. The pain was so fierce he couldn't even keep hold of his gun, and it slipped from his grasp and fell to the floor as he shrieked in agony.

My brother crawled over and picked up the gun.

"You killed the line camp hand who was livin' here," he said. "Why?"

Buck seemed to be fighting to catch his breath, maybe so he could talk instead of scream, but he couldn't quite do it. All he had to communicate with were his eyes—eyes filled with equal parts hatred and pleading. He pressed his hands to his round, heaving belly and wailed louder than ever.

I nearly jumped out of my boots when another cry answered his from just outside the cabin.

Our friends the wolves hadn't left.

"Ain't nothin' we can do about that wound, Buck," Gustav said, raising his voice to be heard above the awful chorus of howls. "You're gonna die. And the pain's only gonna get worse before you do. You know that."

Buck's head quivered and jerked, and at first I thought he was going into his death rattle. Then I realized he was nodding. He was telling my brother "yes." Giving his permission.

Old Red stood, took a step back and shot him dead. He did

it calmly, with absolute economy, not wasting the slightest bit of energy on flourish or emotion. He was simply doing what needed to be done, like killing a mad dog. No matter that the mad dog used to be a man.

The second the shot rang out, the howling stopped, both inside and out.

"Gustav," I said, "what the hell just happened?"

My brother took in a deep breath and let it out again with a cough.

"Later. Right now we'd better open the door a crack and get some of this smoke out of here. Be careful, though."

"I will," I said. "Ain't no more wolves gettin' in here."

I stood guard by the door, letting frigid, fresh air blow in while Old Red stacked the bodies up in a corner like some kind of macabre woodpile. Neither one of us felt like taking the bed that night, though, and we ended up stretched out on the buffalo blankets before the fire just as Buck and Jonesy had been when we arrived.

"When did you know those two fellers was bad?" I said as we stared over our toes into the flames.

"I didn't *know* it 'til Buck grabbed for his gun. But I was thinkin' on it even before we came in here. The horses out in the barn—that just didn't sit right. Two of those ponies was bein' looked after, two obviously wasn't. If the hands were too damn lazy to do their jobs, *none* of the horses would've been fed or cleaned up after. Why care for two and starve two?"

"Cuz two of the horses ain't yours?" I ventured.

"That's what I was thinkin'. Buck and Jonesy, they weren't plannin' on stayin' long, and they aimed to travel light when they left. Those other two horses—the ones belongin' to the line camp hand—they were useless to 'em."

"Hey . . . what about that line camp hand? Where is he?"

"Think about it, brother. Where'd those wolves go when they stopped sniffin' after us? Why are they still hangin' around the cabin?"

I gave the questions the thought Gustav suggested. I didn't care for where those thoughts took me.

"They found somethin' else to eat."

Old Red nodded. "Buck and Jonesy must've thrown the body out back somewhere. Grounds too icy-hard to dig a grave—not that those two would've bothered tryin'."

"But *why* kill the man? Why be here at all?"

"A rendezvous, I reckon. Remember what outfit Jonesy said they worked for: 'The Crazy 3.' That joke starts to make sense if you figure they were waitin' for somebody."

"Well, damn it—what if that feller comes saunterin' in here now lookin' for his pals? Ain't you worried he might, you know, take offense that we *shot 'em to death?*"

Gustav snuggled in under his blanket and closed his eyes.

"Nope, I ain't particularly worried," he said. "Now grab yourself some winks. We've got a lot of ridin' still to do tomorrow."

Well, there I was shacked up in a snowed-in cabin with two fresh corpses in the corner, another one somewhere outside, a pack of man-eating wolves prowling around nearby and an outlaw fixing to knock on the door any second. You can guess how much sleep I got that night.

The next morning we were treated to a sight we'd been denied all the previous day: the sun. It came up with a bold brightness that made everything beneath it seem beautiful. Almost. There was plenty of ugliness in the shady dark of the cabin, and we decided to bring it out into the sunshine.

I dragged Buck and Jonesy around back while Old Red kept watch with the carbine. It just didn't seem right to let them stink up the cabin, you see, so we left them in a fitting spot—next to the man they'd killed and dragged out back themselves. He wasn't much more than bloody rags and bones by that point, and even his boots had been gnawed into gnarled knots of leather.

We found more of the same an hour later, after we'd backtracked to the spot where we picked up our wolf-pack convoy the day before. They'd been eating something when we'd first spied them, and now I understood why Old Red hadn't been worried about the Crazy 3's third member: *He* was the something the wolves had been snacking on. His mount must have thrown him and escaped, for there was no sign of a horse nearby. But half-buried in the snow not far from the man's chewed-up carcass we did find at least part of the pony's cargo.

It was the shredded remnants of a canvas bag, black lettering still legible on one side. I read the printing out for Gustav.

"'Wells Fargo.' So this was a gang we were up against."

"Nope." And then my brother launched into a quote from Mr. Holmes. "'By a man's finger-nails, by his coat-sleeve, by his boots, by his trouser-knees, by the callosities of his forefinger and thumb, by his expression, by his shirt-cuffs—by each of these things a man's calling is plainly revealed.'"

"So exactly what calling is revealed by *that*," I asked, nodding at the mess in the snow before us.

"Not much. But I saw enough of Buck and Jonesy to know they were drovers, just like us . . . only hungrier," Old Red said. "They must've hit a depot or jumped a courier or somethin'. Got separated. Had an out-of-the-way hideout picked out—a little line camp in the middle of nowhere. Planned on meetin' there to divvy up their haul."

"Well, it got divvied up alright."

I scanned the snow around us for any sign of the money, but there was nary a buck to be seen. The winds had no doubt spread the bag's contents hither and yon, and come spring bluebirds and thrushes across Montana would be building their nests from ten-dollar bills.

I suggested trying to track down the man's mount to see what might still be left in the saddlebags, but Gustav wasn't throwing our next move open to a vote. We had a new string of horses—for we couldn't leave all those ponies behind to die slowly in the cold—and who knew how far to go that day. We got back on the trail and moved as fast as we could northeast. We were looking sharp for wolves the whole time, of course, but we didn't see a one all the way to Miles City.

We sold off the spare horses as soon as we could and sent the money (along with a letter of explanation) to Tommy Sullivan at the Double Bar D. Tommy wouldn't find many greenbacks stuffed in the envelope, though. The bank closings had long since beat us to Miles, and many a new pauper was forced to part with everything he had just to scrape up his next meal. There were so many horses on the market we practically had to pay someone to take those extras off our hands. I suggested that we keep a portion of the meager proceeds as a sort of "handling fee," seeing as the ponies would've died if not for us and we surely needed the cash more than the Double Bar D. My brother wouldn't hear of it. Instead, he had us check in with the Wells Fargo office, hoping to maybe collect a bounty on "The Crazy 3." The fellow running the place denied there'd been any robberies recently, however.

"Them boys must not have got away with much," Old Red said to me as we left. "It's cheaper for the company to save face and pretend nothin' happened."

Unfortunately, our search for employment was every bit as unrewarding. The only possible job openings were with the town marshal's office: Each day brought fresh foreclosures, and they needed a slew of new deputies. I even heard of one new-hired lawman whose first assignment was his own eviction. We held our noses and signed onto the waiting list to become deputies should any positions open up, but the Doolin-Dalton gang would have to ride into town and kill three-quarters of the male population for our names to hit the top of the roster.

That's left us with little to do but think (Old Red's specialty) and drink (when my brother lets me waste a few bits on beer) and write stories for high-class magazines that'll probably never print them anyway. Of course, we still have Gustav's detective tales to help us pass the time, though we've lacked the funds to acquire anything new for our little library. So I've been reading the same stories all over again.

When we circled back around to the first Holmes yarn Gustav

found in *Harper's*, "The Cardboard Box," I took special interest in a passage I'd paid no mind to the first three or four times I read it out for my brother.

"What is the meaning of it, Watson?" Holmes asks after bringing a particularly gruesome case to a not-particularly-happy ending. "What object is served by this circle of misery and violence and fear?"

This was the very question that had been plaguing me ever since that night in the cabin, and once I'd wrapped up the story I had to ask it of Old Red.

My brother took a few long, pensive puffs on his pipe before offering me what answer he could.

"Well, I reckon this is one instance where Mr. Holmes is barkin' up the wrong tree. Ain't no use askin' the meaning of such things. What happened back along the trail . . . . "

Gustav shook his head and shrugged at the same time, for once perfectly willing to admit we faced a mystery no amount of deducifying could solve.

"It's just been a damn hard winter, that's all."

Sincerely,

O.A. Amlingmeyer
Langer House Hotel
Miles City, Montana
February 9, 1893

# DEAR DR. WATSON

Dr. John Watson
*The Strand Magazine*
George Newnes Ltd.
3 to 13 Southampton Street
Strand, London, England

Dear Dr. Watson,

"Better late than never" is one of those supposed truisms that's not always all that true. If you make chicken soup for a sick friend but forget to give it to him, let's say, you'd be ill-advised to serve it to him when he's up and about a month later—unless you're trying to get him sick all over again.

Nevertheless, my brother Gustav and I feel compelled to extend our sympathies to you regarding the loss of your friend, Mr. Sherlock Holmes. Though Mr. Holmes passed more than two years ago, we only learned of it recently, so in addition to sympathies we extend apologies if this missive merely serves to reopen an old wound. Sprinkling on salt is the last thing we'd want to do. Rather, we think (or at least hope) that we can offer some small measure of balm.

I'm sure you've heard again and again that Mr. Holmes isn't really dead. Your remarkable accounts of his cases have graced him with an immortality of sorts, and so long as he's remembered, he's not truly gone. I can testify to the truthfulness of that—and take it a step further.

Mr. Holmes has attained more than fame. For some of us, he's become a way of life.

Not that Gustav and I could claim to be "consulting detectives" like your friend. Being cow-hands in the American West, the only thing we're ever consulted on is which steer to rope and brand next. But my brother's determined to change that. And with the help of your stories, he just might succeed.

A stray copy of *The Strand* first introduced us to you and Mr. Holmes last year. Immediately, Gustav set about studying on the story inside ("The Red-Headed League") the way the college boys at Harvard and Yale study on . . . well, whatever it is they study. My formal education lasted a mere six years, you understand, while Gustav measures his schooling not in years but months. To this day, I have to do all his reading for him. But unlettered though he is, my brother's far from un*brained*, and he soon memorized "The Red-Headed League" and every other Holmes tale we could get a rope on.

Gustav's always been a gloomy sort of fellow—it's why he's known as "Old Red" in drovering circles. He may yet have the fiery-red hair of a young man, but he's prone to the black moods of a bitter, gray-bearded codger. He's still his old dark-tempered self most of the time, but that changes when he gets to talking about your stories. They light him up like a rusty old lantern that's been dusted off and fresh-filled with oil.

Old Red's even begun detecting, in an amateur enthusiast kind of way, and he's actually proved to be quite good at it—though *I'm* not always enthused about the danger his snooping can put us in. All the same, when Gustav set off in search of actual employment as a detective last month, I was riding right alongside him, bouncing from town to town across Montana and Wyoming. Some folks might ask why I'd be so willing to tag along on another fellow's crusade, but I reckon you're the last man on earth I'd have to explain that to.

Sadly, the first dozen or so detectives we encountered welcomed us not with open arms but with open contempt. The symbol of the Pinkerton National Detective Agency might be the great all-seeing eye, yet it may as well be the great butt-kicking boot as far as we're concerned. When we weren't laughed out of town, we were simply ignored. Yet Gustav's determination never wavered.

"Well, that about does it for Montana," he said as we walked out of the Pink office in Missoula.

"Idaho?" I sighed. I closed the door behind me, but I could still hear the Pinkerton men guffawing inside.

Old Red nodded. "Idaho."

I turned for a last look in at the Pinks, intending to do what they'd just done to us. Namely, spit in their eye—in this case, the eye painted on their office window above the words "WE NEVER SLEEP." I saw one of the men inside headed toward us, though, so I thought it best to swallow my pride (and my phlegm) until we heard what he had to say. I poked Gustav with an elbow, and he turned around just as the detective opened the door and leaned outside.

"Hold on! I got a tip for you."

He was a portly man with the round, leering face of a little boy tormenting ants, and I was tempted to offer him a tip of my own: watch his mouth or he'd get it smacked.

"Oh?" I said instead.

The man nodded. "You two might not be fit to be Pinkertons, but I bet you'd make a fine couple of Bloebaums."

"A fine couple of what now?" Old Red asked, obviously unsure to what degree he should be insulted.

The chubby Pink grinned. "You wanna be detectives?" He jerked his big, ham-like head to the left. "Follow your nose."

Then he ducked inside and got back to laughing with his friends.

"You ever hear of a 'blow bomb'?" my brother asked me.

"Nope. But I can tell you this much: It ain't a compliment." I started toward the post where our horses were hitched. "Sorry, fellers. No rest for the weary. It's on to Idaho for the lot of us."

"Not yet, it ain't."

Before I'd even turned around, Gustav was clomping away up the clattering planks of the sidewalk.

"And just where are you goin'?"

"Takin' the man's tip," he said without looking back.

"That weren't no tip. It was a kick in the teeth!"

Old Red kept going. I muttered a curse and set after him.

It didn't take many strides to reach Gustav's side. I'm "Big Red" to my brother's "Old Red," and you don't earn a handle like mine with stumpy legs. But even little Tom Thumb himself would've caught up quick enough, for Gustav suddenly made the sort of stop you come to when walking into a brick wall.

He was staring at something ahead and to the left of us—another office window, I saw when I followed his line of sight. There was a large, pinkish triangle painted on the glass.

"Oh, you gotta be kiddin'," I said when I realized what it was.

The big blob was a nose. There were words printed both above and beneath it, and I read them aloud.

*THE BLOEBAUM NATIONAL DETECTIVE AGENCY*
*WE SNIFF OUT THE TRUTH*
*EST. 1892*

This being June of 1893, of course, I didn't consider the agency's date of establishment much of an endorsement. I also thought its slogan and symbol, in a word, stunk.

None of that slowed Old Red down, though. He marched straight into that office. I followed, because . . . well, I reckon fellows like you and me just kind of get in the habit, don't we?

There wasn't much to the Bloebaum National Detective Agency's Missoula office. Three filing cabinets—battered. Two wicker chairs for clients—shabby. One desk—cluttered.

And one man—surprised.

"Yes?" the man said, jerking his gaze up from a newspaper spread across the desk. He was fortyish, well dressed and good looking, but his suit and his features alike had a washed-out quality, like a pretty picture that's starting to fade. "What do you want?"

There was an edge of fear in the man's voice.

My brother may be the deducifier and the elder of the two of us to boot. But I'm the talker. So Old Red took off his weather-beaten Boss of the Plains and nodded at me.

"Good afternoon, sir," I said, sweeping my own hat off my head. "My name's Otto Amlingmeyer, and this is my brother Gustav. We'd just like a moment of your time to discuss any employment opportunities the Bloebaum Agency might have for . . . . "

There was no point in continuing—not with the man laughing the way he was. It wasn't the scornful hooting we'd been hearing from the Pinks, though. It was a laugh of relief.

Old Red and I were dressed rough, for the trail. We looked like what we were—drifters, grubline riders, saddle bums.

Or gunmen, maybe. Hired toughs.

It wouldn't rise to the level of "deduction" as Mr. Holmes would define it, but I could make a pretty decent guess just then. When we'd walked in, the man assumed we were there to stomp the stuffing out of him.

"You'll have to excuse me," he said, choking off his chuckles. "It's just that . . . . " He shrugged, his manner quickly turning cold and dismissive. "There's no work for you here."

I put my hat back on. We'd just doubled our daily quota of rejection, and I was eager to find someone who'd actually be pleased to see us. The nearest bartender, for instance. But before I could head for the door, Gustav moved in the opposite direction, stepping closer to the man's desk, hat still in hand.

"Doesn't look like there's much work for you either, Mr. Bloebaum."

The man scowled at him a moment, then looked down at his newspaper. "That's none of your business."

"It could be."

Bloebaum (for obviously my brother had him pegged correctly) slowly brought his gaze back up again. "What do you mean?"

"I mean it must be hard for a man in your position—trying to compete with a big outfit like the Pinkertons all by your lonesome.

Folks see a half-empty office, one feller sittin' around readin' the paper, they think penny ante, second rate . . . and they just walk up the street to the Pinks. But it don't have to be like that."

Gustav's usually not one for blowing smoke, but he can be a regular chimneystack when he's detecting—or trying to land a job detecting, apparently.

Bloebaum smirked at him sourly. "So what I really need to do is pay a couple cowboys to run around in here pretending to be my busy staff?"

Old Red shook his head. "I ain't talkin' about pretendin'."

The detective sighed, his smile turning wistful. "Look, I know times are hard. I'm sure you two really need the work, but I can't—"

"I ain't talkin' about workin' for pay, neither."

Bloebaum blinked at him. "You're not?"

"Yeah," I blurted out. "You're not?"

"No. I ain't," Gustav said firmly. "We got us a little nest egg—"

"Hummingbird size, maybe," I cut in.

"—so we can put in a little stretch for free to show you what we can do," my brother plowed on. "We might look like your ordinary, everyday out-of-work waddies, but believe you me—we know a thing or two about deducifyin'. All we need is a chance to prove it."

Bloebaum furrowed his brow. "'Deducifying'?"

"Just think it over. We'll be around."

Gustav put on his hat and headed for the door.

"Thanks for consultin' me, Brother," I said under my breath as I followed him. "I do so appreciate the faith you put in my good judgment and—"

"*Wait.*"

Old Red peeked over at me, lips twisting into his smug little "Ain't I smart?" smile. He turned to face Bloebaum again.

"Yeah?"

"Prove you mean it," the detective said.

"How?"

Bloebaum held out his hands toward the rickety-looking wicker chairs.

"A test," he said.

We sat. We listened.

We began our careers as burglars.

Not that Bloebaum described his "test" as burgling. It was "procuring a document that could compromise a client's good standing in the community." Pilfering an illicit love letter, in other words.

"The lady in question knows the gentleman in question wants the letter back," Bloebaum explained. "The lady in question is powerful—and vindictive. If the recovery of the letter is ever linked to me, she could strike back. It would be easy for someone like the lady in question to have someone like *me* squashed like a bug."

"Perhaps through the husband in question?" Old Red said.

Bloebaum nodded. "There is a husband, yes. An important man. Which is why the gentleman in question is so anxious to get the letter back. If the husband should stumble across it . . . disaster."

"What about the thieves in question?" I asked. "Us. How exactly are we gonna steal something when we don't even know who we're supposed to be stealin' it from?"

"I'll tell you how to find the lady in question's home," Bloebaum said. "You'll be able to *recover* the letter from there Sunday morning, when the lady and her husband will be at church—as will I and the gentleman in question."

"Givin' yourselves perfect . . . whataya call 'em? Allabees."

"Alibis. Yes. Very good." Bloebaum offered my brother an insinuating smile. "You *do* have the mind of a detective, don't you?"

"Too bad he's completely lost it," I wanted to say. But I held my tongue until Gustav and I were reviewing the day's events over nickel beer at a dive saloon.

"You wanna play Sherlock Holmes? Fine. I'm behind you," I said. "But playin' sneak thief's another thing entirely."

Old Red was hunched over our little table like he might just lay down his head on it and take a nap. "I know. But it's just this once. To prove we got the cojones for the work."

I took a pull on my beer, then prodded him with the mug. "How do you *know* it'll be just the once? You ever think about what detectives really do day to day? I know it's the puzzle-bustin' that appeals to you—the Holmesifyin'. But that can't be all there is to the job. There ain't no coin in it. For all we know, snatchin' mash notes back from womenfolk is a workin' detective's bread and butter."

Gustav straightened up and glared at me. "Not for Sherlock Holmes it wasn't."

I shrugged then—and I apologize to you now, sir, for what I said next.

"You sure 'bout that, Brother? We've read what? Eight of Doc Watson's stories? For all we know, ol' Holmes was creepin' into ladies' boudoirs all the time to pilfer some—"

"Holmes didn't 'creep' and he didn't 'pilfer,'" Old Red snapped. "He was a gentleman."

I nodded solemnly, knowing I'd gone too far.

"Sure. Alright. But what about Bloebaum? What about the Pinkertons?" I shrugged again. "Hell, what about *us*?"

Gustav scooped up his beer and downed a big gulp.

"We're doin' what we gotta do." He slammed the mug back on the table and wiped foam from his mustache. "Mr. Holmes would understand."

You'd know best if that was true, I reckon. Me, I kept my big mouth shut, except to guzzle a couple more beers. And I kept on letting the matter lie through most of the next day. We passed the time cleaning the trail dust from our gear, treating ourselves to shaves and hot baths and taking a fine-tooth comb to a story in the latest issue of *Harper's Weekly*—"The Reigate Puzzle" by one John Watson.

"Well, you were right," I said after reading it out for the first time.

Old Red had been stretched out on our creaky little flophouse bed, staring at the ceiling as he listened to your tale. He turned toward me looking both aggravated and befuddled, like a man who's been awakened from a nightmare by a kick to the head.

"Right about what?"

"Ol' Holmes got up to a few tricks there alright, but in the end he rooted out the truth without a single creep or a solitary pilfer," I said. "Yup. I guess that is how a *gentleman* goes about his detectivin'."

"Yeah," Gustav said peevishly. "But did you notice what cracked the mystery open for him in the end?"

I glanced back down at one of the illustrations in the magazine—a reproduction of a torn note from which Holmes claimed he could make twenty-something separate deductions (though he only ladled out a handful in the story).

"I'd say that little slip of paper was the nub of the matter."

"Not just the paper—the writin' on it," Old Red said. "Holmes, he knew what kind of men he was dealin' with just from the way that note was scribbled out."

My brother didn't sound awestruck, as he so often does when speaking of Mr. Holmes's abilities. He sounded miserable. And it wasn't hard to deducify why.

Seeing and thinking—those things Gustav can do as well as anyone (with the exception of Mr. Holmes, of course). But how could he make head or tail from someone's handwriting when he can't even read "A is for apple" printed plain as day in a grade school primer?

"Maybe bein' *gentlemen* is a luxury some of us don't have," Gustav grumbled.

"Well, just you don't forget: Even Holmes couldn't do everything by hisself," I said. "Why do you think he always wanted Watson taggin' along?"

Old Red made a neutral sort of noise—a growly "Hmmm." Then he rolled onto his back again, his eyes pointed straight up. "Let's hear that story again, huh? And slow down when you get to the part about 'the art of detection' . . . . "

I obliged him by reading out "The Reigate Puzzle" again—

and by dropping the question of what a proper detective would or wouldn't do. It was Old Red himself who brought the subject up again.

It was Sunday morning, and he was waking me with a shake.

"Time to go. Decent folks are in church by now."

I opened one eye. My brother was leaning over me, already fully dressed.

"So where are the *indecent* folks goin'?" I asked him.

"To work."

"Any chance I could talk 'em out of it?"

"Nope."

I sighed. "Didn't think so."

I reached for my britches.

Once I was decent (or dressed, anyway), we followed Bloebaum's directions to the outskirts of Missoula, where we found the residence of The Lady In Question and her husband. The In Questions lived in a neighborhood that rode the razor's edge between well-to-do and flat-out stinking rich. The homes weren't quite "mansions," yet they surpassed anything as unassuming as a simple "house." Fortunately, there was no one around to wonder what undesirables like ourselves were doing there—the neighborhood was deserted. We passed no one in the streets, and even the dogs, cats and squirrels seemed to have headed off to church.

Still, Gustav and I did our best to move with casual calm as we approached Casa In Question, affecting the unhurried amble of familiar workmen paying a call to inquire about new yard work or a box of mislaid tools. Naturally, we'd left our holsters, spurs and Stetsons back at the boarding house, as true tradesmen wouldn't visit a respectable home dressed for a roundup. And naturally, we walked around to the servants' entrance and knocked politely on the door.

Less natural was what we did when no one answered: We retrieved the spare key hidden in a window flower box and we let ourselves in.

"Hello?" I called out as I closed the door behind us. "Anyone home?"

From somewhere deep in the bowels of the house there came a "Yip!" and the tappy-scratchy sound of paws scrambling across floorboards.

"Prince Buster sounds pretty perky today," I said.

Old Red took a few uncertain steps deeper into the house. "Let's hope not *too* perky."

"Prince Buster" was the Dog In Question. We knew about him for the same reason we knew about the key. The Lady In Question's maid wouldn't stoop to thieving, Bloebaum had told us, but somehow selling information to thieves didn't violate her scruples. She'd given the detective the lay of the land, and he'd turned around and laid it on us. We could only assume the maid was praying for forgiveness at that very moment, for she too would be attending services that morning.

Which left it to Prince Buster to defend hearth and home alone. He wouldn't be much defense, we'd been assured, as he was a Great Dane of great, *great* age.

"According to the maid, he's nearly deaf—probably won't even wake up when you come in," Bloebaum had said. "But if he does, don't worry. He's friendly enough with most people, apparently. He's more likely to lick your face than go for your throat."

Nevertheless, my brother and I weren't taking any chances with the prince: In my pocket was a bag of pemmican, which I took out and dumped on the kitchen floor. Hopefully, Buster would prefer dried beef to fresh cowboy.

Old Red and I braced ourselves as the sound of claws on wood came closer. From the high pitch of the *clack-clicks*, it sounded like Prince Buster had just had his nails sharpened to needlepoints.

"I swear to God, Gustav," I said, my fingers hovering over the empty spot on my hip where my holster would usually be hanging, "if that dog kills us, I'll never forgive you."

The *clack-clicks* drew ever nearer. My brother and I clustered together by the back door, ready to turn tail and run at the first growl.

When at last the dog appeared, he didn't just growl—he raced forward and lunged at Old Red, practically foaming at the mouth. He sank his teeth into my brother and began thrashing wildly.

I looked down and laughed.

"Well, I'll be," I said. "When Great Danes get old, they *shrink*."

The dog doing his best to tear my brother limb from limb—and not getting anywhere near succeeding—was all of eight inches tall. He was also a Chihuahua. His head was turned sideways, the better to clamp down on Old Red's boot with his little jaws. One big, black eye stared up at us, full of spite.

"Looks like you bit off more than you can chew, little feller," I said to him.

"*Grrrrrorrow*," the dog replied.

Gustav lifted up his leg and tried to shake him loose. The Chihuahua wriggled and writhed like a fish on the line, but he wouldn't let go.

"Give him a whiff of pemmican," I suggested.

"Right."

Old Red hobbled over to the bits of jerked meat, the dog dragging along behind him, fighting his every step.

"Go on," my brother said. "Get you some beef, you little bastard."

But the Chihuahua still preferred the taste of boot leather to pemmican, and he wouldn't let go. Perhaps I could've loosened him with a kick or two, but my brother and I share a soft-heartedness when it comes to all animals other than cows, sheep, chickens and bankers. We'd no sooner kick a dog than we'd brand a baby.

"Look, you can still walk, even with that furry spur at your heel," I pointed out. "Let's just move this along, huh? I wanna get outta here."

Gustav hung his head as if saying a silent prayer for strength.

"*Grrrrorrowrrowrrow*," the dog said.

Old Red sighed.

"Come on."

He headed for the hallway.

It was a fine, fancy house decorated with fine, fancy things, but I didn't pause to admire any of the fine fanciness. I was mesmerized by that dog. He stayed stuck to my brother's boot all the way down the hall and up the stairs.

"That is one scrappy mutt," I said as Gustav limped into the first room at the top of the stairs—the master bedroom, Bloebaum had told us. "He just doesn't know when to give up, does he? Kinda reminds me of you like that."

"Well, hell," my brother grumbled.

I followed him (and the Chihuahua) into the bedroom.

"What's the . . . ? Oh."

Before us was what you'd expect to see in a bedroom: namely, a bed. But we'd been expecting *beds*, his and hers, with a table in between them. The letter would be in a jewelry box in the top drawer.

With only one bed, of course, there's no "in between." And there was no table, either. Not like the one Bloebaum had described.

"Sweet Jesus," I said. "We're in the wrong house."

Old Red shook his head. "The key was where it was supposed to be. The stairs and the bedroom, too."

He took a few more steps into the room and started to bend down to inspect the floor on his knees, Holmes-style.

"I wouldn't do that I was you." I gave the seat of my jeans a pat. "I bet it's bad enough havin' that pesky S.O.B. clamped to your *boot*."

My brother stared down sourly.

"*Grrrrrrrrrrrr*," the dog said.

"*Grrrrrrrrrrrrr*," Old Red said.

"Look, the table's not here, so the letter's not here," I said. "So why are *we* still here?"

"Cuz the table *was* here." Gustav pointed to the right of the bed, at the carpet covering the floor. The plush fabric had been dimpled here and there with small, circular grooves—the kind bed legs and a table would make. "Only question is, where is it now?"

He stalked out to the hallway as quick as he could with his little caboose. He checked the next room (a linen closet) and the next (an indoor w.c.) before he muttered the words that told me he'd found what he was looking for.

"Well, hel-lo . . . . "

The missing bed and table were squeezed into what looked like a disused sewing room down the hall. My brother moved to the bed table, pulled out the top drawer and produced a long, flat box of dark mahogany. The letter was inside, folded in thirds and perched boldly atop The Lady In Question's glittering gewgaws.

"Looks like we did it," I said without much enthusiasm. "Bloebaum's got him a couple apprentice detectives now."

"Yeah . . . I suppose," Old Red mumbled. He picked up the letter gingerly, pinching one corner betwixt thumb and forefinger as if it was something he didn't wish to sully—or it was something that might sully *him*. "The lady sure ain't shy about her two-timin', is she?"

"Don't appear so," I said. "Every time she went to pretty herself up with her baubles, there was that letter sittin' there."

"Yup. Seems like the mister'd be bound to notice it sooner or later . . . . "

My brother's eyes lost their focus, staring at everything and nothing they way they do when his gaze turns inward. Something didn't sit right. Something, in fact, jumped up and down very *wrong*.

Before either of us could say just what, though, our resident ankle biter let loose of Gustav and tore out of the room, barking at full blast.

Old Red grimaced. "That can't be good."

And it wasn't, for the next thing we heard was the jangling clatter of a key in a lock followed by the squeak of an opening door.

" . . . don't mind missing that idiot minister blathering away," a man's voice rumbled down in the foyer. "And we left before the offertory, thank God. But couldn't you even wait till we were standing for a hymn or something? To just jump up and—"

A woman said something in reply, but she spoke too softly for us to hear her clearly over the Chihuahua's frantic yapping.

"Fine. Run off to your little hidey hole, then," the man snarled. "Stay there all day, if you wish. You'll be sparing me a . . . *Christ*, Tubby! Would you *please* shut up!"

Tubby—the dog, presumably—went right on barking.

"A Chihuahua. A Chihuahua!" The man spat out an oath so foul I could practically smell it. "We finally get a chance to own a good, red-blooded *American* dog, but oh no! You had to have a Chihuahua! I swear, I don't know which is going to drive me crazy first, Cassandra—you or that little pop-eyed freak! Maybe that's what you want! It would explain so much! You're *trying* to drive me mad, aren't you?"

"Why should I waste my time, Orville?" Cassandra snapped back, the sound of her quick footsteps echoing up the stairway. "You've already done an admirable job of it yourself."

"Why, you miserable bitch!"

I'm sure there was more—and worse. Thankfully, my brother and I were no longer around to hear it. Instead, we were dropping one by one from the window in the w.c.

We had to hope neither Orville nor Cassandra heard the call of nature before we could make our escape, for of course there was no way to close the window behind us. We had to hope, too, that they didn't hear the thuds, oofs and mumbled curses occasioned by our long drops into the rose bushes lining the back of the house.

"You know what I wish?" I whispered hoarsely as I peeled a long, thorn-covered stem from my posterior. "I wish we were goddamn *gentlemen*."

"We best get to runnin'," Old Red groaned, pushing himself off the freshly decapitated garden cherub that had broken his fall (though not, by some miracle, his ankles). "The lady might've worn some of her trinkets to church . . . and ol' Orville, he might be hungry."

The letter was in my brother's pocket.

The pemmican was still spread across the kitchen floor.

Our horses were stabled a half-mile away.

We ran.

Three hours later, we were sauntering—moseying into Bloebaum's office at the appointed hour laboring to look as relaxed as a couple of swells out for a Sunday stroll in the park. Bloebaum was still in his church duds, hair slicked back, mustache freshly waxed. He goggled at us nervously as we came in but managed to wait until the door was closed to spit out his "So?"

Gustav brought out the letter and gave it a waggle.

Bloebaum sighed and smiled simultaneously. "I was worried. The lady in question and the gentleman in question attend the same church. Apparently, she was so upset when she saw him this morning, she left the service early."

"Not early enough to catch us," I said.

"Excellent." Bloebaum held out his hand. "And now, if you please . . . ."

Old Red shook his head.

"We don't please," I said. "Not without a guarantee, anyway."

Bloebaum's smile wilted. "A guarantee?"

I nodded. "In writin'. A month's trial employment for both of us . . . at two dollars a day."

"That wasn't our agreement," Bloebaum said coldly.

My brother slipped the letter back into his pocket.

"Well, once we gave it some thought, our old agreement didn't seem so agreeable anymore," I said. "Your client'll be payin' *you* when it was *us* who stuck our necks out. So we figure we've earned us a better deal. Course, if we don't get it . . . well, there won't be much to keep us around Missoula. We'll just slip that letter back under the lady's door and ride off to—"

"*Wait.*"

The detective's eyes were so ablaze Gustav could've used them to light his pipe. All the same, he smiled, his grin bitter yet admiring—a bow to a worthy opponent.

"You two are a lot sharper than you look. Alright. Why not put you on the payroll?"

He leaned forward and got to scribbling on a scrap of paper on his desk, reading his words aloud as he wrote.

"I agree to pay Arthur and August Amblingmayer . . . " (Neither Gustav nor I bothered correcting him.) " . . . two dollars a day each for a term of employment of not less than thirty days. Signed, William J. Bloebaum."

He completed his signature with a flourish and thrust the note out toward me. I stepped up to take it, then moved back a few paces to stand with my brother.

"Now," Bloebaum said. "The letter."

Old Red handed it over—to *me*. I snapped the paper open with a flick of the wrist and held it up next to Bloebaum's "guarantee."

"What are you doing? Give me that at once!" Bloebaum thundered. "You have no right to read it! It belongs to my client!"

I looked over at my brother and nodded.

"Who just happens to be *you*," Old Red said to Bloebaum. "*You're* 'the gentleman in question.'"

"Except you ain't much of a gent," I threw in. "Are you, 'Billy Boy'?"

Bloebaum didn't answer—not with words, anyway. He just sank into his chair, going so limp it looked like he was about to drape himself over it like a sheet.

"It struck me as mighty peculiar, the maid not mentionin' that the lady'd got herself a new dog . . . and had moved out of the master bedroom to boot," Gustav said. "It seemed like whoever was passin' along the skinny on the lady's house hadn't actually been there in weeks. But why the lie about a tattlin' maid—unless it was *you* who'd been in that house? *You* who'd be carryin' on with the lady?"

Bloebaum had looked up, his eyes wide, when Old Red mentioned the lady's room switch. But as my brother went on, the detective hunched over and put his head in his hands.

"Course, I couldn't be sure, so we took us a look at that letter 'fore we came over here. You didn't sign your name to it, but I assume the lady's husband could piece together who 'Your Darling

Billy Boy' was if *he* was to see it. Me, I needed some other kinda proof. I don't know much about handwritin' . . . hell, I can't even *do* it. But fortunately—"

"The l's in 'Billy' and 'dollars' and 'William' is what really gave you away," I told Bloebaum. "Even when you're writin' cursive, you make your double-l's with just two straight lines."

Gustav gave me an approving nod. "Good eye, Brother."

"Why, thank you, Brother."

Bloebaum finally looked up at us again. "Cassandra . . . the lady. You say she's in her own bedroom now?"

"Yup," Old Red said. "I don't know if it's got anything to do with that letter, though. Maybe the husband noticed it, maybe not. I reckon she gave him every chance to see it, though."

"Oh, yes. That she did," Bloebaum mumbled miserably. "It's one of the ways they torture each other—leaving around little hints of their indiscretions. She showed me where she was keeping my letter. She thought it was funny. I didn't. If it ever came out that I'd betrayed a client—"

"Whoa," I broke in. "Client?"

"Oh, Mr. Bloebaum," Old Red said, shaking his head with doleful reproach. "The husband hired you?"

Bloebaum nodded reluctantly, shame-faced, like a schoolgirl caught passing notes. "He's preparing a case for divorce. He needs solid proof that Cassandra's committed adultery. He hired me to get it. It was the first decent job to come my way since I left the Pinkertons."

"'Left'?" Gustav said, cocking an eyebrow.

Bloebaum cleared his throat. "Was asked to leave," he muttered.

"Well, I reckon you got the proof the husband wanted," I said. "You just picked a hell of a way to go about it."

Bloebaum shrugged lethargically, as if he could barely muster the energy to lift his shoulders. "I couldn't help it. Following a woman, watching her . . . it can bewitch a man. Eventually, I approached her, told her what her husband was up to. She . . . . "

He cleared his throat and shifted his gaze downward, to an empty spot atop his desk. "She made me a counter-offer. I broke it off last month, when I finally realized what a fool I'd been. But it's been eating me alive ever since. That letter—it could destroy me. I couldn't work up the nerve to get it back myself, though. Prince Buster hated me. It wouldn't surprise me if one of Cassandra's other beaux finally poisoned the big . . . . "

A piece of paper fluttered through the air and settled onto the desk before Bloebaum.

"Take it," Old Red said. "Makes my hands feel dirty just holdin' the thing."

Bloebaum snatched up the letter, clutching it tight in trembling hands. He gazed at my brother in wonderment a moment . . . before ripping the paper into a hundred pieces. When he was done, he sighed contentedly, then looked back over at us.

"Thank you. Truly. But . . . I'm sorry. I really can't afford to hire you. Not with—"

Gustav barked out a scoffing laugh.

"Mister, if you think we'd still wanna work for the likes of you, you're as dumb as you are dishonest," I said.

As we headed for the door, I did to Bloebaum's "guarantee" what he'd done to his love letter.

"Well," I said once we were outside again, "what now?"

"You know what now."

I crooked a thumb back at Bloebaum's office. "That don't give you second thoughts about detectivin' for a livin'?"

Old Red scowled at me like I'd just asked if he had second thoughts as to the sky being blue or the grass green. "Bloebaum there might've been a disappointment, but our Holmesifyin'—that came through again, didn't it?"

"I suppose so," I said, surprised to hear my brother mention *our* Holmesifying. He usually speaks of Holmes as something that belongs to him alone. "We did get things untangled . . . eventually."

Old Red nodded firmly. "There you go then."

And that was that. His faith remained unshaken.

Or maybe I shouldn't call it "faith," since that's something you're supposed to hold to in lieu of proof. And we've seen proof aplenty, because we've put Holmes's methods to the test time and time again, and they haven't failed yet.

We still haven't found jobs as detectives—or run across anyone who could hold a candle to Holmes. But that doesn't mean your friend's flame has flickered out. You helped it burn all the brighter when he was alive, I have no doubt, and you're keeping it ablaze today with your stories. I wouldn't be so presumptuous as to say the torch has been passed to my brother and me, but I will say this: We've seen the light.

For that, we both thank you.

Sincerely,

O.A. Amlingmeyer
Coeur d'Alene, Idaho
June 21, 1893

# THE WATER INDIAN

Mr. William Brackwell
c/o The Sussex Land & Cattle Co.
Somerset House
London, England

Dear. Mr. Brackwell:

I trust your journey back to Merry Old was a smooth one and you met with fewer of the, shall we say, surprises that were so commonplace during your stay in Montana. (By "surprises," of course, I mean dead folks.) I do hope you won't let the carnage you witnessed at the Bar VR color your view of the American West. Such goings-on are hardly the norm, no matter what your experience (or the dime novels) might lead you to believe. I mean, here my brother and I are in Utah, and we haven't witnessed a murder in *minutes*!

Not that our travels have been boring. Nope, that would hardly do it justice. Tedious—now that hits closer to the mark. Monotonous, wearying and mind-numbing, too.

Except for when it was blood-curdlingly, hair-raisingly, pants-fillingly terrifying. And for about twenty-four hours up in the Rocky Mountains, that's exactly what it was.

When we parted ways a couple months back, you asked that I keep you apprised of whatever progress we might make toward my brother's goal. But I didn't bother writing before now, as there was no progress to report. And there's still not. In lieu of news, though, let me present you with this: something you can trot out the next time you're in need of a spook story to entertain your friends of a dark, stormy evening by the fire. You can tell them one of your American cowboy pals passed it on to you, and such men aren't given to balderdash or exaggeration. Ever. Any of them. Why, the last time a drover was caught in a lie was 1876, and the scoundrel was immediately stripped of his spurs and sent east to become a banker.

Anyway—on to the yarn.

As you'll recall, Old Red and I planned to hit the trail in search of jobs as Pinkertons. *And we've succeeded!* In hitting the trail in search of jobs as Pinkertons, that is. As for actually *finding* jobs as Pinks . . . there we've utterly failed. Believe it or not, when a couple dusty saddle-tramps stumble into a Pinkerton office intent on joining the payroll, they are *not* received with open arms. (Though when one of said saddle-tramps tries to explain that he's actually a "top-rail deducifier" thanks to all the Sherlock Holmes stories he's studied on, the pair is greeted warmly indeed—with gales of laughter.)

As if this wouldn't be tiresome enough, it took us days and sometimes weeks to reach each fresh humiliation. Hailing from Kansas Grangers as we do, we were raised to view the Southern Pacific as Satan, the Union Pacific as Lucifer and the Central Pacific as Beelzebub—different names for the same, great evil—and my brother refused to bankroll the bastards with even a penny from our meager kitty.

Conscience rarely comes without a cost, though, and in this case it was paid mainly by our backsides. After leaving the Bar VR, we journeyed first west across Montana then southeast through Idaho, all of it on horseback. By the time we were skirting around Bear Lake into Utah, my saddlewarmer was bruised black as an anvil.

Now, this wasn't just Utah Territory we were riding into—it was Mormon Territory. And given the clashes of years past, a couple drifting Gentiles like ourselves could hardly assume we'd be welcome, or even tolerated. So we kept to ourselves as we wound down through the Bear Lake Valley, steering clear of the main towns thereabouts.

I didn't mind missing out on the saggy, smelly, lice-infested boarding house beds we'd have no doubt found in places like Pickleville and Fish Haven. Once you've been on a few cattle drives, camping out seems like a positive luxury when there's no night herding to do and no belly cheater waking you at the crack of dawn banging a stew pot over your head. And the Bear Lake Valley made "roughing it" none-too-rough, what with its well-worn trails, ample trees for shade and tinder, and teeming cutthroat trout practically fighting each other for the honor of gracing your frying pan.

In short, the place was Eden without the serpent . . . or Eve. Or so it seemed.

Our first clue that all was not paradisiacal came as we rounded the southwestern corner of the lake. Just off the trail was a rotten, falling-down fence and, beyond it, what might have been a field of alfalfa before weeds and grass were allowed to overtake it. It wasn't long before we spotted an abandoned farmhouse—and then another soon after with its own fields choked with wildflowers and thistle.

This was beautiful country, good for grazing cattle or raising crops either or, and it was a puzzlement to me that farming folk should ever give it up.

"There ain't never been no Indian troubles up thisaway . . . have there?" I asked my brother, eyeing the tree line nervously.

Of course, these days "Indian troubles" are suffered almost entirely by the Indians alone, and they run to starvation and disease rather than raiding and killing. Yet the bloodshed isn't so far behind us the thought of braves on the warpath can't still chill the blood.

"Nothin' but Shoshone and Ute 'round these parts . . . provided you could still find 'em. Friendly ones, they are." Old Red leaned out from his saddle and spat. "Too friendly for their own good, I expect."

"Well, where'd everybody go, then?"

"What you really mean is *why'd* they go. And you know what I say to that."

I did indeed. I'd heard him say it often enough. "It is a capital mistake to theorize before you have all the evidence"—my brother's favorite quote from his hero, your famous countryman, Sherlock Holmes. Most drovers want to be Charles Goodnight or Buffalo Bill Cody if they have any ambition at all, but Old Red's always been a contrarian (or just plain contrary, anyway). The Holmes of the Range—that's what he's set out to be.

We were to rendezvous with ol' Holmes shortly, as it turned out . . . and be in need of his particular brand of wisdom, as well.

As we were passing our third deserted farm, the sun was sinking below the mountains behind us, and my brother made a most sensible (though not entirely welcome) decision: We would spend the night in the abandoned homestead visible just off the trail.

It felt a little like a violation, a desecration even, settling into someone else's house. They hadn't been gone long—no more than a couple years, Old Red judged by the cobwebs and dust and dry rot—and they'd left some of their furniture behind. A table and chairs hewn from local pine, a bed with a finely crafted headboard of mahogany, even a battered foot-pump organ. I half-expected the rightful occupants to barge in any minute, slack-jawed to find a couple presumptuous cowpokes lighting up kindling in their fireplace.

Yet I might actually have welcomed the intrusion, provided nobody felt the need to shoot us. Old Red's far from the chattiest man around—very, *very* far—and whatever topics of conversation we had to chew over had been gnawed down to the bone weeks before. Fresh company would've been mightily appreciated. As it was, we had to rely on the old, dog-eared variety: my brother's stack of Holmes stories.

Old Red requested a rereading of *A Study in Scarlet*, no doubt because it takes as its backdrop a bloody feud betwixt Utah

Mormons. I obliged him, like I always do (my brother, you'll recall, being as short on schooling as he is long on smarts).

Round about the spot in the story where Doc Watson gets to writing about "The Country of the Saints," my brother interrupted me—with his snores. So I put down the magazine I'd been orating from and closed my eyes myself.

Even stretched out there on the floor by the hearth (for the bed frame had no mattress) I was more warm and snug than I'd been any night in weeks. Yet sleep didn't come. I still had that creepy feeling we didn't belong there . . . and that someone might come along to confirm it, loudly and forcefully, at any time.

After what seemed like hours, I finally drifted off to the Land of Nod—only to be yanked back to the Land of Here and Now by a noise outside.

Something was moving in the woods a stone's throw from the front door. And not just *moving* in it. Crashing through it and tearing it down, by the sound of things.

"Hey," I groaned groggily.

"I hear it," my brother said, sounding so crisp and alert he might've been polishing off a pot of coffee at high noon.

We lay there a moment, listening to the creaking of tree limbs and the *shush-shush* of movement through the brush.

"Big," I said.

"Yup."

"Bear?"

"Maybe." Old Red sat up, ear cocked. "Horses ain't spooked."

There was a *snap* outside, loud.

"Yet," I said.

My brother reached down for the Winchester lying next to him on the floor.

"Better have us a look."

Together, we crept to the nearest window and peeked outside warily, careful not to create silhouettes against the ember-glow from the fireplace. Mighty good targets, those would make. And if what we were hearing outside was horses—from a party of the faithful come to root out Gentile squatters, let's say—targets we could well be.

Our own ponies were stabled in a dilapidated barn about a quarter-mile off, and that's where we directed our squints first. My brother and I were safe enough from bear, puma or wolf long as we stayed inside, but we couldn't just cower there while something big and hungry made a midnight snack of our mounts. We might yet have to venture out for a face-to-face with who-knew-what.

There was just enough moonlight to make out a shimmying in the trees near the barn, branches dancing in the half-darkness. The movement was high up—nine or ten feet off the ground. Beyond it, a single star flickered in the nighttime sky.

Only it couldn't have been a star. It was too low on the horizon, not in the sky at all.

Then I saw the *other* star—another perfect pinprick of yellow light, right beside the first. And that's when I knew what they were.

Glowing eyes, at least a foot apart. Eyes that were staring straight at us.

"Sweet Jesus," I gasped. "If that's a hoot owl, it's got a wingspan as wide as Texas."

"Ain't no owl," Old Red growled, and he moved to the door, threw it open and stepped outside.

I came out behind him, Colt in hand, as he took aim.

The lights jerked downward, then disappeared entirely. There was another rustle of quick movement in the trees, and then . . . nothing. No eyes, no motion, no sound for the next two minutes.

"Well," Old Red finally sighed, "we'd best pass the rest of the night out with the horses. Just in case."

I looked back wistfully at our cozy spots by the fire.

"Can't we bring 'em in here with us?"

My brother just went inside and started gathering up his bedroll.

We split the hours till dawn into watches, but we needn't have bothered. *You* try sleeping with only a few planks of knotty, warped barn wood between you and some monstrous whatsis stalking around in the dark. Not that we ever heard the beast come back. But one visit was more than enough to keep me jumping at every cricket chirp all the way to daybreak.

"Well?" I said as my brother and I finally stepped out into the orange-yellow light of early morning.

"Well, what?"

Old Red moved off toward the trees, eyes down, scanning the ground.

"Well, what was that thing?"

"I have no earthly idea."

"You got an *unearthly* one?"

My brother glanced back just long enough to shoot me a scowl. "You know I don't believe in spooks."

"Me neither . . . usually. And last night sure as hell wasn't usual."

Old Red knelt and picked a broken branch out of the underbrush. It was maybe three feet long and still studded with fresh, green pine needles. One end was splintered, and in the middle was a notched groove cut into the bark, as if the branch had been torn down by one powerful, clutching claw.

My brother looked up, then pointed at something above him.

A broken stub stuck out from a pine tree a dozen feet up.

"Spooks don't tear down tree limbs."

"Granted," I said. "*So what does?*"

"'It is a capital mistake to—'"

"Oh, for chrissakes!" I spat. "You wanna make a capital mistake? Quote Sherlock Holmes to me after I spent the night lyin' around waitin' to be eaten by the bogey man."

Old Red put down the branch and moved further into the brush. "Ain't no such thing as . . . hel-lo."

He stopped cold.

"What is it?"

"Tracks."

"What kind?" I asked, already feeling relieved. If it steps with paw, hoof or foot, my brother'll know what it is. I've seen him identify not just a cow's breed but its age, weight and even brand from one long stare at the pies it left behind.

"Never seen the likes of this," Old Red announced. He started off again, still crouching low. "Bogey man tracks, maybe."

"Ho ho. Thanks a lot," I grumbled, following him into the forest to have a look for myself. I assumed he was guying me . . . till I laid eyes on those tracks.

There were two footprints pressed into the soft, mossy sod beneath the tree, right where we'd spotted those eyes shining in the night. They were side by side, a right and a left, plain as day. What wasn't plain, though—not plain at all—was what could have made them.

Whatever it was, it had big pads and claws, like a bear. But there was something stretching from toe to toe, mashing the earth down into little humps. Webbing, it looked like, as one might see on a duck or frog or beaver—a water-critter.

"There's more over thisaway," Old Red said. "Coming and going."

He stopped, but his gaze kept on moving along the forest floor, following a trail I was blind to. Soon he was staring straight into the sun streaming down through the trees.

To the east. Toward the lake.

Old Red started off again.

"Uhhh . . . shouldn't we be movin' along?" I called after him. "Salt Lake City ain't gonna come to us, y'know."

"Exactly. It ain't goin' nowhere," my brother muttered. "Which means it'll still be waitin' for us when I'm done here."

I sighed, then started after him—but only after dashing back to the barn to collect the Winchester.

It was a comfort having it at hand, for the deeper we went into the woods, the stronger grew the feeling that we weren't alone. And we weren't, of course: There were chipmunks and squirrels and songbirds all around us. But they went on about their business in their usual jumpy, oblivious way, whereas the presence I sensed was steady, quiet, watchful.

And purely imaginary. Or so I tried to tell myself.

It wasn't long before the lake came into view ahead of us. I hadn't spied much more than the occasional dimple in the sod or trampled twig after the first set of prints, but that changed as we approached the shoreline. There were tracks in the bank so deep and well-defined even a bottom-rail, bat-blind sign-reader like myself couldn't miss them.

One set led one-two, one-two straight into the water.

The other led *out* of the water.

"You know what I just realized?" I said.

"What's that?"

"Whatever made them prints . . . it walks on two feet."

Old Red shook his head sadly, as if—through my keen powers of observation and deducification—I'd just surmised that mud is brown and water wet.

"You don't say," he mumbled.

The tracks ran parallel to a big, rotten cottonwood that looked like it had toppled into the lake a half dozen years before, and my brother stepped up onto the trunk and walked along it, using it as a pier. The water was crystal clear back toward the bank, but the further out Old Red went, the more it deepened and darkened until you couldn't see what might be beneath the surface.

The tree dipped under my brother's weight, tilting further forward with his each step until the water was swirling over his feet.

"You wanna know what else I just realized?" I said.

"Yeah?"

"I wanna get the hell outta here."

"What are you still doing here, then?" a voice boomed out behind me.

I jumped so high I was wearing the sky for a hat.

"Easy," the voice warned when my feet touched ground again. "Put the rifle down and turn around. *Slow.*"

I did as I was told and found myself facing a big-boned, pot-bellied man of perhaps fifty-five years. He had a long, white, wild beard and even wilder eyes—which were glaring at me, incidentally, over the leveled barrels of a scattergun.

"You," he said to Old Red. "Keep your hands where I can see 'em."

"Ain't got nothin' to do with 'em anyways," my brother said.

We'd left our gun belts back at the barn.

"Listen, mister—you wanna do us all a favor?" I said. "Point that cannon of yours at the water. You won't be gettin' any trouble out of me and my brother, but that there lake I ain't so sure about."

Rip Van Winkle didn't oblige me. He was about thirty yards off—far enough that a shotgun blast might not kill me outright, but close enough that he couldn't miss if he tried.

"Oh, ho. Seen something, have we?" he said, and for the first time I noticed a hint of brogue in his voice.

"We seen *something*, alright—something that come outta the lake, from the look of things."

"You got a notion as to what our something mighta been?" Old Red asked. He was still balanced precariously on the end of that log with dark water lapping up around his ankles.

"At the moment, I'm more interested in who *you* are," Rip told him.

"Amlingmeyer's the name," I said. "Otto and Gustav— Big Red and Old Red to our friends." I grinned as genially as a preacher passing out how-do-you-dos at an ice-cream social. "That could include you, provided you point your artillery some other direction."

The old man tightened his grip on his shotgun. "Your kind and mine can never be friends."

"Now, now—let's not be so hasty," I said (hastily). "I've known cats and dogs that come to be bosom chums, by and by."

"Which 'kind' is it you're thinkin' of, mister?" my brother asked.

"What do you think? Gentiles and Mormons."

"Oh. *Those* kinds." I did my best to look guileless. "And which might you be?"

Rip narrowed his eyes. "Which are *you*?"

# Dear Mr. Holmes

Never in my schooling days (all six years of them) had I ever faced a quiz as weighty as this. Stand up and spell "danger" with a j, and the worst you'll get is laughed at. But answer wrong now and the punishment might be a bellyful of buckshot.

I peeked over at my brother, hoping he'd Holmesed out which faith it was Rip seemed to hold so dear. As you well know, it's amazing the things Old Red can tell about a fellow from little more than a quick glimpse and some careful cogitation. A man's trade, his home life, his hopes and fears—my brother can see it all in a hang-nail and a dirty collar. I've often told him he could clean up as a sideshow fortune teller if only he didn't have his heart set on detecting.

And yet all I got from him now was a shake of the head.

I couldn't bullshit our way out of this. I'd have to gamble on honesty.

I hate when that happens.

"I suppose we'd be Gentiles, as Mormons reckon it. We was raised Lutheran, but ain't neither of us seen the inside of a church in a coon's age." I looked heavenward, palms pressed together as in prayer. "Sorry 'bout that. No hard feelin's . . . I hope."

Apparently, He was in a forgiving mood: Rip lowered his scattergun and favored us with a grin wide enough to spy even through the white thicket of his beard.

"Well, then—welcome to Kennedyville, boys!" he said. "I'm Kennedy."

There were handshakes all around (my brother having been allowed at last to come ashore) while Kennedy made apologies for the less-than-hospitable way he'd originally greeted us.

"Me and my kids, we're the last Gentiles left around here. The other families pulled up stakes after the valley got to overflowing with Mormons. I've just been waiting for the day the Brethren turn up to claim all the old homesteads. And when they do . . . . "

His grin actually grew wider, though there was no amusement to be seen in it. It almost looked like he was a bearing his fangs.

"So what brings you two through these parts?"

I laid out a judiciously expurgated account of our travels, saying only that we were out-of-work drovers headed south in search of jobs. The truth of it—that we'd set out to become sleuths—tends to get folks eyeing you like you're foaming at the mouth.

"Cow-hands, are you?" Kennedy asked, seeming pleased. "So you've worked on ranches."

"Ranches, cattle drives, farms," I said. "We've had dealings with animals about every way you can without joining the circus."

Old Red cleared his throat. He'd opted for his usual greeting when shaking hands—a grunt—but now he had something to say.

"Speakin' of animals . . . ."

He nodded down at the peculiar tracks leading into and out of the lake.

Kennedy nodded, his expression turning grim.

"Oh, yes. We'll talk more about that."

Then he brightened again—and I did, too, when I heard what he said next.

"Why not over breakfast? I can have the girls whip up hotcakes and bacon."

Hotcakes, bacon . . . *and girls?* God had most definitely forgiven me.

I rubbed my hands together and tried to keep from drooling on my shirt.

"Lead the way, Mr. Kennedy."

And so he did, cutting back through the woods to a spread no more than a quarter-mile from the farmhouse we'd stayed in the night before. As we tromped past rows of summer-gold wheat, Kennedy and I chatted amiably about his daughters, Fiona and Eileen. ("Pretty as a picture, the pair of 'em," he boasted. "If there was anything but Brethren around here, they would've been married off ages ago.") Old Red remained silent, though, his gaze darting from side to side as if he might catch a glimpse of our giant, web-footed friend out for a morning stroll.

"Wait here for a minute while I run ahead," Kennedy said as

we approached a tidy little cottage. "The girls would never forgive me if I brought home gentlemen callers without giving 'em a chance to pretty up, first!"

He scuttled on into the house, leaving me and my brother out front with the chickens strutting to and fro hunting for grubs.

"Mighty hospitable feller, once he decides not to kill you." I eyed the henhouse nearby. "When's the last time we had us some eggs, anyway?"

"That all you can think about? Food?"

"Nope," I said. "I'm mighty anxious to meet them gals, too."

Old Red rolled his eyes—then turned them back toward the forest.

"You're wastin' your time, Brother," I said. "Bogey men don't get around much afore dusk."

Yet I was feeling it, too, for all my tomfoolery. That presence again, lurking, watching, waiting.

There were patches back in those trees where the thicket and leaves left it black as night at highest noon. Who knows? Maybe that'd be darkness enough for a bogey man to do his prowlings, even though the sun might still shine.

Neither Old Red nor myself were superstitious men. But, then again, it's not a superstition if something's *real*. And those tracks sure weren't an old wives' tale.

Something was out there. Something . . . .

I forced myself to turn toward the henhouse again.

"Back to more important questions," I said. "Such as, 'Scrambled or fried?'"

"Scrambled, I reckon," Old Red sighed. "Like your brains."

"Oh, no, Brother—*you're* the egghead of the two of us, remember?"

Kennedy stepped out of the house and gave us a pinwheeling wave of the arm.

"Come on in, boys! It's time you met the best cooks in Kennedyville!"

Fiona and Eileen proved to be the prettiest girls, too—and

might have been even if they weren't the only ones. Willowy, raven-haired, bright-eyed and smiling, they were visions of loveliness such as a drover carries with him for a thousand miles. By the (alluring) look of them, they fell in age somewhere between myself and my brother—in their mid-twenties—and though they teetered on the brink of what some would call old maidhood, their charms had not faded but rather deepened with time.

Then again, I always have been partial to older women.

And younger ones.

And skinny ones, plumps ones and all the ones in between.

Oh, hell—let's just face it. I'm gal crazy.

Old Red, on the other hand, is crazy about women in his own way . . . which is crazy-scared. I doubt if that whatever-it-was in the woods could spook him half as much as a wink from a pretty lady. The more Fiona and Eileen fawned over us—taking our hats, pouring us coffee, asking (Huzzah!) how we'd like our eggs—the more Old Red lived up to his handle by blushing as scarlet as a pimpernel.

(I will admit to you here, Mr. Brackwell, that I don't know what a "pimpernel" actually is. I gather from my readings that some come in scarlet, however.)

"You are a lucky man, Mr. Kennedy," I said, slathering butter over a stack of flapjacks that stretched half-way to the roof. "Having two such daughters to look after you here."

Kennedy nodded, his obvious pride slowly giving way to sadness.

"Lucky, I am . . . though I'd think myself luckier if their mother were still with us."

Eileen was hurrying past with a pitcher of milk, and she stopped behind him and put a hand on his shoulder.

Kennedy reached up and smothered her fingers under his big paw.

"She died bringing my youngest into the world. It's been just the three of us ever since."

"I'm sorry," I said.

Kennedy gave his daughter's hand a squeeze, then let go.

"Oh, we get along fine. It's only in the last few years things have turned lonely."

"With the other families leavin', you mean," Old Red said. "There any reason they cleared out other than the Mormons was movin' in?"

Kennedy gave my brother a somber nod. "There's another reason, alright. One I gather you two know about first-hand."

My mouth was stuffed full of griddlecake and bacon, but that didn't stop me from offering a reply.

"Well, there weren't no hands—nor *claws*—involved, thank the Lord. But yeah, we saw something mighty strange last night. And then there was them tracks we was followin' when you, uhhhh . . . stepped out and introduced yourself."

"What's goin' on around here, Mr. Kennedy?" Old Red said.

The old man took in a deep breath. He seemed reluctant to speak, and once he got to going I figured I knew why: He was afraid we'd take him for a madman.

"I suppose the simplest way to put it is this," he said. "We've got ourselves a monster."

Kennedy's daughters stopped their bustling in the kitchen, listening along with my brother and me as their father told his tale.

"The Utes called it a Pawapict—a Water Indian. A spirit that lives in the lake. A lonely, ghostly thing, they said. Coaxes you in, then never lets you go. They can come to you as a snake, a baby, even a beautiful woman . . . or so the legend goes. I never put any stock in it myself. Redskin twaddle, that's all I took it for. But then those Latter Day heretics swarmed in, and before long they were claiming the Indians were right. Some of the Brethren started saying they'd seen a sea serpent up near Fish Haven. The Bear Lake Monster, they called it. Of course, it was obvious what they were trying to do—scare us 'Gentiles' off our land. But we just laughed . . . until we started seeing the thing ourselves. A giant with great, glowing eyes prowling around our farms, frightening our women and children. Well . . . first the Mormons, and now *this*? It was more than most people could take. Argyle—that's what the town called itself then—it just drifted away, scattering like dandelion seeds on the wind until it was all gone."

Now, if we'd heard such a windy as this around some cattle-drive campfire, I know how Old Red would've received it: He'd snort, roll his eyes and quickly compare it to the fresh little mounds dotting the ground all around the cows bedded down for the night.

My brother heard Kennedy out quietly, thoughtfully, though. He wasn't quaking in his boots over that "Water Indian," yet he wasn't cutting loose with any sneers, either.

"Argyle ain't *all* gone, though, is it?" he said.

Kennedy shook his head and chuckled. "No. Not so long as Kennedyville's still here. And here it'll stay. Here *we'll* stay."

"Why?" I asked. "I mean, you got a nice spread and all, don't get me wrong. But it must be awful lonesome up here with all your old neighbors gone."

Over in the kitchen, behind their father's back, Eileen and Fiona exchanged a little look. Raised brows, widened eyes, tight lips.

The question I'd just raised—"Why stay?"—seemed to be one they'd done some thinking on themselves.

Eileen caught me watching, and I beamed a grin at her, turning my attentions into something flirtatious.

"And I can't say I care much for your one new neighbor, from what we've seen of him," I said. "I don't guess you'd be too happy should *he* come a-callin'."

"Oh, I don't know," Eileen replied, her voice, like her father's, honeyed with just a drop of brogue. "We're grateful for whatever company we get."

"Very grateful," her sister added, mooning at Old Red.

My brother felt the sudden need to re-butter his hotcakes.

"Lonely or not," Kennedy said sternly, going stiff-backed in his chair, "we won't abandon our land. Not to the Mormons, we won't."

Old Red peeked up from his pancakes.

"And not to a monster?"

"Ah! That's all the more reason to stay." Kennedy leaned forward toward my brother. "I'm going to catch the rascal!"

That was enough to slow even *my* chewing.

"You aim to catch a 'Water Indian'?"

"Why not? Whatever it really is, it's solid enough—you've seen the tracks. Why shouldn't a trap catch it the same as any other animal? And Mr. Barnum . . . he'd pay thousands for such a thing, wouldn't he?"

"Maybe he would've," I said. "But ol' P.T.'s been dead goin' on two years now."

"Oh. Well." Kennedy shrugged. "Some other huckster, then. It hardly matters who. Get your hands on a living, breathing monster, and the showmen'll line up for the chance to buy him. We'll be *rich*."

I tried for another sneaky peep at the women to see what they thought of their father's beast-wrangling scheme. But they were ready for me this time with faces as blank as a fresh-wiped chalkboard.

"Of course, it's not easy without any help." Kennedy slumped and shook his head. "It's hard enough to manage the farming, just me and the girls. There's not much time for tracking or trapping. Still, I've come close to catching the big devil. More than once, I have. And one day . . . . "

Kennedy slapped a palm on the table.

"But look at me!" he boomed, suddenly jolly. "Keeping guests from their feed with all my blather. Eat up, boys! Eat up! Then, when you're done, I'd like to show you around the place, if I may."

Right on cue, Fiona and Eileen hustled over to re-load our plates with heaps of steaming-hot grub, and when my brother and I stood up fifteen minutes later, my belly sagged out over my belt like an overfilled sandbag. Yet somehow I found the strength to drag my new-found girth around after Kennedy as he gave us a tour of his spread.

He had plenty to be proud of there: acres of wheat, garden

vegetables growing in neat rows, a small but hearty assortment of livestock. And the pens, the barn, the water pump—all of it in good repair.

I was amazed one old man and two women could manage so well on their own. But then I learned of the toll it took, and it seemed to make a little more sense.

Behind the barn, in the midst of a small stand of firs, was a single grave marker. Kennedy noticed us eyeing it as he led us past.

"My wife," he said.

Old Red moved closer to the lonely little family plot. Kennedy and I followed him.

When we reached the cool shade of the trees, we all stopped and doffed our hats.

"A good woman," Kennedy said. "Been gone many a year now."

But not as many as I would've thought. Carved into the dark, knotty old wood were these words, which I read aloud for my brother's benefit:

ABIGAIL KENNEDY
BELOVED WIFE & MOTHER
DECEMBER 1, 1847 - MARCH 15, 1875

Which meant Eileen wasn't three or four years my elder, as I'd reckoned. If her mother died birthing her, she was three years *younger* than me. Pretty though she still was, at the rate she was going she'd be a bent-backed, snaggle-toothed crone by the time she hit thirty.

The Kennedys may have been surviving as a trio, but to thrive they'd need to be a quartet or quintet, at least. If the Water Indian didn't kill them, the drudgery would.

Well, the only decent thing to do was help out in whatever way we could. It was Old Red who volunteered us, actually, though I'd been just about to do so myself. Kennedy tried to look surprised, but it was plain he'd been hoping all along we'd offer to take on some chores. "No need for that" gave way to "You could nut a couple bull calves for me" in two seconds flat.

The rest of the day passed as so many once had for me and my brother. Collecting prairie oysters, milking cows, slopping hogs, chopping wood. It was our childhood all over again, right down to the women-folk. Instead of our dear *Mutter* and sisters toiling away beside us, though, it was Eileen and Fiona. Wherever we were, whatever we were doing, they were somewhere nearby, chattering, singing songs, bringing us cool water and warm smiles.

Hard though the work was, it felt comfortable. Right. Seductive, you might even call it. I'd thought farming was about the last thing I ever wanted to do—all sodbusting ever brought our family was aches, pains and early graves. But the Kennedys did their best to make it seem pleasant.

And pleasant it was . . . except for the flutter in my stomach, the itch at the back of my scalp, the creepy-crawly feeling that kept pulling my gaze to the woods.

*Something's out there.*

The thought stayed stuck in my mind like a bit of gristle in your teeth you keep worrying with your tongue.

Yet Old Red didn't seem edgy in the least. Even more unlike him, he appeared to be enjoying himself, hotfooting from chore to chore with such cheerful obliviousness I almost expected him to start skipping and whistling. Knowing my brother as you do, you might doubt me more on this than on my sighting of the lake creature, but I swear I saw it with my own eyes: At one point, he approached Fiona—not just voluntarily, but *smiling*—and offered to help her hang out the washing.

Soon after that, Kennedy invited us to stay the night. It was an offer we all knew was coming, as the sun was practically down in the treetops, and the shadows from the forest were stretching out ever longer and darker. My brother and I had already brought our horses over to be watered and fed, so there was nothing to do but say yes.

Kennedy seemed pleased—ecstatic, almost—and he

immediately set his daughters to cooking up a regular feast. When us men came in at dusk, we found the kitchen table laden with baked ham, mashed yams, green beans in butter and fresh bread.

I felt a mite guilty about the sumptuousness of it all, these being folks who probably made do with vegetable stew and squirrel meat, most nights. Yet declining such hospitality would be a grievous insult, I told myself. Good manners dictated—nay, *demanded*—that I stuff myself like (and with) a pig. Which I did my utmost to do.

Yet my utmost, for once, wasn't up to the task. My stomach was already full . . . of butterflies. A whole swarm, it felt like, all of them a-flapping and a-fluttering and generally giving me the collywobbles. What I did get down my gullet, I barely tasted.

"You don't like the food?" Eileen asked me from across the table.

I looked up—realizing only then that I'd been staring out the window—and found her pouting at me prettily.

"Like it? Nope." I popped a forkful of ham into my mouth. "I *love* it! Why, with you two here to work the stove for him, it's a wonder your pa don't weigh a thousand pounds."

"I'm getting close!" Kennedy chortled, and he leaned back in his chair and gave his big belly a playful pat.

"So I noticed," my brother shot back with (for him) uncommon impishness. He'd just been picking at his vittles, like me, though for him this was the norm. Most days, Old Red doesn't eat enough to put fat on a consumptive flea.

"You're one to talk!" Kennedy joshed him. "You look like you're about to dry up and blow away. What you need is a good woman cooking for you like this every day."

Fiona was seated next to him, across from my brother, and she turned and gave the old man a swat on the arm.

"*Dad* . . . ."

She peeked over at Old Red and batted her eyes.

"I'm just saying," her father went on, "our friends here should settle down. Drifting from town to town, job to job—that's all well and good for a young buck, but a *man* needs more. Sooner or later, you have to put down roots."

"We used to have roots," I said. "Then the whole danged family tree up and died on us."

"We'll put us down some new roots one day," Old Red added, looking at me—almost making me a promise, it seemed. Then he shifted his gaze back to Kennedy and Fiona. "But the thing about roots is, they don't just hold you steady. They hold you still. Almost like . . . . "

*Chains*, I think he was about to say. He amended himself at the last second, though.

" . . . an anchor."

"Ahhh, but there's nothing wrong with dropping anchor when you've found calm waters," Kennedy said. "Stormy seas, my younger days were. Up here I finally found safe harbor."

"Safe harbor? With your Mormon troubles and your . . . "

I couldn't quite bring myself to say "monster," so I jerked my head at the door—and the blackness beyond it.

" . . . exotic wildlife."

Kennedy chuckled in a dismissive sort of way.

"Oh, well, as much as I might complain about the Brethren, the worst of those troubles is long past. And as for the Water Indian, whatever it is, it's never harmed anyone. It's frightening, yes. But dangerous? That I haven't seen."

"There's a first time for everything," I said.

"Not for *everything*," Kennedy replied. "Not if I can't catch the thing. Then there's no way to know what it's really like. Or what it's really worth." The old man cocked his head to one side, his eyes flashing so fiery-bright it's a wonder his puffy white eyebrows didn't burst into flame. "But if I were to have some help . . . . "

I couldn't stop myself—I jumped. Not that the old man's words were so shocking. It was the dainty foot stroking my calf under the table that startled me.

"Something the matter?" Eileen asked, all dewy-eyed innocence even as her foot snaked its way up toward my thigh.

I blocked her with clenched knees. Flirting's all well and good, but even I'm not dumb enough to let a gal toe-tease me when her father's five feet away and a shotgun's nine.

"'scuse me." I gave my chest a little thump. "Hiccups."

And then I jumped again—as did everyone else.

Outside, twigs were snapping, branches creaking, leaves shushing.

Inside, I was quivering.

"Set out another plate, Eileen," Kennedy said, his voice hardly more than a whisper. "We've got more company."

Eileen didn't move.

"All we have to do is wait," her sister said, voice atremor. "It'll go away eventually."

"We'll be fine as long as we stay inside," Eileen added, so straight and stiff in her chair she could've been carved out of wood herself. "In the light."

"That's right. The night-time's his," Kennedy said. "But we can track him tomorrow, when the sun's out. With three of us to look, maybe we could finally find his lair. And once we've got that, we've got *him*."

"Oh, please," Old Red snapped. "That's bunk, and you know it."

The old man, Fiona, Eileen, *me*—we all gaped at him.

"Excuse me?" Kennedy said.

"You're really just scared to face that thing, ain't you?" my brother sneered at him. "Well, I'm not. Now's our chance, and I'm gonna take it."

Old Red pushed his chair back from the table and came to his feet, his expression a scowling gumbo of fear and anger and defiance. There was a wildness in his eyes I'd never seen before. In any other man, I would've called it bloodlust.

He stomped to the nearest window and peered out through glass so black it could've been a mirror dipped in pitch.

"'His lair'? 'His *lair*'?" Old Red barked out an incredulous laugh. "His lair's at the bottom of the damned lake. Ain't no way we could ever . . . a-ha!"

He jabbed a finger at the window. Even from my spot at the table, I could see what he was pointing at: twin pinpricks of light glowing in the darkness high in the trees outside.

Old Red whirled around to face us.

"I don't care what kinda critter that is," he said, and he marched over and snatched up Kennedy's scattergun. "Two barrels in the gut'll kill it quick enough."

"No, no, no," the old man spluttered. "We need it alive, remember? To sell."

"I think we oughta listen to the man, Brother," I said.

But Old Red was already striding off again.

"Can't sell it if we never catch it. And a body'll fetch a pretty penny, too."

He threw open the front door and stepped out onto the porch.

Kennedy hurled himself from his chair and stumbled after him.

"Noooooo!" he howled.

Old Red took aim.

Fiona and Eileen screamed.

Out in the darkness, the lights dropped downward, then disappeared.

Old Red pulled the triggers, and the shotgun spat fire into the night—but not where the lights had been. At the last second, my brother had jerked the shotgun up, spraying buckshot at the stars.

When my ears stopped ringing, I heard a new sound: whimpering. From the women. And from somewhere out in the forest, too.

"Mr. Kennedy," Old Red said coolly, all trace of his killing frenzy suddenly gone, "why don't you tell your boy to stop playin' games and come on inside?"

"My . . . boy . . . ?"

"Your son, sir." Old Red turned back toward the woods. "And bring them special moccasins of yours with you! And your rig for the candles! Y'all owe us a look at 'em, I'd say."

And with that, he handed Kennedy the shotgun, sauntered inside and retook his seat at the table.

"That was a cruel thing to do!" Eileen spat at him.

"Oh, I'm sorry. Did he frighten you?" I shot back, matching her venom with acid. "Not a pleasant sensation, is it?"

I still didn't know all the hows and whys, but the *what* was plain enough: The clan Kennedy had taken my brother and me for fools. And, alas, they'd been half right.

Fiona and Eileen glowered back at me, sullen and silent.

"Keeley! Keeley, boy! Are you alright?" the old man called out from the porch.

A sniffling "I'm fine" drifted from the darkness of the trees, and then the Water Indian himself emerged from the shadows—a slender, slouching teenage boy. As he and his father shuffled inside, I saw that the kid was carrying a length of rope. Tied to it was a wooden rod sporting a snuffed candle on each end.

"Take those ridiculous things off," Fiona muttered at the boy. She waved a hand at his feet, which were encased it what looked like Goliath's furry bed slippers. "You're not going to track mud all over my clean floor."

Keeley nodded glumly, wiped his nose on his sleeve, and shuffled back out to the porch.

"Make those yourself?" Old Red asked as the kid kicked off "those ridiculous things."

"Yessir," the boy said, managing a sad little smile. He held up his fuzzy fake feet, both embarrassed and proud. "Bear paws and rawhide."

"Neat bit of workmanship. You might have a future as a cobbler," I told him. "Providin' your career as a confidence man don't pan out."

The boy slinked over to the table and took the last empty seat—the one to my left, at the head of the table opposite his father. The rope and rod he put on the table next to the ham.

"Well, isn't this cozy?" I said. "Y'all got any more kin out scarin' the bejesus out of strangers? Cuz if you do, may as well bring 'em on in. There's still plenty of eats to go around."

"We're sorry, alright?" Eileen snapped. She pointed dagger-eyes at her father. "It wasn't our idea."

The old man had slumped into his seat so limp he could've been a scarecrow stuffed with pudding. But his daughter's spiteful tone brought him up ramrod straight, and he met her glare head on.

Eileen's backbone slowly lost its starch until at last *she* was the one hunched in her chair looking wilted. It was as if her father's gaze had sucked the life right out of her.

Kennedy turned to my brother.

"Tell me. How did you know?"

"Well, sir, usually I make it a point not to have any prejudices and to just let the facts lead me where they will," Old Red said, paraphrasing a line from his hero's latest adventure in *Harper's Weekly*. ("The Reigate Puzzle," should you care to look it up.) "But it turns out I've got me one prejudice I can't shake: I don't believe in spooks and monsters. So that's what's been leadin' me today."

My brother looked at the other end of the table, at the boy.

"Led me to notice how them tracks of yours just happened to go in and out of the lake next to a big ol' log—which somebody could use to climb out of the water without leaving more footprints on the shore. And led me to notice a notch in a broken tree limb where the 'Water Indian' had been skulkin' around." He nodded at the rope coiled up on the table. "The kinda notch *that* might make if it was thrown over and used to shake the branches way up high. Or to dangle something up there. A couple candle 'eyes,' let's say."

The boy nodded, looking awestruck. Old Red hadn't shot wide of the target once.

My brother turned back to the old man.

"Course, it didn't have to be y'all playin' bogey man. At first, I thought it might be someone tryin' to scare *you* off—some of 'the Brethren' hopin' to clear out Kennedyville for good. But when you run on ahead this morning to tell your family we was comin'? Seemed like a good time to cook up some flimflam. And when you told us your wife died birthing your youngest . . . and then the gravestone said she passed in 1875?"

Old Red threw Eileen a quick, there-and-gone glance.

"I'm sorry, Miss, but there just ain't no way you're eighteen."

Eileen perked up just enough to shoot him a hateful scowl.

"So I volunteered to help you hang out the washin'," my brother went on, turning to Fiona. "Pinned up some shirts and britches a big, bluff man like your father would bust at the seams. Looked like clothes for a smaller feller. Younger, maybe. Like eighteen, perhaps."

"My, my . . . you're smarter than you look, aren't you?" Fiona said. "But I bet there's still one thing you haven't figured out."

"That's right," Old Red said. "Why?"

Fiona jerked her head at her father.

"Because the king of Kennedyville commands it, that's why."

Then more words spilled out of her, coming so fast, in such a floodburst, she couldn't even take the time to breathe.

"At first, he sent Keeley out to scare you off. That's what he does whenever any Mormons try to stay the night around here. But when he found out you were Gentiles, he thought we could trick you into *staying*. Permanently. As part of the family. Keeley would have to keep out of sight for a while, but that wouldn't last long—just until my father caught one of you in the act."

"Caught us—?"

"—in *what* act?" I'd been about to ask. But then suddenly I knew, and all I could whisper was, "Oh, my."

Caught one of us with one of them, she'd meant. With her or her sister.

I couldn't help myself then: I shivered. When it comes to sheer blood-freezing terror, a lake monster's got nothing on a shotgun wedding.

"You know," Old Red said, "if y'all are this desperate to, uhhh . . . expand the family, I'd say it's time you moved on to greener pastures, courtin'-wise."

"Don't you think we know that?" Eileen cried out, her voice

quavering, on the verge of becoming a sob. "Don't you think that's what we—"

"*No!*"

Her father slammed down a fist with such force every plate on the table jumped an inch in the air.

"I was here before those bloody Mormon heathens, and I'll still be here after they're gone! This is my home! My land! My lake! My family! And I'll never give any of it up! *Never!*"

When Kennedy was done, Fiona, Eileen and Keeley were all looking down, silent and still, like worshippers in church competing to seem the most pious. Hate the man as they might— and I suspected they did—a little blustering and table-thumping and they were utterly in his thrall.

"Well," Old Red said quietly, "I think we best be leavin'."

The old man blinked at him. "What? You can't leave now. It's dark out."

"Oh, don't worry about us," I said. My brother and I stood and started backing away from the table. "We've done plenty of night-herding. We won't break out necks."

"Look . . . . " Kennedy tried out an unconvincing smile. "I'm sorry about the tricks. The lies. Let us make it up to you. A good night's sleep indoors and a hearty breakfast before you hit the trail. What do you say?"

*I say you're insane*, I thought.

For obvious reasons, I kept this to myself.

Kennedy's smile went lopsided and slowly sank.

"You can have your pick of spreads . . . . "

The old man stood and took a staggering step after us. He stopped next to the spot where he'd left his shotgun propped up against the wall.

"Your pick of *wives*. Just stay. Please. You won't regret it."

We kept backing away.

Kennedy took another step toward us. Beyond him, his daughters and son just watched from their seats, unmoving, unblinking, glassy eyed. They seemed strangely sleepy, as if what they were seeing was merely a dream they'd had before and would no doubt have again.

Old Red and I reached the door.

"Don't go," Kennedy said, his voice half-pleading, half-demanding. "We need you here. *I* need you . . . . "

"Goodbye," my brother told the old man.

"And good luck," I said to his children.

And then we were outside in the gloom.

We saddled up quick as we could by lantern light. I kept expecting Kennedy to come out and tell us again to stay. Or try to *make* us. Yet when it came time to swing up atop my mount, I found myself lingering, waiting.

Old Red horsed himself without pausing a jot.

"They ain't comin', Brother," he told me.

He knew what I was thinking: Maybe the boy or one of the women would dart out after us, beg to be brought along. And we could—maybe should—help them out. After all, we knew what it was like to be trapped on a farm, tied down by obligation and expectation. And Old Red, at least, knew what it was like to escape.

He hit the cow-trails at eighteen and never saw the family farm again. And in a way, I felt like he was running from the old homestead even still. You can't get much further removed from the dreary toil of sodbusting than a gentleman deducifier cracking mysteries in well-appointed drawing rooms.

Old Red had freed himself from the past—or was trying to, anyhow, which maybe amounts to the same thing. So if he looked at Fiona and Eileen and Keeley and didn't see the strength there to do likewise, I suppose it wasn't there to be seen.

I pulled myself up into my saddle.

"Think they'll ever get away from here? The gals? Or the kid?"

"Not till the old man's dead." My brother gave his pony his heels. "Maybe not even then."

The horses ambled slowly out toward the trail, finding their way by memory as much as moonlight. It could have been a short journey—all we had to do was head north fifteen minutes and bed down in the same abandoned farmhouse we'd been in the night before. But Old Red and I agreed to push south a ways instead. More than ever before in all our ramblings, we both felt the need to *move on*.

I looked back just the once. All I could see was the dull yellow glow from the cottage windows aflicker through the trees like a sunset shimmering on dark, rippling water. Then a turn in the trail blotted it out, and the last of the light was swallowed into the black depths of the forest.

Should you ever make it to America again, Mr. Brackwell, I'd urge you to visit the Bear Lake Valley. It's beautiful country, and friendly, too. Lord knows they like their visitors.

If it should be ten years before you pass that way—heck, a *hundred*—I feel like you'd find "Kennedyville" there still, utterly unchanged.

Population: Four . . . but always room for more, if you're of the right frame of mind.

Yours faithfully,

O. A. Amlingmeyer
Logan, Utah
July 4, 1893

Steve Hockensmith

# THE DEVIL'S ACRE

Urias Smythe
Smythe & Associates Publishing, Ltd.
175 Fifth Avenue
New York, New York

Dear Mr. Smythe:

I trust this letter finds you and your associates well. I can only assume it finds the lot of you mighty *busy*, as I have yet to hear your reaction to the book I submitted to you last month: *On the Wrong Track, or Lockhart's Last Stand, An Adventure of the Rails.*

Not that I am in the slightest impatient to have you get to it. Quite the contrary. Like a fine wine—or, to be more democratically minded, a jug of corn mash moonshine—my book can but ripen with age. Though I could perhaps add that the public's interest in sampling said concoction might likely diminish as the events that precipitated its distilling recede ever further into the past. Even as dazzling an episode as the commandeering of a Southern Pacific express train fades with time, just as fine wine and moonshine alike eventually turn to vinegar.

But why point this out to you? As a successful publisher, you are no doubt well aware of the importance of striking while the (in this case, railroad) iron is hot. So I leave it to you to proceed at what I assume is your usual measured, deliberate, dawdling pace.

By no means rush yourselves on my account—or your own!

# Dear Mr. Holmes

No, I write to you today not to urge undue (or due) haste in your reply. Rather, it's because, while my book has lain fallow, I have not.

As I mentioned in my last letter to you, based on sheer quantity of thrills, chills and close scrapes, the heroes of your own *Deadwood Dick Magazine* and *Billy Steele—Boy Detective* seem like elderly shut-in spinsters compared to my brother and myself. While ol' Dick or little Billy manage to get themselves into some kind of dust-up each and every month, hardly a day passes without a new threat to life and limb for me and Gustav. Why, I'm sometimes reluctant to so much as get out of bed to make water for fear I'll be attacked by rampaging Apaches or kidnapped by pirates on my way to the privy.

As a case in point, allow me to relate the latest near-calamity to befall us—a tale, incidentally, that I think would fit quite snugly in the pages of one of your magazines. *Jesse James Library*, say. Or, even better, *Big Red and Old Red Library*.

To refresh your memory, Big Red and Old Red would be me and my elder brother Gustav. We picked up our nicknames on the cattle trails we once worked as cowboys, though our handles have little of the drover's usual irony about them. A fat cowhand may be "Skinny," a thin one "Tubby" or a dumb one "Professor," but I am with no uncertainty about it *big*. Old Red's not old per se, having put in a mere twenty seven years on this earth of ours, but he does tend to act aged, often coming across as crotchety as Methuselah suffering a flare-up of lumbago. As for the "Red," our hair accounts for that, it being . . . well, as you might assume, not exactly powder blue.

Having recently lost our jobs as Southern Pacific rail dicks (the railroad frowning upon the mislaying of company property, be it a coffee mug, a signal lantern or—*ahem*—a locomotive), Old Red and I recently found ourselves jobless, friendless and near-penniless in the S.P.'s home town: San Francisco. Naturally, we wouldn't be welcome at the Palace Hotel along with the Rockefellers and the Rothschilds and whichever other visiting fat cats might be on hand. So we ended up instead in the neighborhood known as "the Barbary Coast" . . . along with the sailors and the macks and the rest of the wharf rats.

Of course, the Coast has a certain reputation, what with its dance-halls, deadfalls, footpads, floozies and all-around atmosphere of iniquity. And it lives up to said reputation—or perhaps I should say sinks *down* to it. But once you've seen a pack of young drovers cut their wolves loose at the end of a five-month cattle drive, there's little in the way of wildness that can shock you anymore. Take Dodge City of a Saturday night, switch all the Stetsons to sailor's caps and derbies, and multiply the noise and chaos by a factor of four, and you'll get the Barbary Coast. We figured we could handle it.

We chose for our lodgings a rooming house on Pacific invitingly named The Cowboy's Rest. The *Cockroach's* Rest would have been more accurate, as we saw more cucarachas than cowpokes thereabouts. But shoddy and shanty-ish though the place might be, it offered several advantages as a base of operations, the foremost being (in my brother's mind) the cheapness of its rooms and (in mine) the cheapness of the drinks served in the saloon downstairs. The Rest is also a mere twenty-minute walk from the local office of the Pinkerton National Detective Agency, and it was there we intended to go as soon as the scrapes and bruises we'd collected during our brief run as railroad detectives had healed.

Old Red, you'll recall (assuming you've read my book by now and are merely in the process of securing the huge sums of money required to properly publicize its publication), had it in his head that he'd make a top-rail sleuth. He'd picked up this seemingly peculiar notion from the tales of the late, great Sherlock Holmes that have been appearing of late in the pages of one of your competitors. I say *seemingly* peculiar because, as it turns out, Gustav really does have a natural talent for detecting . . . even if his attempts to prove it tend to end in disaster.

Come to think of it, they can *begin* disastrously, too—which was almost the case here.

# Dear Mr. Holmes

When not sniffing around after an actual mystery, you see, Old Red likes to practice his craft on strangers, sizing them up for clues he can use to piece together the particulars of their lives. "Just got throwed out by his wife," he might say to me, nodding at a glum-looking gent with rouge on his cheek and a wrinkled shirt-tail hanging from his carpet bag. Or "Best lock up the silver when she's in to clean" as we pass a shifty-eyed woman in a maid's uniform—just before she veers off into a pawn shop, a muffled, metallic clinking coming from the bundle tucked under one arm.

It was with this pastime in mind that Gustav and I secured for ourselves a corner table in the bar-room of the Cowboy's Rest the other day. My brother would sharpen his wits with observation and deducification, I would dull mine with steam beer, and thus we might while away a pleasant afternoon.

And pleasant it was, too . . . right up to the moment someone got it in his head to kill us.

The someone in question was a fellow of the type the Frisco papers have taken to calling a "hoodlum"—a young, oily haired hooligan wearing an oversized frock coat, a red velvet vest, a rakishly tilted felt hat and a plain old-fashioned sneer. He'd been seated with a similarly slicked-up and scowly compadre a few tables over, and their hissy whispers and low, dark laughter had about them a most definitive air of skullduggery. This, of course, attracted my brother's undivided attention. So undivided, in fact, it eventually drew some attention itself.

"What's your problem, m_____?" one of the hoodlums snarled, addressing my brother with a term your typesetters would no doubt refuse to put in print.

"I ain't got no problem," Gustav replied.

"You sure as h___ do."

The hood rose from his chair. He probably topped out at a mere five foot four . . . but when he whipped out his six-inch knife he may as well have been Goliath.

"Why you been staring at us, a_____?"

"Look, friend," I cut in, "I can't speak for the a_____ here, but *I'm* starin' at one heck of a big pigsticker. And frankly, I'd rather I wasn't. So why not put it away and let me buy you a beer, huh?"

"Shut up, c_____. I was taking to *him*." The young thug took a step toward our table, his glare locked on my brother. "Why the eyeballing? You some kind of g_____ copper?"

"Nope," Old Red said . . . and said no more. My brother may be a mighty slick thinker, but when it comes to talking there are times he's about as slick as flypaper. Not that it really mattered just then.

As the hood took another step toward us, his friend stood to join him. This second fellow was bigger than his buddy, and a gold band gleamed across one of his curled fists—brass knuckles. Maybe not quite so deadly as a knife, yet still a good sight more dangerous than the bare skin-and-bone knuckles we had to defend ourselves with.

Obviously, *slick* wasn't going to get us spit with these hombres. The only thing they'd understand was *rough*. So that's what I aimed to give them.

"Alright, you stupid q\_\_\_\_-b_____ z_____s," I growled, coming to my feet. "You asked for it."

The hoodlums froze, looking confused. Apparently, they'd never been called q\_\_\_\_-b_____ z_____s before.

I picked up my chair.

"Y'all might wanna clear out," I said to the only other patrons in the place—a pair of pea-coated sailors who sat leering at our little standoff like we were the cancan dancers at one of the melodeons up the street. "There's gonna be an awful lotta wood and brain and such flyin' around here in a second."

The sailors scooted their seats back a few feet.

"Thank you." I pivoted and swung the chair up over my head, facing the hoodlums like a baseball batter awaiting the first pitch. "I do like to have me a little extra elbow room when I'm about to serve up a whuppin'."

"Put down the chair, Brother."

I peeked back at Old Red. Not only was he still in his chair, he sat so motionless he could have been mistaken for a piece of furniture himself.

"For a feller who prides himself on his powers of observation, you seem to be missin' something a tad obvious," I said. "Like, for instance, that those ain't fresh-picked posies them b_____s got in their hands."

"Oh, I ain't worried about them two," my brother said.

The smaller of the two hooligans spat out a cackle. "You oughta be, f_____."

"Nope. Y'all ain't gonna lay a hand on us." Gustav jerked his head to the left. "It's that scattergun makes me nervous."

"Scattergun?"

I craned my head around to get a better look over my shoulder.

There was our landlady, one "Cowboy Mag," standing behind the bar with a sawed-off shotgun in her hands.

"It might be pointed at you two, but still . . . ," Old Red went on, talking to the hoods. "Them things got quite a spray to 'em. Never know who's gonna pick up a pellet when the buckshot flies."

"Ma'am," I said with a polite nod to Mag, and I set my chair gently on the floor and took a seat.

"Ha!" the thug with the blade barked without bothering to turn for a look himself. "Like I'm gonna fall for that!"

"Listen up, you p_____ v_____s!" Mag boomed, and just in case she wasn't speaking loud enough, she let her shotgun get in a word, too—by thumbing back the hammers. "No h_____ f_____s gonna l_____ with my j___-y_____ customers in my w_____ place. So you'd better t____ s_____ your v_____ r_____s outta here . . . and you can go l____ your u____ g____s up your d____ m____s while you're at it!"

Now, we drovers might not be the worldliest fellows, but when it comes to cursing we're as learned an any man jack on this earth. "Q____-b_____ z_____s" not something you'll pick up on any old street corner, you know.

For sheer width and breadth of filth, though, Cowboy Mag had me beat by a country mile. To be truthful, I didn't understand half of what the woman had just said.

Her intentions were clear enough, though: If those hoods didn't skedaddle, they'd soon find their "d____ m____s" filled with lead.

The hoods skedaddled—*pronto.*

"G_____," Mag chuckled as she put her double-barreled bouncer back beneath the bar. "That'll teach those t_____ h_____s to p_____ around in my b_____ m_____."

(As I assume you have by now fully absorbed the flavor of conversation in the Coast, I won't bother with any more _____s. Just insert your own d___ or s___ or some such between every other word and you'll be getting the talk pretty much as Gustav and I heard it.)

"Thanks kindly for the help," I said.

Mag leaned forward onto the bar. She was an oversized woman in body as well as spirit, and for a moment there it looked like her décolletage was about to spill from her low-cut dress like twin pumpkins from a cornucopia.

"If I thought you two were coppers, it's *you* I would've run off," she said. "Cowboys, ain't you?"

"Ma'am," I said, "you are a regular Sherlock Holmes."

Old Red rolled his eyes . . . beneath his big white Boss of the Plains. We may have been spitting distance from the Pacific, yet he still insisted on dressing like we were moving cattle up the Chisholm Trail. And while I'd tried to citify myself with a cheap suit and a new bowler, I knew I couldn't pass for a slicker just yet— not with my Plains drawl and sun-darkened skin.

"Got a soft spot for punchers, do you?" I said to Mag.

"Ol' Mag's nothing *but* soft spots!" she roared back, giving her shoulders a shake that set her bosom to quivering like we were in the midst of a California "earth-quake." "But yeah. They don't call me 'Cowboy Mag' cuz I'm crazy about *tailors*. Used to have hands coming through the Coast all the time, bringing cattle in from Monterey and Sonoma. Not so much anymore. Which is why I'm so pleased to have a couple real buckaroos like yourselves around for a while. What brings you thisaway, anyhow?"

"Bad luck, mostly," I said, and I offered up a heavily expurgated version of our woes (the full tale being offered exclusively to Smythe & Associates . . . for the moment).

"So now you're broke, huh?" Mag said when I was done.

As "Would we be stayin' in this dump if we weren't?" struck me as more than a trifle rude, I offered up a simple "Yup" instead.

"Well, I can help you with that. Cowboys can always get work on the docks, you know. You're handy with knots and ain't afraid to work up a little sweat. Tell you what—" Mag produced a stubby pencil from somewhere in her voluminous gray-black hair and began scribbling across the front page of that day's *Morning Call*. "Just say Cowboy Mag sent you."

She ripped off a strip of paper and held it out to me. On it, I saw once I'd walked up to take it, were scrawled these words:

*NO. 35 PACIFIC STREET*
*ASK FOR JOHNNY*

"Feel like tryin' your luck as a dockhand?" I said to Old Red.

My brother shrugged. "I reckon I don't feel like starvin'." I finished my beer with a gulp, Gustav took two to polish off his, and away we went.

Outside, the sky above was clear and blue—and the street below it crowded and befouled. Our little corner of the Coast was so jam-packed with dens of sin, folks had dubbed it "the Devil's Acre," and certainly this day it had every appearance of being one of Hell's more swarming quarters. Great herds of drunken men staggered from saloon to dance-hall, dance-hall to brothel, and then brothel back to saloon to begin the cycle anew. They paused only to piss, puke or pass out, and no matter which it was they were likely relieved of their wallets in the process. For once, it was almost an advantage being flat busted, as the pickpockets had little to pick from ours but lint.

It took us nearly a quarter hour to slog through this quagmire of corruption to No. 35 Pacific Street, and in that time we laid eyes on more decadence and depravity than most Christians see in a lifetime. I wasn't sure exactly what to expect at journey's end—a union hall or shipping office, maybe. So when it turned out to be yet another dive drinkery, I was surprised less by this discovery than by my own naiveté. The natives wouldn't have stood for an actual place of work in the Barbary Coast. It would be an affront to community standards.

"After you," I said to Old Red—which meant I was kept waiting on the sidewalk a spell, for my brother made no move to go inside. He just stood there staring at the entrance to that watering hole.

"It's called a 'door,'" I explained. "Folks put 'em in the sides of buildings so you don't have to climb down the chimney to get inside. Wanna give it a try?"

Gustav nodded at the saloon. It was a dead-fall—an unlicensed groggery of the sort that so skimps on pretense it doesn't even bother having a name. You know it's a place for drinking simply because a steady stream of men stumble in drunk and stumble out drunker.

"Kinda seedy, ain't it?" Old Red said.

"As a watermelon. But that'd be about right for fellers workin' the piers, wouldn't it?"

"Them and certain others."

"You got a certain 'certain others' in mind?"

My brother shook his head. "Not *certain* certain, no."

"What is it, then? Your Holmesifyin' givin' you pause somehow?"

"Nope. Just my gut." Old Red turned to spit in the street, then squinted again at the door to the dead-fall. "You know how there's *certain* roadhouses, *certain* ranches you hear whispers about. The ones the smart fellers ride around."

"Sure."

"Well . . . ."

Gustav spat again—then reached up and tugged my bowler down hard over my ears.

"Hey!" I protested.

My brother leaned first to the right, then to the left, examining the back of my head.

"Naw, that won't do at all. Them little derbies ain't got enough brim to 'em."

"What in the world are you babblin' about?"

Old Red tilted my hat back so it rode up high on my forehead.

"Your hair," he said. "I'd try to hide mine, but that wouldn't do us no good with my mustache to give us away."

He scowled at me a moment, then nodded gruffly.

"Alright. I reckon that just might work. It's a good thing we don't look much alike, aside from bein' redheads."

"Yeah, I thank the good Lord for it every day. Now you wanna tell me what you're playin' mad hatter for? Why's it so important to cover up my hair?" "Cuz we ain't goin' into that there dive together."

"We ain't?"

"No, we ain't. I'll go in first and do me a little scout before askin' for 'Johnny,' whoever he is. Then you mosey in a little later and make like we don't know each other. If everything looks to be on the up and up, I'll take off my hat, and you can just come on over and introduce yourself. But up till then, I want you hangin' back. Just in case."

"Just in case *what*? Ain't nothin' gonna happen to us in a saloon in the middle of the d___ day."

Gustav turned toward the dead-fall again.

"We'll see what kinda day it is," he said grimly. Then he went inside.

I passed the next few minutes watching the half-clothed strumpets across the street try to entice passersby into their cathouse "cribs" for a little "fun." I'm not opposed to fun on general principle—far from it—but personally I don't consider a raging case of crabs to be a barrel of laughs. I was not tempted.

In any event, I reckoned Old Red didn't need much time for his reconnoiter: From the outside, at least, that saloon looked about as roomy as your average outhouse. You could probably scout the place out without so much as turning your head.

So soon enough, I was striding inside—and quickly realizing I'd been only half right. Sure, the place was small, with only five or six scattered tables, a bar barely the length of a couple coffins and a ceiling so low it'd put splinters in my lid if I walked with too much spring in my step. But it was dark and noisy in there, too, and I needed a moment to get my bearings before I could even begin to look for my brother.

If ever there was a tavern intended exclusively for the use of bats and hoot-owls, this was it, for it was hard to believe anyone else could be expected to navigate in such a gloom. I stumbled to the bar and ordered a beer from a man I could barely see, and when he plonked it down a moment later I found it more by sound than sight.

My eyes adjusted to the murk as I worked on my beer, though, and after a few sips I spied Old Red. He was at the far end of the bar, on the other side of a dark-suited man so broad, squat and round he could've passed for a pickle barrel. I assumed this was "Johnny," as he and Gustav were hunched over the bar together, sipping drinks and talking in low voices.

My brother's Boss of the Plains was still perched atop his head.

So I nursed my beer and did my darnedest to eavesdrop. Unfortunately, the boisterous har-har-haring of the other patrons—most of them foreign sailors, local drunks or the hoodlums who made both their prey—drowned out whatever it was Old Red and Johnny were whispering.

After I'd been there maybe five minutes, tippling with the dainty sips of a society dame at a tea party, the bartender stopped across from me and shook a dirty finger at my glass.

"You drinkin' that or waitin' for it to evaporate?"

I scooped up my beer, poured it down my throat and slapped a nickel on the bar.

"Another please."

The barkeeper filled my glass from a froth-topped pitcher that was almost—*almost*—as grimy as he was himself.

"This is a bar," he snarled, putting the pitcher down hard. "You just want something to lean against, go find yourself a streetlamp."

I nodded and took a healthy gulp of my fresh beer. (Well, freshly poured, anyhow. It tasted so stale I wouldn't have been surprised to learn it had come to America aboard the Mayflower.) As the bartender stalked away, I sneaked a peek to my right, hoping I hadn't drawn too much attention to myself by *not* behaving like a boozy ass.

Johnny was turned away from me, toward Gustav, his wide back blocking my view. As for my brother, all I could see of him was his hat. He was still wearing it, that much I could tell, but the angle of it seemed odd. It was tilted forward, the brim almost in a straight line up and down, as though Old Red was hunched over the bar to read something—which I knew couldn't be the case, since he reads about as well as a catfish plays poker.

I was just about to lean back and try for a better look when the barkeep barked out, "Keys! *Keys!*"

I followed his gaze to a scratched-up old piano at the back of the room. A gangly, unshaven oldtimer was drooping on a stool beside it, head on chest, eyes closed.

"Wake up, Keys!" the bartender roared. "Time to earn your keep!"

"Yeah, come on!" someone shouted. "Play us a tune, Keys!"

"How about 'Auld Lang Syne'?" someone else called out.

Most of the customers roared with laughter. The rest—like me—watched with wary half-smiles as Keys blinked himself blearily awake and began dragging his stool around to the front of the piano. This was apparently part of some comical custom of the place, but the guffaws had a cruel edge to them, like the cheers at a bull fight.

The old man brought his long arms up over his head, held them there a moment, then crashed his hands down upon the keyboard.

He wasn't just banging away, though. He'd struck a chord—one with a low, ominous tone. He repeated it twice, loud and quick, then let it float there in the air like a black cloud.

Then came a ray of sunshine cutting through the gloom—a bright melody that echoed out of the piano ragged and off-tune yet still merrily, almost manically, jaunty.

"London Bridge Is Falling Down."

There was more laughter, and a few men actually started to sing along. But the recital didn't last long. One quick run-through of the song and Keys was done. He dragged his stool back around to his resting spot, slumped against the piano and closed his eyes.

As floor shows go, it was pretty pathetic. Certainly, the Bella Union and the other big concert saloons had nothing to fear from this place. Yet the performance brought down the house: Men were still clapping and stomping their feet even as the geezer slipped back into his slumber.

I glanced toward the end of the bar, thinking I might share a little eye roll or shrug with my brother. But there was nothing to share—because there was no one to share it with.

Old Red was gone.

Johnny was leaning over to share a whispered word with the barman, and I could finally see around his stout frame just fine. Yet all I saw was wall. I jerked my head this way and that, searching the rest of the room. In vain.

It had been all of a minute since I'd turned to watch Keys tickle the ivories (or give them a good beating, more like), and in that time Old Red had left somehow. Yet he couldn't have gone out the front door without walking right past me, and the back door was over by the piano. I'd have seen him leave thataway, too.

Now, my brother can be cantankerous, and I'll admit there have been moments I wished he'd just go away. But never had I ever dreamed he might actually up and do it—simply vanish without so much as a puff of smoke. So sudden was his disappearance, in fact, that I might have doubted my own sanity, worrying that this "Gustav" was a figment of my imagination much as my crazy Uncle Franz once befriended a potato he addressed as "Herr Berenson."

I quickly spotted proof that I wasn't loco, though—and that

something foul was afoot.

When I glanced back where Old Red had been standing, I noticed that there were two half-full glasses on the bar next to big, burly Johnny. The barkeep picked one up, emptied it out beneath the bar, then began giving the glass a vigorous spit-shine with a filthy rag.

If my brother had heard the call of nature and slipped off to the w.c. (or, given the character of the place, the back alley), why would the bartender be cleaning out his glass? And if Gustav had simply elected to leave, why wouldn't he have collected me on the way out?

Which meant Old Red was gone, but he hadn't left. He'd been *taken*.

I looked down at the bartender's feet, leaning forward far as I could without tipping head over heels and landing atop his brogans. Unlikely as it was, I had to make sure Gustav wasn't down there behind the bar trussed up like a beef ready for the brand.

He wasn't, of course. All I saw was a slop bucket, what looked like a tap handle (perhaps for the secret stock of *drinkable* beer squirreled away for specially favored patrons), boxes filled with assorted bottles and—good information to have—a short-barreled shotgun just like Cowboy Mag's. It must be a regulation in *The Barkeeper's Handbook*, right between "Water down whiskey" and "No credit to cowboys": "Keep scattergun under bar."

The bartender caught me gaping his way and shot me a glower so sour he could have poured it out and sold it as lemonade.

I forced myself to smile.

"Don't worry about me, mister. I learned my lesson." I picked up my beer and splashed half of it over my tonsils. "Glug glug glug, right?"

The barman didn't bother responding, which was fine by me. What I needed right then was to be ignored. I had me some heavy-duty thinking to do, *fast*.

Of course, the person best suited to bust such a puzzle was Old Red himself, and I couldn't very well consult with him on his own kidnapping. And turning to the law wasn't an option. The Barbary Coast's a precarious place for policemen, and they usually don't go there at all except in squads of ten or more. I'd probably walk a dozen blocks before I saw a single cop.

Yet there was someone I could turn to, I realized, though he wasn't on hand, either: Mr. Sherlock Holmes. True, Gustav was the expert on Holmes, but he only knew of the man through me. I read him John Watson's tales of the great detective each and every night. Whatever my brother had heard about deducifying, I'd heard, too. It was just a matter of putting it to work.

I closed my eyes and dredged up Old Red's favorite Holmes quotes.

"It is a capital mistake to theorize before you have all the evidence."

Useless.

"Little things are infinitely the most important."

Useless.

"There is nothing more deceptive than an obvious fact."

Useless . . . and pretty danged silly.

"When you have excluded the impossible, whatever remains, however improbable, must be the truth."

Which might lead me to conclude that—as my brother could not have flown through the ceiling or dug down through the floorboards—Johnny and the bartender must have *eaten him* while I had my back turned.

Useless useless useless.

Unless . . . .

I had turned my back, hadn't I? And why? To watch a sorry old sot flail away at a piano . . . *because the barkeep told him to.*

Keys' little routine might have been a distraction. But a distraction from what? He hadn't blocked anyone's view of either door. He'd just made a lot of noise.

So maybe it wasn't the sight of something he was covering up so much as the sound. The opening of a hidden door, perhaps, or the workings of some secret mechanism.

# Dear Mr. Holmes

"Exclude the impossible," Holmes had said. Alright. If my brother hadn't been taken out to the left or the right, that left only up or down. Maybe one wasn't so impossible after all.

I threw back my head to guzzle the last of my beer—and get a peek up at the ceiling over the spot where Gustav had been standing. There was nothing to see but rafters and cobwebs.

I put down my glass and dug a dime from my pocket.

"Shot of rye for the road," I said to the bartender. Then "Dagnabbit" as I let the coin slip betwixt my fingers. After bending down to retrieve my money, I took a good look at the floor at the far end of the bar.

When I stood up again, I was grinning—and gritting my teeth.

"Here you go, my good sir," I said with as much cheer as I could muster considering how badly I wanted to pop off the barman's head like the cork from a bottle. I dropped the dime in front of him. "And you'll see no sippin' from me this time, I promise you."

Silent, scowling, the bartender thumped down a shot glass and sloshed it full of liquid the color of tobacco juice. Which was pretty much what it tasted like, too.

I tossed it down with one swiping swig and set the glass back on the bar.

"Keep the change."

I got no thanks. The barkeep just snatched up my shot glass, gave it a single swipe with his ratty little rag and set it aside, ready for the next paying customer. He was drifting back toward his big buddy Johnny as I turned to go.

Heading for the door, I kept myself to an easy amble when what I really wanted to do was dash. It was torture not glancing back to see if Johnny and the barman were watching me—and maybe noticing the wisps of short-cropped cherry-red hair peeking out from under my bowler. But if little things *are* the most important, then even such a trifling show of nerves might be all it would take to arouse suspicion and squash what slight chance I had of saving my brother.

I finally knew where he was, and I couldn't get there myself with a bucketload of buckshot in my back.

I managed to keep my gaze straight ahead.

The sunshine was blinding-bright when I stepped outside, but a few blinks and the ink spots disappeared. I set off down the street still keeping myself to a mosey, just in case.

Before I reached the first corner, though, I finally allowed myself that look over the shoulder. I saw drunks, chippies and rowdies aplenty, but no sign of Johnny or the barman.

I spun around and hustled back toward the dead-fall.

I didn't go inside again, though. Instead, I turned down a narrow alley that ran along the side of the saloon. A dozen quick strides brought me to an angled doorway jutting out from the building—the entrance to a storm cellar. I bent down and gave the rickety twin doors a cautious tug.

Locked. Bolted from the inside.

I paused to consider my options. A moment later, I sighed when I realized how badly the best one stunk. Still, the best is the best, even when it's awful.

So I knocked. Lightly, politely at first, then harder when I remembered that nobody did anything politely in the Barbary Coast.

"Who is it?" a man called out from down below.

I chanced an answer, praying it didn't call for a brogue or falsetto or some other giveaway trait.

"Johnny."

"Already?" Muffled, shuffling footsteps drew closer to the door. "Bit early, ain't it?"

"So?" I grunted, hoping Johnny didn't have a lisp.

The doors rattled.

I stepped back, rattled myself but knowing there was but one way to proceed.

"It's just that it ain't dark yet . . . ," the man said.

The doors began to swing open.

" . . . and we've only got four *EEP!*"

By the time he saw my face, my kick had almost reached his.

As Old Red is fond of pointing out, I manage to put my foot in my mouth pretty regular-like. This was the first time I'd ever put it in someone else's, though. It didn't go in far, of course. Just enough to send the man flying back into the cellar minus his front teeth.

I jumped down after him, giving him a toe to the stomach twice before he could so much as let out his first groan. He was a scrawny, grubby little fellow, and I might've felt bad about treating him so rough if not for what I spied piled up in the shadows further back in the basement.

Men. Four of them, splayed out on a rotten old mattress directly below the lines I'd noticed in the saloon floor—the trap door. From underneath, I could see the wooden slat that pulled out to drop it open and the jointed rods leading up through the ceiling, perhaps to that extra "beer tap" tucked away beneath the bar.

I didn't care about the how just then, though. It was the who that truly troubled me, for stretched out atop that mound of men was my brother, his body as limp and lifeless as the barman's rag.

I glowered down at the little fellow I'd just put the boot to and brought my foot up again without so much as thinking to do it. I can't even say what thoughts were in my head at that moment. It's as if there were no thoughts at all, just an explosion of red and black and a great, awful noise like the scream of a steam whistle. I'm not sure what I was about to do—stomp the poor pipsqueak to a pulp, I suppose. Certainly, that's what *he* assumed.

"No, mishter! Shtop!" he cried out, mush-mouthed with blood. "They ain't dead! I work for the Chicken!"

I froze with one foot hovering over the man's face, wondering if my first kick hadn't knocked something lose in his head.

"What are you talkin' about?"

"The Chicken—the *Shanghai* Chicken! Johnny Devine! Thish ish hish plashe! We're crimpsh, not killersh!"

I set my foot back down on the dirt floor.

"Crimps?"

The word tickled a memory of newspaper and magazine articles I'd read about the Coast. "Shanghai," too.

"You mean you aimed to sell them fellers off to crew sea ships?"

The little man nodded. "Jusht got an order from a Norwegian whaler. A dozen men jumped ship the shecond they made port, and they need replashementsh."

I stared hard at Gustav and the men beneath him, noticing only now the slight up-down of their chests and the raspy sound of ragged breathing.

"We jusht drug 'em. Laudanum in their drinksh. They wake up later with headachesh, that'sh all."

"Yeah, sure," I said, starting toward my brother. "Wake up on some leaky tub in the middle of the Pacific, you mean."

As I drew closer to "the Chicken's" victims, I noticed another pile in a darkened corner beyond them—a heap of a good two dozen *hats*, with my brother's white Stetson up top like the snowcap on a mountain.

Then I saw the swollen purple bump on Gustav's forehead. Those headaches weren't brought on by laudanum alone.

I spun around just as the little crimp staggered to his feet and started toward me with his blackjack raised high.

"Thank you, friend," I said. "Now I don't have to feel bad about *this*."

"*This*" being a swift kick to the unmentionables followed by a roundhouse that flattened the man's nose and blew out his candle.

I left the crimp lying in Old Red's spot atop the stack of soon-to-be sailors. I wasn't happy about leaving those other fellows to the Chicken's not so tender mercies, but even so large a man as me can only manage so much dead weight at once, and acts of charity would only get us Shanghaied all over again . . . or worse.

I toted Gustav home draped over my back, something that surely would've aroused a touch of curiosity just about anywhere else. This being the Barbary Coast, though, all I got was the occasional wisecrack along the lines of "Good thing *one* of you can handle his liquor!" By the time we were back in our room at the Cowboy's Rest, Old Red was starting to stir.

"You alright, Brother?" I asked once I had him stretched out on our bed.

Gustav's eyelids fluttered, then went wide. He pushed himself up to a sit, one hand pressed to his head.

"What the h___ are we doin' *here*?" he groaned.

That's right: "What the h___ are we doin' here?" Not "Thank you, Brother." Not "How'd you find me?" Not "I owe you my eternal gratitude and will never give you guff again so long as I shall live."

"What are we doin'?" I said. "Well, you are sittin' up when you should be lyin' down. And me, I'm thinkin' I liked you better unconscious."

Old Red waved a limp hand at the war bags we kept piled up in the corner.

"Best get those packed up quick. We gotta go."

I started to ask "Why?" but didn't even make it through the "Wh-."

"Oh," I said. And I set to packing.

Not five minutes later, I was helping Gustav hobble down the stairs. Our clomping drew Cowboy Mag from her bar-room.

"How about a little hair of the dog, boys?" she asked, friendly as can be—until she noticed the bags I was dragging behind us. Lickety-split, her smile spun around into a frown.

"Ain't no dog done my brother like this. It was a Chicken . . . and a snake," I said. "Speakin' of which, I been tryin' to remember. How'd you say you got your nickname again?"

Cowboy Mag planted herself before the door. With her plump arms and legs akimbo, she made a formidable roadblock.

"Don't think you're leavin' without settlin' up with me first."

"We wouldn't dream of it," Old Red said, his voice still hoarse and trembly. He gave me a pat on the back. "Brother, would you mind?"

"Certainly not."

And I propped him up against the wall, put down our bags and truly settled accounts with ol' Mag.

Now, for the record, let me state that I have never struck a lady, and I never will.

Let me add, however, one obvious and important fact: Cowboy Mag was no lady.

With best wishes of (and hopes for) publishing success,

O.A. Amlingmeyer
The Cosmopolitan House (Hotel)
Oakland, Calif.
August 8, 1893

# GREETINGS FROM PURGATORY!

Urias Smythe
Smythe & Associates Publishing, Ltd.
175 Fifth Avenue
New York, New York

Dear Mr. Smythe:

Greetings from Purgatory! Or, as it's known locally, Lovelock, Nevada. My brother and I are floating here in Limbo (another alias for the place) until we can catch a train out. So far no luck, for we'd literally have to *catch* a train—as in throw a rope 'round the smokestack and yank it off the tracks—to get one to stop. Expresses just blow the place by, and even the local runs don't slow down unless they need coal or water.

One nice thing you can say about Purgatory, though: It's a fine place to get some writing done. There certainly aren't any distractions. A train station little bigger than an outhouse, a smattering of abandoned shacks and a mud puddle that passes for the town square—that's about all Lovelock has to offer. I don't even think there's any paint around for a man to watch dry. So I may as well tell you how we came to be here. With a little puffery, it might even make a decent tale for one of your detective magazines.

It was actually you, sir, who set us on the trail here. When I learned I finally had an actual publisher—who'd pay me in actual cash!—I told my brother we could use the money to go anywhere and do anything his heart desired. Which was a pretty safe offer to make, I figured, seeing as Gustav's one and only desire the past year has been to be a detective. I assumed he'd have us push on to some new city (having soured on San Francisco for reasons detailed in my last submission to you, *The Black Dove*) where we could try once again to land work as Pinkertons.

I have now learned my lesson regarding "safe bets" when it comes to second-guessing Gustav "Old Red" Amlingmeyer.

We were going, he announced, to San Marcos, Texas. And he left it at that . . . because he knew he could. He may be the champion deducifier of the two of us, but even I could solve this puzzle. It had but two pieces to put together: San Marcos and Old Red.

Before we took up drovering together, Gustav had worked a ranch down San Marcos way. And, as cowboys so often will, he fell in love with a "soiled dove"—a cathouse chippy whose name I don't even know, so reluctant has my tight-lipped brother been to speak of her. But whoring's as rough and risky a job as punching cattle, in its own way, and this much I do know: Somebody up and killed that girl. And Gustav finally aimed to find out who.

First, though, we'd have to trade our current San (Francisco) for the old one (Marcos). And that involved more than a stroll around the corner and up the block. Two thousand miles lay between us and the answers my brother had set his sights on—half of those miles over mountains and through desert. That was more trail than even a couple hard-riding saddle bums like ourselves could ever hope to cover. We'd have to go by train.

Now, as you know well from the first book you purchased from me, traveling by rail would present certain challenges for us. The likelihood of near-constant *vomiting*, for one. What syrup of ipecac is to babies, trains are to Old Red. And the feeling's mutual, in a way. The one railroad that could get us directly across the Sierra Nevadas was the Southern Pacific, the very company that oh-so-briefly employed us as private detectives. Given that we got the boot after an S.P. special under our care *flew off a cliff*, it was unlikely we'd be welcomed back with complimentary tickets for a private Pullman. I didn't think we'd be allowed aboard so much as a cattle car should the S.P. Railroad Police learn we were angling for a berth.

So it was decided (and when I use that phrase, of course, it was my elder brother doing the deciding) that we would purchase the cheapest seats on the slowest local out of Oakland.

"If we don't wanna bump into any S.P. dicks, that's the way to go," Gustav reasoned. "Any special's gonna have an express car and high-class sleepers—and spotters to keep an eye on 'em. But a little local run ain't no one gonna bother with, bandits or railroad bulls either or."

"True enough," I conceded. "But I'd have thought you'd want this trip over quick, what with your flip-floppy stomach and all."

Old Red added a big squeeze of lemon to his already sour expression.

"You let me worry about my stomach."

"I'd like to do that, really I would." I ran a hand over the well-tailored sleeve of my new sack coat, fresh-purchased with the first payment from my beloved publisher. "Only I've got something to worry about myself: a thirty dollar suit. And I ain't keen on seeing it covered in upchuck the next seven days solid."

"Just go buy the damn tickets," Gustav grumbled.

As I reckon it, I won the argument. I can never actually convince Old Red to change his mind, of course, but if I can get him to tell me to shut up, that at least means he concedes I've got a point.

When dealing with my mule-headed brother, it's important to keep your goals realistic.

So it was that we said a not entirely fond farewell to San Francisco and environs and set off on a rattling, clattering local that pulled off onto side tracks for what seemed like every other train in the state. It took us half a day just to reach Sacramento, and there we bought tickets for Ogden, Utah, on the other side of the Sierras. We'd managed to put a hundred miles of flatland behind us. Now came seven hundred more of twisty track spiraling up rocky peaks over cavernous gorges.

Gustav (and my new suit) survived the first leg of this journey unsullied thanks to liberal doses of (A) stomach-soothing peppermints and (B) mind-diverting Sherlock Holmes (as orated by yours truly—Old Red, you'll no doubt recall, having the letters to read nothing more complicated than a cattle brand).

My brother's devotion to the late, great detective I've written of many times, so you might think I had nothing new to say of it. But alas, that is not so. That "Black Dove" business had taught him a bitter lesson—truth and justice are not always the same thing—and his faith in St. Sherlock had taken a bit of a beating as a result.

"Very neat," he'd mutter sullenly after I read out another Holmes tale. "Very tidy."

Tidiness being something we had yet to experience in our own adventures as detectives. Messiness—that had been the way of things for us.

Still, Old Red never told me to stop reading from *The Adventures of Sherlock Holmes*.

The conductor, on the other hand, did. And none too politely, at that.

At the time, Gustav and I were more than twenty-four hours into our trek through the mountains, having survived (barely) a sleepless night squeezed together on what the railroad, with what I can only assume was snickering sarcasm, described as our seat. "The rack," that's what I would've called it.

This was no luxury express like the one we'd come to California on three months before. There were no becurtained sleeping berths. Just small, unpadded wooden benches pressed back to back so as to ensure minimum waste of space and maximum discomfort.

That Old Red and I had made it as far as we had without

one of us killing the other was a miracle—one I attributed entirely to the powers of almighty Holmes. Without the gospel of John Watson for balm, it was just a question of which would get to flying first, the fur or the contents of my brother's stomach.

And yet here was the conductor asking me to bottle that balm up. Or *telling me to*, more like.

"Alright, that's enough. This isn't a theater, and you're not Edwin Booth"—those were his exact words. It was the first thing I'd heard the grim-faced, gray-haired man speak other than "All aboard" and "Tickets, please" . . . and half the time he hadn't bothered with the "please." In general, he seemed to regard his passengers—an admittedly motley assortment of patch-kneed farmers, vagabond drummers, and miners fresh from blowing their pannings in the Barbary Coast—as unfit for even this, surely the rustiest, mustiest, shaky-and-quakiest sardine can in service to the Southern Pacific.

"I'm sorry, captain," I said ever so politely, smooching a little extra heinie with the honorific conductors feel is their due. "But ridin' the rails don't agree with my brother, and these here stories sure do help the miles slide by a little smoother."

Now, as a lot, conductors aren't overly fond of cowboys, my former profession tending toward young rowdies ill equipped for long stretches cooped up in what is basically a bunkhouse on wheels. And though I was sporting my fine new Frisco-bought suit, Old Red still insisted on dressing like a dollar-a-day ranch hand. Which might explain why the conductor was grimacing at Gustav like a vulture circling something so yuck-ugly even it wouldn't swoop in for a taste.

"That's not my problem," the man sneered.

Regrettable sartorial choices aside, of course, Gustav and I had been taking pains not to draw attention to ourselves. So I might not have put up an argument but for two things. Firstly, it was dusk, and after a few more minutes of "The Musgrave Ritual" the snow-topped peaks and yawning chasms passing by the windows would be safely swallowed by darkness—and the few crumbs my brother had swallowed that day would have a better chance of staying swallowed, Holmes or no.

And secondly . . . well, the conductor was a high-handed S.O.B., and it just plain got on my nerves.

"It *will* be your problem, sir, when half the passengers in this car are screamin' for scrub brushes to scrape off the spew. And the longer I read, the less the chance that's gonna happen."

The conductor was a gaunt man with the glowing, healthy hue of your average cadaver. But his sunken cheeks flushed red now, and his disdain-deadened eyes flared to angry life.

"There've been complaints from the other passengers already—about you and your incessant babbling."

"Complaints? Really? I ain't heard nobody complainin'." I looked over at the bushy-bearded Hebrew merchants in the seat opposite ours. "We botherin' you?"

They looked at each other and shrugged.

"*Vos?*" one of them said to me.

They'd been chattering away in English half the day—with Texas accents, no less—but now they wanted to pretend they didn't speak English.

Very wise of them, actually.

I turned to the folks sitting behind us, a big Mormon clan on their way back to Salt Lake City.

"Have we been disturbin' you all?"

"Oh, no!" said the youngest of the brood, a tow-haired nipper of maybe eight years. "I wanna hear the ending!"

The dour, gray-bearded family patriarch eyed me gravely, then looked at the conductor.

"So long as he's not reading 'A Study in Scarlet,'" he said, "it's no bother to us."

(In fact, I'd tabled the very tale in question, as Doc Watson painted the Mormons with the same brush most dime-novel scribes set aside for bloodthirsty "redskins" and jungle-dwelling cannibals.)

"You see?" I said to the conductor. "Ain't no objections if I keep at it."

The conductor thumped a thumb into his own spindly chest.

"*I* object, and that's all that matters. We'll be turning the lights down soon, and I don't want you keeping everyone up half the night. Now put the book down and shut up."

I was indeed thinking of putting the book down—down the officious jackass's scrawny throat—when Old Red finally piped up.

"It's alright, Brother," he croaked. "I know how it comes out anyhow."

He was sallow and slick with sweat, and his gaze kept darting to the men's lavatory, as if he was gauging how quick he could get there in a dash.

"You sure?" I asked him.

"Am I ever not?" he snapped back.

I closed the book.

"Awwwww," the kid behind us moaned.

The conductor snorted with scornful satisfaction, then moved on down the aisle without another word.

I jerked a thumb at the mountains going orange-tinged with twilight outside.

"You don't need a distraction from all that?"

"I'll be fine so long as you stop *pointin' at it*," Gustav grated out.

I didn't like the twitchy-flinchy squint of his eyes, though, or the way he pressed both hands over his taut washboard of a stomach as if he could wrestle the thing into submission.

"Alright, then," I said. "Let's find something to focus on in here." I made a quick study of the passengers in our line of sight. "Four rows up, other side of the car, on the aisle, facing us."

Old Red took all of a second to size up the man I was singling out—a young drover about my own age.

"Feh," he said. "You wanna distract me with some Holmesin', you gotta throw me more of a challenge that that."

"Really?" I shrugged. "Prove it."

My brother shook his head and sighed . . . then reeled out his deducifications all the same.

"Feet, face and hands—that's what tells the story of a man, no matter the duds he's sportin'. And that feller's feet, face and hands don't just tell the story. They shout it. Why, even from here I can see he ain't got dirt under his nails. And he fancies himself a cowboy, but he ain't got the tan you'd find on a soda jerk. His boots ain't got no crease nor fade, and they're big ol' things, too—for a flat-footed feller who's walked everywhere his whole life 'stead of ridin' there in a saddle. And his hat's still stiff and clean. Ain't never been rained on or used to hold water or oats for a horse. Naw, right there you got a city boy who's got his head filled up with Buffalo Bill bull. He's runnin' off to try his hand at punchin' somewhere on the Plains, only he don't even know this is the worst time of year to do it. Fall round-ups'll be over by the time he even makes it to a ranch. His mother—she's a left-handed Irish-born charwoman, by the by—she tried to stop him, but . . . . ." My brother cut himself off with another grunted "Feh" and a dismissive swipe of the hand. "It deduces itself."

"Yeah, I reckon you're right," I said—though that was all the reckoning I could truly have claimed to make. I hadn't pegged the kid for a greenhorn at all. "Let's try something different. 'Spot the Spotter.' Instead of me pointin' someone out, you look over everyone in the car and tell me if any are S.P. dicks."

Old Red shook his head.

"I been playin' that game since we set foot on this train, and there ain't no spotters to spot. It's like I figured in the first place: The railroad ain't gonna bother with guards or spies on a penny ante run like this." My brother jerked his chin at the conductor, who'd moved on to more important business at the far end of the car: giving a young mother guff about her bawling baby. "That's probably why he's such a bitter son of a gun. He's used to better things. Better days."

"What makes you say that?"

"Oh, just the fact that it's obvious. See how baggy-butted his uniform is? And loose around the breadbasket? The man's lost a lot of weight lately. On account of the booze, maybe."

Unfortunately, I didn't quite hide my astonishment quick enough.

"You didn't notice the whiskey on his breath? Or the flask in his pocket?" my brother marveled. "Good god, I give up. It's like tryin' to teach detectin' to a tree stump."

He settled back in our seat as far as he could—which wasn't far—and tipped his Boss of the Plains over his face. Given a choice between talking to me and staring at the inside of a hat, he chose the latter.

So I set myself to admiring the scenery while there was still scenery to admire. The last rays of the dying day were sparkling atop a huge, pine-fringed lake thousands of feet below us, the water flashing orange, then going gray, then slipping into blackness along with everything else outside.

And everything *inside*, as well, it so happened, for the conductor kept the car's gas lights so low I could barely see the end of my own nose. The night before, he'd left just enough light on to read by, and I'd spent hours whispering John Watson's words to my jittery brother. I'd have no such option this night, though, and even so much as a trip to the w.c. would require a lit match, a map and a lot of luck.

I leaned against the window and tried to sleep, but the rattling and swaying of the car kept jostling me awake. The whole train was tilted, unmistakably headed downward, winding its way fast out of the Sierras. By morning, we'd be skirting a whole new set of peaks—the Humboldt Range. Which just happened to be home to the Give-'em-Hell Boys, the most notorious train robbers since the James gang . . . and no friends of ours, as you'll recall from my magnum opus (and your great publishing success, I do hope) *On the Wrong Track*. Of course, the Give-'em-Hell Boys aren't what they used to be, seeing as Old Red and I *killed* the brains of the bunch. All the same, I had no desire to encounter the surviving brawn. I had a sneaking suspicion they were the grudge-holding types.

Eventually, I heard snores coming from beneath Gustav's

Stetson, and the sound shamed me. If my brother could fall asleep along this stretch of track even with all the butterflies bouncing around in his stomach, what the heck was I doing awake? I fixed my mind on a happier memory from our last train trip—befriending a certain young lady who graces my idle imaginings often now—and let pleasant musings about our next meeting lull me to sleep.

Unfortunately, the Give-'em-Hell Boys are a pushy lot, and they managed to bully their way back into my head, tragically ruining a dream so sweet Whitman's could box it up with their chocolates. There was much nightmarish yahooing and firing off of guns and a sudden, lurching stop to the train that felt so real it woke me up . . . sprawled across the Israelites sitting across from us.

I'd been thrown from my seat.

The sudden stop was no dream.

"Ohhhh, mister," one of the men under me groaned. "You got me right in the *beytsim*."

"*Vos?*" I was tempted to say, but I gave him a simple "Sorry" instead. From the way he doubled up once I was off him, I knew just what his "*beytsim*" were, and getting got there is no laughing matter.

"That didn't feel like no stop for coal," I said to Old Red as I slid in next to him again.

"Nope. That it didn't." My brother was little more than a hazy gray outline in the muted glow of the dimmed lamps, yet still I could see said outline gesture at the window. "And there ain't no coal to get, anyhow."

I turned to take a look outside. There was enough moonlight to make out a rocky slope, scattered trees, a winding black ribbon that might have been a creek bed up ahead. But there was no platform, no station house, no water tank, no buildings at all.

I swiveled around, peering over at the window on the opposite side of the car. Through it, I saw the same thing. Which was nothing. No town. We'd stopped in the middle of nowhere.

"You think maybe . . . ?" I said to Gustav.

His outline shrugged.

I reached under the seat and pulled out my carpetbag.

"Don't," Old Red said before I even had the bag unsnapped.

He knew what I was going for: my forty-five. His own Colt was tucked away in a valise underneath his keister. Yet he made no move for it.

"This ain't no place for a fracas like that," he said. "If it's you-know-who . . . well . . . we'll just have to handle 'em someways else."

My hands kept working as my brother spoke, undoing the clasps, digging around for the feel of coiled leather and cold steel. Something brushed against my ear as I searched, and I glanced aside to find the little Mormon boy leaning over the back of our seat, staring down into my carpetbag with wide eyes.

He couldn't wait for me to draw out that Peacemaker. A shootout would be just what a kid would want to see . . . right up to the moment a bullet split his skull.

"Sorry, son," I said. "Nothing in here but long johns and undarned socks."

And, a moment later, a wad of cash: As a precaution, I stuffed most of our bankroll into one of my holey socks.

Just as I got the carpetbag stowed again, there was a clatter at the front of the car, followed by the sound of scuffling footsteps. Someone was coming through the vestibule from the passenger compartment ahead of ours. A few somebodies, actually, though it was too dark to make out how many and who.

"Lights!" one of the somebodies snapped.

The gas lamps suddenly flared up full, momentarily blinding me (and, I could tell from the moans and curses all around, everyone else). Then the lamps dimmed down again just as quick, settling on a low glow just a shade up from the darkness we'd been riding in all night. Or so it seemed. It was hard to tell with all the black splotches floating before my eyes.

I knew what I'd see up by the vestibule before the spots even cleared. The gasps and screams told me that. It was just a question of how many there'd be and whether they looked familiar . . . and whether Old Red and I looked familiar to *them*.

The bandits—there were just two of them, it turned out—were wearing handkerchief masks and long coats and gloves. Big Stetsons were pulled down tight just over their eyes. They seemed neater and cleaner than the ratty, dust-covered Give-'em-Hell gang we'd run into a few months before. But who could say? Maybe they'd hired someone to do their washing since the last time we met.

As desperadoes will, of course, they were holding guns. One was pointing his down the aisle, swiveling it from left to right, right to left, showing he could put a pill through any passenger he pleased.

The other fellow had the business end of his gun jammed up against the conductor's head.

"P-p-please, everyone," our "captain" stammered. "Just do as they say!"

"Listen to the man!" the bandito behind him barked out. "Any of you gives us trouble, I'll blow his brains out . . . and then it'll be your turn!"

He apparently heard enough sobs and snivels from around the car to feel his words had been taken to heart, for he looked over at his compadre and nodded.

The other gunman was holding a gunnysack in his left hand, and he held it out before him as he stepped toward the nearest row of seats.

"Money and valuables in the sack! Quick quick *quick*!"

Farmers and peddlers and family men aren't much for putting up a fuss when iron's getting waved around, and the robbing went quick quick *quick* indeed. The only fellow I thought might kick was the dude "cowboy" my brother had practiced his Holmesing on—the lad's head might be so filled up with dime-novel twaddle he'd try something heroic. But he just dropped his cash in the bag like everyone else, his eyes abrim with tears.

Something tickled my intuition as the bandit hovered over him, but I couldn't pin down what it was. Heck, it was hard to remember to breathe, I was so jumpy. The gunman with the bag had almost reached our row, and if these fellows *were* part of the Give-'em-Hell gang . . . and if they recognized us . . . .

"Make him reach for it," Gustav whispered to me.

"Are you crazy?" I protested (quietly). "I don't want him lookin' at me more than—"

"You heard me."

As did the bandit with the bag, it turned out.

"Keep your mouths shut!" he snarled, looming up over us at last. I half expected him to follow up with something on the order of "Oh ho . . . we meet again." But all he did was give his sack a shake.

I leaned over and dropped in the few greenbacks I hadn't stashed away in my valise.

Old Red glared at me.

The gunman did, too.

"You can afford a suit like that," he said to me, "yet you're gonna travel half-way across the country with four dollars in your pocket?"

I shrugged.

"How do you think I could afford the suit? I'm a very frugal man."

"Feh," my brother grumbled, shaking his head. "You and your damn city clothes . . . . "

"What's going on back there?" the robber at the front of the car called out.

"Got a dumbass holding out on us!"

"Oh, good." The other bandit cocked his forty-five—which was still nuzzled up just over the conductor's right ear. "I was hoping I'd have an excuse to kill this sorry piece of—"

"For God's sake!" the conductor wailed, pleading eyes locked on me. "Give them what they want!"

"Alright, alright!" I pulled out my carpetbag and opened it up again. "Just don't get all jumpy if you catch sight of some iron in here."

I slowly reached in and pulled out our nest egg—every blessed buck we had left over from the money you yourself sent me, sir. Without it, the only way we were getting to Texas was on foot. Which would take us approximately two-hundred seventy-six years. Give or take.

The cash was snatched from my hand.

By Old Red.

"Listen, friend," he said to the outlaw looming up over us. He held the roll of bills away from himself, just out of the man's reach. "This is all the wampum we got to make it to St. Louis for our dear sister's funeral, and if you take it, we won't have a cent for her darlin' little orphaned—"

"Shut up," the gunman sneered, and he stabbed out the hand holding the swag bag and used a couple gloved fingers to clumsily snag the cash. The stretch brought his left wrist poking out from his coat sleeve, exposing all of two inches of skin not covered by cloth or leather. But two inches was plenty.

The skin was black.

I peered up at the strip of flesh visible between the top of the man's mask and the brim of his hat.

The skin was white.

Old Red, meanwhile, stole a quick glance down, staring at (I noticed when I followed his gaze) the outlaw's clunky, dark, square-toed work shoes.

Feet, face and hands—those had been the key to understanding a man, my brother had said. And even with gloves over one and a mask on the other, I'd just seen enough of this "bandit" to know exactly who he was.

I waited for him to relieve our Hebrew neighbors of their folding money and move on down the aisle before daring another whisper Gustav's way.

"You notice the—?"

"Of course."

"I can't believe it."

"I believe what I see."

"Well, what're we gonna do about it?"

"What do you think?"

"*Shut up back there!*" the gunman at the front of the car hollered.

"Please," the conductor whimpered. "Stop provoking them!"

After that, Old Red and I just sat there trying to look as scared as everyone else. We had no intention of provoking anyone to do anything. Yet.

Soon enough, the robber with the bag of ill-gotten goods reached the end of the car, and his pal shove-marched the conductor down the aisle to join him.

"No one follows us, no one steps outside, no one opens a window or *this man dies!*" the one with the gun on the conductor bellowed.

And then both bandits disappeared into the vestibule, dragging the captain with them. They'd been fast—in and out of our compartment in less than five minutes. Now they were on to the third and final passenger car. Just a few more ticks of the clock, and they'd vanish into the night with every cent we had.

I reached under my seat.

My brother reached under his.

We weren't reaching for our socks.

When the gang returned to its secret lair a little later, we were already there waiting for them, Colts in hand. And if you're wondering how we got there ahead of them without horses—or how we knew where their hideout was in the first place—the explanation's simple enough. The "lair" was less than a hundred feet from our seat.

It was the train's locomotive.

"Welcome home," I said.

"Drop 'em," said Old Red.

We were up in the engine cab at the time, and even in the dim light of the moon I could see the robbers' eyes pop wide above their masks.

"Are you insane?" one of them snapped. He'd been walking

beside the conductor, and he whipped his gun up to the man's head again. "*You* drop 'em, or I'll blow this S.O.B.'s brains out."

"Be my guest," I said. "But personally, I don't think he's got any brains to blow. Not if this was his idea."

Gunman and captive alike blinked at me in disbelief.

"Huh?" the bandit said.

The other masked man got it a lot quicker.

"Dammit, Phil," he moaned forlornly, gun slipping from his limp fingers, "you *swore* there weren't any spotters aboard."

And he turned a look of mournful reproach on the conductor.

"Shut up, Ed," "Phil" hissed at him.

"Oh, don't worry about Ed there spillin' the beans," Gustav said. "They been out of the can quite a spell. Ain't that right?"

My brother threw a glance my way, offering me the honor of Holmesing it through.

"Indeedy," I said. "You boys wanna masquerade as long riders, I suggest you weather your coats and hats a mite first. The ones you're wearin' ain't got a wrinkle to 'em, let alone any trail dust. Like you just bought the things yesterday . . . which I assume you did. And them big, black, bricky work shoes you railroaders wear would barely fit through a stirrup. *And* whichever of you was out collectin' the booty . . . ? He must surely be the fireman, cuz gloves and coat or no, we caught sight of coal dust blackin' up his arms."

"And we had us a few suspicions before then, too," Old Red threw in—by "us," of course, meaning himself alone. "The way you was fussin' at folks to quiet down tonight struck me odd, captain . . . and then doubly so when you kept the cars nearly pitch black after the sun went down. I reckon you wanted as many folks asleep as could be—the better to discombobulate the lot of us when the 'gang' came aboard. Flashin' the lights up so bright for a second was a good idea. It had me seein' spots sure enough. But in the end, y'all didn't get the job done fast enough for it to help you."

"Ed" looked down and kicked at a rock that may or may not have been there at all, it was too dark to say.

"Jesus," he groaned, "you know the plan better than I did."

His fellow bandito still had his artillery aimed at the conductor. And from the look in his eyes, he was mad enough to use it, too—though on the captain or us, I wasn't sure. After a little quiet seething, though, he finally tossed his gun in the dirt.

As for Capt. Phil, he looked enraged not to be a hostage any longer. Any and all pretense that he was an innocent party—or an honorable "captain"—was gone, and he glared at us with a white-hot hate that practically lit him up like a lantern.

"Faking motion sickness. That was real cute," he spat. "I never suspected for a second you two were S.P. dicks."

"There's a reason for that," Old Red said. "We *ain't* S.P. dicks."

"Well, we *were*," I quibbled. "For all of three days."

"Huh?" the still-nameless bandit/railroadman said again. It seemed to be all he was capable of, aside from threats.

"We ain't the law," I said to him. "We're just here for that."

I pointed at the bulging bag in his left hand.

"You're not going to arrest us?" Ed asked.

My brother shrugged.

"Can't very well arrest you with no badges. And anyway, the S.P. ain't no friend of ours. I doubt they'd even appreciate us doin' 'em the favor. So just hand back the cash, and we'll call it square."

The three men looked at each other, silently debating.

"Oh, for Christ's sake, Raymond," Ed finally snapped. He pulled down his mask with an angry tug, revealing a round, soft, soot-smeared face that had not a hint of hardened outlaw about it. "Give 'em the damn bag. It was a stupid idea to begin with."

"Raymond" grumbled something unintelligible (and no doubt unprintable) under his breath. Then he cinched the sack tight and swung it up toward the cab.

It landed in my waiting arms.

"Wise decision, gents. The first you made tonight," Gustav said. "I hope you've learned your lesson."

The conductor replied with a bit of obscene advice Old Red's heard often, though he's never put it to use. For all the popularity of the phrase in certain quarters, the act it describes isn't physically possible.

My brother and I hopped down from the cab and started back toward the passenger cars—though Gustav kept his gun on Ed and Raymond as we went.

"Come on, Phil," I said, waving for the conductor to join us. "And try to look a little cheerier, would you? After all, we just rescued you from the Give-'em-Hell Boys."

Phil followed along, as ordered. He never did manage to look cheery, though. Or anything less than murderous.

Of course, there were smiles aplenty from our fellow passengers. Some had tried talking us out of leaving the car earlier, but they were all more than happy to claim their cash. I was just glad I took ours out first, for the bag was empty before we made it half-way through the last car.

Not all thieves bother with masks.

Soon enough, the train started up again (Old Red and I having supposedly released the bound-and-gagged engine crew after chasing off the outlaws). Yet while the passengers around us settled back into their seats and their sleep with remarkable speed, Gustav and I remained awake, on guard.

For a fellow we'd just "rescued," Phil sure was giving us dirty looks.

"It'd be a big risk to him, lettin' us walk off knowin' what we know," I whispered to Old Red as the conductor eyed us ominously from the front of the car.

"I know."

"And he's seen how much cash we got on us. If he hatched up that dumb scheme cuz he's got money problems, he might be tempted to solve 'em yet."

"I know."

"And that Raymond feller—he didn't seem so inclined to give up easy."

"I know."

"Long as we're on this train, we ain't safe."

"*I know*, dammit. And I know what we gotta do, too, so don't feel you gotta lead me there by the nose."

I stopped pointing out the obvious, and both my brother and I sank back in our seat, hats over our eyes. When Gustav's elbow dug into my side a few minutes later, I peeked out to find Phil gone.

"Let's go," Old Red said. He pulled out his carpetbag yet again, and I did the same.

Now, seventy-two hours isn't long to work for a railroad, but it was enough for my brother and me to pick up a trick or two. The one coming in handy just then being this: how to jump from a moving train without breaking your neck.

We landed amidst sandy-yellow dirt and scrub brush.

"You alright?" I asked Gustav as I pushed myself to my feet.

"I'm alive, anyway," my brother grumbled. He'd rolled to a stop atop a particularly thistly-looking patch of chaparral. "These days, that's as much as I let myself hope for."

He extracted himself from the thicket and made a survey of the terrain.

To the east, the train was chugging away toward a sun fresh-risen over barren nothing.

To the north was rocky-mountainous nothing.

To the south was flat-desert nothing.

To the west, behind us, was gloomy gray nothing.

Old Red sighed and started trudging along the track, headed east. Of the four points of the compass, it was the least nothingy. And after a few hours walking, we did indeed hit *something*—though, as noted earlier, Lovelock only barely qualifies as such.

Here we remain even as night starts to fall. The local stationmaster, a surly old goat we found asleep under his desk, assures us a train'll stop by and by . . . when a crew feels like it. Which doesn't seem very promising to me. *I* certainly wouldn't stop here if I had a say in the matter.

A train coming out of the west, from the Sierras and California—that's what we're waiting for. Yet often I've spied my brother gazing glumly eastward. It's where the tracks lead he's thinking of, I'm sure. Texas and whatever answers await us there, if any. As quests go, this one certainly isn't off to an auspicious start.

"You know," I said, setting my pencil aside but a few minutes ago, "that was some mighty sharp deducifyin' you did on the train."

I was just trying to buck my brother up. And as usual, he was having none of it.

"Oh, sure," Gustav growled. "Just look how neat things ended up. Look how tidy."

We were lollygagging around the train station, waiting in vain as we had all day, and Old Red waved a limp hand at the seemingly limitless emptiness that stretched from the tracks all the way out to the sky.

I have no doubt we'll escape this sun-baked Limbo sooner or later. Yet my brother won't be truly free until we get to Texas . . . and maybe, I fear, not even then.

Keep an eye out for the next correspondence from me, Mr. Smythe. The postmark will read "San Marcos, Texas." But whether the letter will be mailed from Purgatory, Heaven or Hell, I can't yet say.

Your humble junior partner in publishing,

O.A. Amlingmeyer
Lovelock, Nevada (though God only knows where I'll end up posting this from)
September 24, 1893

# ABOUT THE AUTHOR

Steve Hockensmith is the New York Times best-selling author of *Pride and Prejudice and Zombies: Dawn of the Dreadfuls.* His first novel, *Holmes on the Range,* was a finalist for the Edgar, Shamus, Anthony and Dilys awards, and its heroes went on to star in four sequels (*On the Wrong Track, The Black Dove, The Crack in the Lens* and *World's Greatest Sleuth!*). Oh, and they have their own collection of short stories, too. But surely you know that already, seeing as you just read it. You can find Hockensmith online at www.stevehockensmith.com. Well, you can find him all over the Web, thanks to Google, but stevehockensmith.com is where he *wants* you to go. And from there he wants you go to Amazon. In a buying mood.